THE MEANING OF HOME

THE MEANING OF HOME

A Novel

— SCOTT I. FEGLEY —

The Meaning Of Home © 2018 by **Scott I. Fegley**

All rights reserved. No part of the this publication may be reproduced, stored in or introduced into a retrieval system, or transmitted, in any form, or by any means (electronic, mechanical, photocopying, recording, or otherwise), without the prior written permission of the publisher.

This is a work of fiction. All of the characters, organizations, and events portrayed in this novel are either products of the author's imagination or are used fictitiously.

The scanning, uploading and distribution of this book via the Internet or via any other means without the permission of the publisher is illegal and punishable by law. Please purchase only authorized electronic editions, and do not participate in or encourage electronic piracy of copyright materials. Your support of the author's rights is appreciated.

ISBN: 978-1-7313-7443-1

First edition November 2018

Cover & Interior Design by ARC MANOR, LLC.

For my parents, Harry and Carol Fegley, V. M. D.

Whoever saves a life, saves the world entire.
—THE TALMUD

I

Without second chances, who among us, canine or human, could say they had lived a full life? Second chances are the squares in the patchwork quilt of my life stitched together by the humans who shared it with me. My story cannot be told without theirs any more than theirs is complete without mine. Only when the threads are woven together, and bonds are formed, will anything I tell you truly make sense. In this world, there are as many lost humans as there are lost dogs. This is a story of how we are found.

My name is Charlie. What kind of dog am I? Good question. I have seen my reflection on occasion in glass doors and mirrors, and I have heard myself described by humans as part Pomeranian, part fox. What I am is handsome.

My coat is the glistening, golden and white color of a toasted marshmallow, and as soft as goose down. My tail of long, white hair curls up in the Pomeranian fashion and splashes across my back. From my fox lineage, I inherited an elongated body, triangular face with narrow, pointed ears and nose, and inquisitive dark brown eyes. Humans often wonder aloud how a dog as handsome as I could ever be found living on the streets. It's not hard to understand really. Most of the humans I met on the streets did not choose to be there either. Sometimes it's just bad luck.

You might say my life started out as bad luck for my mother. She was a pure-bred Pomeranian and a champion show dog. I never met my father. Often with dogs, as it is with humans, conception is not the result of a willing intention and careful breeding, but rather a casual acquaintance and a moment in heat. And often with dogs, as it is with humans, the offspring in the latter case are unwanted, bestowed at the moment of birth with the heavy baggage of being labeled a mixed breed, a mistake.

For a short time after I opened my eyes in this world, my home was a comfortable room with a sofa and bookshelves adorned with my mother's trophies and ribbons. I was blissfully ignorant of my imperfect pedigree and the intentions of my mother's human companion, a short, round woman with gray hair. My mother showered my brothers and sisters and I with affection and kept us clean and well fed. In those early weeks, I spent my time in the folds of blankets in a large wicker basket by the sofa. My mother lay on the sofa above us and kept watch. She would hop down into the basket when it came time to feed us. As we became more mobile, she followed us around the room and carried us back to the basket when our legs gave out. I have no doubt my mother wanted us, but the decision to keep us was not hers to make.

The last day I saw my mother, I had just become co-ordinated enough to hold my own against my brothers and sisters in play. The five of us were a writhing, wrestling ball of fur rolling around the room, nipping at each other's feet and ears and yelping with glee. In the midst of our tumbling, three humans entered the room—the woman with the gray hair, a young woman and a young man—through a door that led to the Great Unknown. It rarely opened, and when it did, my brothers and sisters and I were not allowed through.

I had seen my mother's human companion often enough. She brought us food and water and cleaned up our messes. On occasion, she held us up and examined us, but with cold hands and little emotion. Sometimes, she took my mother with her when she left the room as she did earlier that day, but she had always brought her back. This time, she entered the room empty-handed. The young couple came in behind her.

Anytime a human entered the room, my brothers and sisters and I rushed to greet them. Humans we hadn't met excited us more. I suppose it is instinctive in us as Man's best friend and is perhaps fueled in part by our innate curiosity about humans and their behavior.

My brothers and sisters went to the older woman first. They danced around her legs and whined shamelessly for her attention. I found myself drawn to the mysterious young woman. She was slender with long, black hair she brushed back from her face as she knelt down to pet me, and she carried about her a bouquet of scents, a delightful blend of sweet fragrances, soft leather, and washed clothes. I circled her and indulged in the scent of the knee-high tan leather boots she wore.

"Ooohhh, you are soooooo cute!" she crooned. "*Ven Aqui!* Come here, puppy!"

The sound of her voice struck an instinctively pleasing chord. I didn't need to know the words to understand she wanted me. I looked up into a pleasing face full of warmth and color so different from the loose jowls and perpetual scowl of my mother's human companion. She had delicate features—a narrow nose in between high cheek bones, curved red lips, and exquisite eyes as dark as my mother's.

I sniffed the fringe of her brown leather jacket worn over a white blouse tucked into her jeans and licked the hand she held out to me. I wanted her all to myself. To be sure my brothers and sisters would know I claimed her first, I squatted over the toe of one of her boots and let out just a little urine.

"*Ay! Que haces?*" the young woman squealed and jumped up.

When the older woman saw what I had done, she scolded me. She picked me up and carried me toward another door on the other side of the room. This door was almost always open. It led to a smaller room where my brothers and sisters and I were supposed to go when we had to relieve ourselves. The room had a hard, cold floor and a spongy mat the older woman made us sit on until we peed.

But the room had another purpose. Punishment. Whenever I forgot to use the mat and relieved myself on the carpet in the large room, the older woman shut me in the small room for a little while. I assumed it was what she intended to do then, but she stopped and turned around when the young woman spoke to her in a soft voice.

"It was nothing. May I hold him?" She walked over to the woman with the gray hair and took me from her arms.

I seized the opportunity to make amends and wiggled and wagged and licked. If my paws were on the ground, I would have been running.

"Obviously, he'll have to be neutered when he's older," the woman with the gray hair grumbled.

The more I wiggled and licked, the more the young woman laughed. "We're friends!" she said. "He's quite a character."

"I'd say he's the most outgoing of the litter."

"And the chunkiest." The young woman held me out at arm's length. "Look at that belly!"

"Are you sure you want to do this?" asked the young man who had been silent until then. He had black hair, too, but his face was not pleasing to me. His eyes were dull and uncaring, he didn't smile, and he didn't show any interest in my brothers and sisters or me. The young man leaned against the wall by the door to the Great Unknown with his hands buried in the pockets of his black leather jacket. I didn't like the tone of his voice either. It was unwanting and reminded me of the way the woman with the gray hair spoke to me at times.

"Yes." The young woman looked me over again. "Yes, he's the one."

"Then he's your responsibility," the young man said. "Don't expect me to get up and walk him or clean up his crap."

"I am tired of working in an empty apartment all day," she said. She nuzzled my face with hers. "He'll keep me company when you're not there."

"Suit yourself," the young man replied. "Just remember I said this wasn't a good idea."

While the humans were talking, I gazed down at my brothers and sisters who were still circling the humans' feet. For once, I was getting all the attention and I felt special. I wanted them to envy me.

The young woman moved toward the door to the Great Unknown. My heart raced. I was going somewhere my brothers and sisters had never been and I felt extra-special. Maybe they were taking me to see my mother? She was nearby. I could smell her. She had been through the hallway and on the stairs the young woman walked down after we left the room.

My mother barked faintly above the louder, higher pitched squeals of my brothers and sisters. Her bark had a tone of worry and concern the way it did in the dark when something aroused her. I answered to let her know how excited I was to be outside the room, but it only seemed to upset her more. Her sound and her scent faded when the young couple left the home where I was born.

I had never been outdoors. At first, I thought I was in the largest room a dog could imagine. The ceiling was a magnificent blue and white like the walls of the room inside my home, but so much higher. And the smells! There were so many smells in the air carried along by a gentle breeze, each one more tantalizing than the last. Although the young woman held me close to her chest, I stretched out my neck away from the smell of her leather jacket to breathe in each new odor.

The young woman carried me through yet another door into the smallest room a dog could imagine. It was so small, she had to sit down to get in. The man walked around the room and entered through a door on the other side. He had to sit down, too. In front of us was a big window above a smooth surface that smelled of leather. The young man sat in front of a wheel. When he grabbed the wheel, the room made noise, a loud noise which both scared and excited me at the same time. And then the room moved.

Plenty of new smells inside the moving room kept me guessing for a little while. I matched some to a crumpled, white bag lying on the floor by the young woman's feet. I quickly distinguished and memorized the different smells I associated with her—the fragrant smell of her hair and skin, the pungent smell of her leather jacket and boots, and a fair scent underneath all the others that was just hers.

The man took a short white stick from inside his jacket, stuck it in his mouth, and set one end on fire. I recognized the smell from his clothes earlier, but it was much stronger now and irritated my nose. I pressed my nose against the cold glass of the moving room.

"You could have waited until we were home," the young woman said. "It bothers him." She lowered the glass and the wind rushed in my face. It chased away the foul smoke and brought with it a shock of smells all tumbling and rolling around in one gust like my brothers and sisters and I when we wrestled. The sensation was exhilarating.

When the young man finally stopped breathing in on the white stick and crushed it in a bowl, the woman closed the glass. My exhilaration turned to boredom. I lay quietly in her lap for a while until my stomach began to grumble. It was well past my feeding time and I wanted to return to the room with my food and my basket. After all the excitement, I was ready for a meal and a nap. I barked respectfully to let the young woman know, but she sat quietly while the room kept moving.

As the pangs in my stomach grew sharper, I fidgeted in her lap and cried.

"He must be hungry," the young woman said.

The man said nothing.

She reached down and picked up the white paper bag, unwrinkled it, and stuck her hand inside. She offered me some cold, salty yellow sticks. I gently took them from her hand and ate them in her lap.

"That's all I have now," she said, "but everything's waiting for you at home." The young woman ran her hands over my coat. Back then, my hair wasn't very long, but it was soft. "You'll have your own bed, your own supper dish. You'll have the place all to yourself."

I liked listening to her voice. It was a voice that soothed. But the longer I stayed inside the moving room, the more uneasy I felt and the less likely it seemed I would return to the room where my mother and my brothers and sisters lived. Our past separations had been brief and our reunions joyful. The possibility of not seeing them again had never entered my mind until that moment. I moved about in the young woman's lap and whined more.

The young woman scratched my head. "We'll be home soon," she said, but it did not stop me from whining.

"I told you this wasn't a good idea," the man said gruffly.

Home. What did that mean?

I was to learn, in life, a dog can have many homes. Good homes. Bad homes. And sometimes no home at all. Just like humans.

II

The young woman's name was Mira. Her apartment was high up in a tall building that looked out over a city. I began to understand the difference between outside and inside and day and night as I watched the sky outside the glass of her apartment change colors and turn from blue and white to shades of red and orange and then black.

Inside the apartment, the light stayed on. Mira and the young man she called Mark were able to control the light inside the apartment, even making the light appear and disappear room by room. The light outside the glass had changed gradually on its own. Even when the color outside the glass had turned to black, it was not as dark inside Mira's apartment as it had been at times in the room where I was born. Beneath us, a carpet of light spread out until it met the edge of the blackness I learned was the night sky. Tiny lights in the night sky Mira called stars and a larger light she called 'the moon' also let light into the apartment.

Mira left me free to explore. A hallway led from the door to the apartment into a large open room where the sky outside seemed to make up an entire wall. I smelled Mira's leather and Mark's smoking stick in the carpet and wondered if they rolled around on the floor like my brothers and sisters and I had done in our room. I sniffed around a sofa and chairs that were smooth and slippery and smelled like Mira's jacket, and stared up at trees growing out of large pots.

Across the space from the sky wall, a light hung down from the ceiling over a table and chairs. There was carpet underneath the table and chairs, too. But nearby, in an area I heard Mira call the kitchen, the floor was hard and slippery. Half a wall stood between the kitchen and the carpeted area, tall for me, but not for Mira or Mark. Mira opened a shiny silver door in the kitchen, brought out a can, and scooped its contents into a bowl she set on the floor for me. I trotted over and smelled the food, smells I would later learn to distinguish as beef and chicken. It was moist and so much more pleasing to me than the dry pebbles the woman with the gray hair left in our dish.

"*Oye!*" Mira said. "*Pequeño.*" Little one. "Not so fast. You'll give yourself a tummy ache." She laughed while I licked the bowl until I could no longer taste the beef or chicken on its smooth sides.

For a time, a full belly and the sights and smells of Mira's apartment kept me from dwelling on the lengthening separation from my mother and my brothers and sisters. Mark sat on the sofa and watched humans talking inside a box that hung like a picture on another wall.

Mira sat next to him holding me in her lap. When Mark got up, he made the box turn dark, and left the room. Mira picked me up and carried me into the kitchen. She sat me on a spongy mat and clapped her hands and told me I was a good boy. I understood what she wanted me to do, so I let out a little stream of urine. Mira squealed with delight and clapped harder.

"Good boy! You're such a good boy!"

I will never understand why performing this simple act gives humans so much pleasure when done in one place, but so much anger when done in another.

Mira picked me up and put me in a large box with a door made of metal bars that stood in the kitchen by the half wall.

"Sweet dreams, Pequeño," she said as she closed the door. "Don't be afraid."

I watched her walk away. I sensed I was being punished and did not understand why. Even though there was a comfortable blanket inside the box, and a snack, it was a very small space, much smaller than the punishment room. The older woman with the gray hair confined me there only when I peed where I wasn't supposed to. But I had done exactly what Mira had asked. Humans are complex creatures, some of whom I had difficulty understanding even after much time as their companion. But that first night with Mira, I had barely three months of living in my skin and little knowledge to go along with it. I was confused, lonely, and without my mother or my brothers and sisters for comfort, I was scared.

I whined and whimpered and made sounds that had always earned me a sympathetic nuzzle or lick from my mother. The kitchen remained silent but for the faint sound of distant honking horns and humming from the big box with the silver door. I scratched at the sides of the box and whined more. Still, Mira did not come. A sound I had never made before startled me. It started as a low rumble in my throat, then rose to a high wail and filled the room. I inhaled gulps of air and did it again and again. Mira came running.

"Oye! Oye! Pequeño!" In another room, Mark was yelling. Mira opened the door made of metal bars and I rushed into her arms. She wasn't wearing her white blouse anymore, but a thin, white dress that showed more of her skin and smelled just as sweet. Her black hair curled in a braid around her neck and I nuzzled and licked and squirmed against her as much as if I had been at my mother's teats.

"I thought you'd like your own bed," Mira said. "La Señora told me to get this box for you. I should have known better."

Mira carried me through the apartment past the glass that looked out on a night filled with lights to another room where the light did not come in. As my eyes adjusted to the darkness, I saw shapes along one wall like the bookshelves that held my mother's trophies. Another shape as large and long as a bookshelf lay on the floor. Mira sat down on it and let me sit on it, too. She laid me among sheets as soft as my mother's fur and just as warm, and I rolled and wriggled to find just the right spot. Then I heard Mark's voice.

"Are you loco?" he shouted. "Get that dog out of my bed."

"He's scared," Mira said.

"*Mierda. El cobarde.* The coward. Let him find his courage in the kitchen."

"You told me to shut him up," Mira replied. "Now he's quiet."

"In the *barrio* where I grew up, dogs were filthy creatures. They ran wild in the streets. They fouled themselves and then licked themselves and made us sick. Get it out of my bed."

"We're not in a *barrio*," Mira said quietly.

"I let a dog in my house for you," Mark replied. "Not in my bed."

Mira lifted me out of the folds of the sheets just as I had finished creating my own basket of sorts. I juggled my disappointment upon leaving the bedroom with relief when I saw she was not taking me back to the kitchen and the box with the metal bars on the door. She carried me down the hallway into another room just as dark, but much smaller. I could not see shapes of any furniture inside except a sofa along one wall. Mira curled up on the sofa with me clutched to her chest. She reached up and pulled a blanket lying on the sofa down overtop us. She was soft. I was warm. And I was content enough to be quiet.

As I listened to Mira breathing, I remembered the sounds my brothers and sisters had made as we slept in our basket. Not as pleasant, of course, but comforting in their own way. My eyelids drooped close with the fatigue of a day that began in familiarity and ended in uncertainty. I breathed in Mira's scent and understood she would be my companion from now on, but I could not rid myself of the sense that even this relationship would not last. I would not have peace in my surroundings as long as un-wanting existed within them.

III

Mira made pretty clothes during the day. I lay on the floor of the room she called a studio while she put clothes on human shapes, tied strings around them, and stuck them with pins. These humans did not talk, and I suppose it was because they did not have faces. They didn't have legs either. Mira guided them out of a closet every morning and walked them back into the closet in the late afternoon when she finished her work.

The studio had its own wall of glass that showed us the sky. The floor was hardwood. Except for a few tables, a white chair on wheels, and a shelf with many rolls of cloth, the studio was bare of furniture. Two walls were covered with pictures of clothing, paper cut-outs in a variety of shapes, and boards with pins stuck in squares of colored cloth. Mira spent the day moving back and forth from the tables to the walls and the shelf, sometimes drawing, sometimes cutting. She cut the paper and then the cloth and held the cloth up against the silent humans.

"What do you think, Pequeño?" she would ask. I'd wag my tail and smile every time Mira spoke to me. If her voice was happy, I was happy. "You're right. I don't like it, either." The cloth dropped to the floor where several other pieces lay. Mira went back to the table and started drawing again.

Sometimes she opened the closet where the silent humans slept and pulled out a strange, white machine that stood on a table with wheels. She sat by the machine on the white chair and used it to join several pieces of cloth back together. I wanted to ask Mira why she cut the pieces of cloth in the first place if she was only going to join them back together, but I guessed it was a game she liked to play. The noise the machine made during the game bothered my ears. I usually left the room while it was on. When it stopped, I'd return to see Mira standing by a silent human clothed in a new garment.

"There, Pequeño." She smiled. "This will be the one all the girls wear."

Mira and I became inseparable. Dogs were meant to live in packs and Mira was my alpha female. Mark was the alpha male we tolerated. We went for a walk every day except when the sky was the color of the older woman's hair. Mira made me wear a ring around my neck that smelled of leather. She attached a long string to it she called a leash and held the other end. I did not like it but endured it for the privilege of the walk.

The world outside the apartment intrigued me. The city seemed to be home to as many dogs as it was for humans. Big dogs almost as large as humans. Dogs with long hair like me. Others that seemed to have no hair at all. Short, long, thin, fat, big ears, big noses, smiles and growls. And I observed it was the same with humans. There were as many unique features about them as there were in the dogs who were their companions. The more I learned about humans, the more I understood the many similarities between humans and dogs.

Other dogs lived inside our building. I could smell their scents in the hallway outside Mira's apartment, in the tiny room she called an elevator, and the larger room called a lobby, each one distinctive like the many sets of clothes Mira wore. In this way, dogs and humans are different. Humans have the ability to change the way they smell. Dogs do not. Nevertheless, each human still carries with him or her a distinctive odor. No matter how many people crowded around us outside the building, I always found Mira's scent among them.

The sidewalks outside the apartment building were a forest of human legs. I had to pay attention to avoid being stepped on. Humans on the sidewalks always seemed to be going somewhere fast and their eyes were several feet above me looking ahead. The younger ones often had strings hanging from their ears attached to a shiny object they held in their hands. Sometimes, they sang while they walked, or talked to the shiny object. In either case, they seldom looked where they were going. Mira had one of the shiny objects, too. She called it a phone and held it to her ear with one hand while she held on to the end of my leash with the other.

Each walk was an opportunity to refresh and expand my scent trail of the city. It began with the trash can just outside the front doors of the apartment building and followed a line of trees growing out of circles cut in the sidewalk down to a tall pole at the corner. We often had to wait there for the moving rooms Mira called cars to move along their path and stop before we had another turn to move along ours.

Up another sidewalk, benches, bus stops, curb blocks, bike racks, and, of course, fire hydrants were all guideposts and keepers of my scent. Dogs do not jettison their urine haphazardly. We cannot draw ourselves a map with ink and paper like humans. We follow our noses and no scent is more recognizable than one's own.

Our destination on most of our walks was a park several corners away from the apartment building with wide, grassy areas, tall trees, and a pond with a water spout in the middle. Creatures with long necks and large wings lived around the pond's edge and swam in its water. Something came over me the first time I saw them, something primal that had not been refined through my breeding and it said 'food.'

I ran toward them with a burst of speed that took Mira by surprise. The leash flew from her hand and, unencumbered by the restraint, I ran even faster. I heard Mira's yells above the squawking of the great birds, but instinct compelled me to ignore her. Birds were running in all directions. Some had taken to the air or set out upon the water with a thunderous flapping of wings. But I needed to catch only one.

A pair of birds had veered off up a grass covered hill away from the pond. Though their wings were flapping, they had not taken to the air and their short legs and funny-looking feet could not carry them as fast as I could run. I was on them in a heartbeat, my nose full of their scent and my snapping jaws just inches from one of the great birds' tail feathers, when the other bird turned and attacked. With its wings spread, it coiled its long neck and struck.

The bird bit my ear. He bit it hard, and it hurt. The shock and pain made me forget my pursuit of the bird's companion long enough for the second bird to gather up its courage and go for my haunches. The furious flapping of the birds' wings in my face confused me. After several jolts of pain from their pecking at my face and ribs, I decided I wasn't having fun anymore and I wasn't that hungry after all. I turned and ran off toward a pair of humans who were standing at the top of the hill calling me. I found all humans fascinating and, clearly, these humans wanted me. So I went to find out why.

"Come, boy! Good dog!" They seemed to become happier and more excited the closer I approached. "Good boy! Good dog!" I basked in their praise and jumped up and down around their feet. A young man in a t-shirt and shorts reached for me. I jumped away wanting to play a game of chase, but the woman with him grabbed the leash that was still trailing behind me and my freedom came to an end. She scooped me up, held me tightly in her arms, and scratched me where the birds had pecked. It made my hind legs kick.

When I saw Mira walking up the hill, I barked and squirmed in the strange woman's grasp, but she did not let go.

"Oye, Pequeño!" Mira said when she reached us. "Are you loco?" Her chest was heaving, and her skin glistened with moisture. She took a piece of cloth from the bag she always carried and wiped her face with it. "Thank you," she said to the woman holding me.

"He's handsome," the woman said. "He looks like he's part fox." It was the first time I heard a human speak of me that way. "That would explain his interest in the geese," the man said.

The woman handed me to Mira but did not let go until Mira had the leash wrapped around her hand several times. Once in Mira's arms, I wiggled and licked her face. I sensed she was unhappy with me, but not unhappy enough to yell at me the way Mark did. She still wanted me. She squeezed me tightly and buried her face in my fur.

"Don't ever do that again, Pequeño," she said. "If you ran away, I'd miss you so much my heart would break."

A dog can sense whether a human can be trusted. Humans give away much of their unspoken thought through their eyes and body movements just as dogs do. I did not trust Mark and it was more than his un-wanting of me. It was a certain coldness in his expression, a sharpness in his tone of voice, and the dullness of his eyes that revealed a hidden discontent. The discontent showed itself at times in the evenings when Mark came home from his work. He sat in the room with the sky wall drinking from cans while he watched people talking inside the box on the wall Mira called a TV. Drinking from the cans made him yell at Mira in a loud voice.

"Why haven't you made dinner yet, Mira? I'm hungry."

Mira yelled back. "I've been working all day, too. You're drunk. *Boracho!*"

Sometimes the yelling faded away to a chilly silence. I'd follow quietly at Mira's heels as she moved about the apartment while Mark opened and slammed the silver door in the kitchen and took food into the room with the TV. But sometimes Mark turned violent. He'd yell more. And he'd throw the cans across the room and turn over chairs and call Mira names until she cried.

Whenever Mark was violent, I went inside the box with the door made of metal bars and stayed there until the apartment was quiet again. I don't know why. Mira never made me go inside the box anymore when she left me alone in the apartment. I had never chewed anything I wasn't supposed to, and I had learned to use the spongy mat. Mostly, I napped in a bed Mira left on the floor in the room with the sky wall. It was a big basket with warm blankets that reminded me of the wicker basket I was born in. But when Mark yelled, or when the sky outside the glass turned dark and flashed with lightning and the glass shook with the boom of thunder, I went in the box until it stopped.

There were days I wanted to trust Mark. On days he did not have to work, he sometimes accompanied Mira and me on our walks. He made Mira laugh and put his arm around her shoulders or held her hand. They touched their lips together like Mira did with me when Mark wasn't around, but they didn't use their tongues. When they stopped and bought food from the silver carts on the street corners, Mark dropped scraps on the ground for me, although he never fed me from his hand like Mira did. But the days Mark was kind were not plentiful enough.

Every night after Mark turned off the TV and went into their bedroom, I hopped in my bed and listened to the sounds of the city outside the sky wall. The apartment was never completely quiet even with the TV off. I had become accustomed to certain sounds like the different horns of the cars on the streets below and the occasional loud wail of the cars and trucks with the flashing lights. Birds with lights made noise, too, as they flew high above the apartment building. At night, the city itself seemed to hum. In the first weeks of my life sleeping inside the wicker basket, the only sounds I had heard were my brothers and sisters grunting and snoring and passing gas.

One night after Mark and Mira had argued, Mira went into their bedroom and closed the door. Mark watched the TV for a while, but then he got up, turned off the TV and the lights, and went into the bedroom, too. I left the box in the kitchen and went over to my basket. I lay in bed listening to the usual night sounds intermingled with Mark and Mira's voices. They spoke softly at first. Mark spoke in a kind voice—and gently—but then Mira's voice changed. It had a strange tone I had not heard before, a high, short sigh that caused me to sit up in my bed. I had heard dogs make similar noises when they were frightened and wondered if Mark was hurting her.

As Mira's voice grew louder, the sound turned into a long moan like the sound I had made myself the first night in the apartment. The memory of how awful I felt when she left me in the box with the door shut sent chills rippling through my body, and I sensed Mark must be punishing her for arguing with him. I ran down the hall to the bedroom and began to howl outside the closed door, but Mira's howling was even louder than mine. I kept howling and scratched at the door until Mira's howling finally stopped. Then I heard Mark's angry voice.

"El Diablo." The Devil. "I am going to beat that dog!"

Mira was laughing. Her laughter confused me. She opened the bedroom door wearing her thin, white dress and smelling heavily of her scent. "Oye! Pequeño." Her voice was unafraid. *"Estoy bien. No te preocupes."* I am fine. Don't worry. She laughed again and walked with me back to my bed. She knelt down beside me and gave me belly scratches when I rolled on my back.

My ears stood up long after Mira returned to her bedroom and I shook in my bed despite the belly scratches. Because I did not trust Mark, I could not be sure he would not hurt her.

I envy humans' ability to think of the strangest things and then create them.

"Oye! Pequeño," Mira called to me one day. I was stretched out on the floor of her studio basking in a patch of sunlight. "Wouldn't you look handsome in clothes, too?" By then, my cream-colored hair had grown to its full length. I stood a bench seat high from the floor to the tip of my ears and was nearly a door's width in length, longer with my tail straight instead of curled up over my back. I had never considered myself lacking for looks, but I did sometimes wonder what I might look like in a different coat.

Mira laughed at herself. I sat up and wagged my tail as I always did. Then Mira stopped laughing and stared at me with a finger pressed against her lips. It was the same sign she used whenever I spoke too loud and Mark began to yell. But Mark wasn't there, and I wasn't speaking. I laid my ears back and looked away from her. Experiencing Mira's displeasure was bad enough when I deserved it.

Mira walked around me in a circle. Suddenly, she scooped me up and set me down on one of her tables. She took her string and stretched it across my body from the tip of my nose to my tail. Then she wrapped it around my chest and my belly and wrote on a piece of paper lying on the table. It was the oddest human behavior I had experienced up to that point in my life, but if tying string around me made Mira happy, I was happy to play the game with her.

After she set me down on the floor, Mira began drawing and cutting again. She worked without even looking at me or out at the sky. She worked past the time we usually went for our walk. I grew restless and began to walk back and forth by the door. When I eventually caught her attention, she grabbed my leash and collar and stomped over to the studio door. I waited for her to bend over and put the collar around my neck, but Mira simply stared at the collar in her hand as though she had forgotten what it was for. I barked and danced and shimmied to show her how much I wanted to go for a walk.

"Go use your mat, Pequeño," she said. My heart sank as she turned and walked back to her table. I scurried into the kitchen to use the mat before I found myself in deeper trouble.

When I returned to the studio, Mira was still working. I lay on the floor in the patch of sunlight and dozed until her voice awakened me.

"Try this on, Pequeño," she said. Mira had made me a new coat. It was long across my back and wrapped around and fastened underneath my belly. There were openings for my front legs, but it stopped short of my hind legs, so I could still lift a leg to pee. The piece around my neck was much softer and wider than my old collar. On the underside, Mira had sewn a bowtie between two small flaps. She attached my leash to a ring she had fastened to the top.

"Now you are even more handsome!" Mira said. She smiled. "Let's go for a walk!"

Out on the city sidewalks, I was very proud of my new coat. I walked up to other dogs we met to allow them to sniff if Mira let me. Mira was proud of my new coat, too. She often stopped to talk to other humans with small dogs who did not have a human-made coat and she picked me up to give them a closer look. I felt much warmer in my new coat and discovered I could breathe easier without the old, narrow collar pressing against my throat. Mira's creation seemed to impress everyone except Mark. I was still prancing around the apartment in my new coat when Mark came home that evening.

"He looks ridiculous," Mark said. Mira simply ignored him.

Mira began making me more clothes. Then she made clothes in bigger and smaller sizes for other dogs to wear. It seemed to me she was making more clothes in her studio for dogs than she was for humans. The faceless, silent humans did not come out of their closet for quite a while.

One day, several humans I had not met before came to the apartment to see the clothes Mira made for dogs. I will always remember that day as the happiest I ever saw Mira.

She wore a dress she had made with brightly colored flowers and had me dressed in an outfit she called a suit with buttons and a bowtie. One of the humans set up a couple of white umbrellas inside the studio even though it was sunny outside, and it had never rained inside the apartment even once. There were bright lights inside the umbrellas. The man set up large screens to block the light from the sky wall so the light from the umbrellas was the only light in the room.

Mira and I stood underneath the umbrellas. She said they were going to take our pictures. The other humans took many pictures that day, pictures of Mira and I wearing many different clothes. She said we were color-coordinated, but I distinguished the different clothing by the scents they held. The pictures were going into a book to be given away to other humans interested in Mira's clothing. In the weeks ahead, Mira spent much more time in her studio, often working late into the night long after Mark had turned off the TV and gone into their bedroom alone. I heard them arguing about how much time Mira spent in her studio.

"Come to bed, Mira," Mark said.

"I have to finish these new orders," she replied.

"You always have more orders," Mark said. "What do I have to do to get you to come to bed?"

"We aren't behind with our bills anymore," Mira said. "Maybe we can save up enough money to buy a house! I've always loved those brick homes on Lombard Street with the wrought iron railings and all those shady trees."

"There's nothing wrong with this apartment."

"Lombard Street is a nicer place to start a family."

"We'll never start a family if you don't come to bed."

"Soon. I'll be there soon."

But it wasn't soon. I fell asleep in my basket and awakened as the sky began to lighten outside the sky wall. I went into the studio and found Mira still working at a table.

"Hola, Pequeño," Mira said softly. "I wish I could teach you how to make clothes. I can't make all the clothes people want." She looked sad.

She rolled the white chair back from the table and I jumped in her lap. For a little while, Mira held me and whispered to me about orders and deadlines, a home on Lombard street, and how she wished Mark understood.

When she heard him stirring in the bedroom, she pushed me off her lap and returned to her work.

Sometimes I wonder how my life might have been different if Mira had never made me a new coat. Perhaps the three of us would have continued living in the apartment and, despite Mark's uncaring, I would have never wanted for food or shelter or a human's care.

Mira's pet clothing became so popular, she had to move her studio to another building on another street. Instead of just the two of us in the apartment, several humans worked in the new studio, a much bigger room with many more tables and shelves of cloth. Mira and the other humans sat in front of silent TVs she called computers creating pictures. Often, Mira asked one of the other humans to take me for my walk, a woman she called Cindy.

Cindy had long hair the same color as mine, but she put a tie in hers. It was only long in back and it looked like she had a tail like me. Cindy talked to me and took me for my walks to the city park. As we walked along a sidewalk one day past the ground floor of a tall building, Cindy stopped and showed me a picture in the glass as big as the sky wall in the apartment. I barked. I recognized Mira and the largest reflection of myself I had ever seen.

"Look, Pequeño," Cindy said. "You're famous! Your picture is in all the pet stores."

I kept barking. I wanted Mira to come out of the glass and walk with us, but she simply stared at me with an expression that never changed. Even my own reflection did not come with me as it usually did.

I wondered what it meant to be famous. If it meant being without Mira, I was not sure it was something I wanted. Although Cindy was kind and I knew she cared about me, she wasn't Mira. I missed being with Mira every moment of the day as we had been in the apartment. Most of all, I missed the way she made me feel wanted.

I think it is worse for humans to feel unwanted than for dogs. When humans feel unwanted, they sometimes say and do horrible things. The last night Mark and Mira were together in the apartment, Mira and I had arrived home well after the sun's light left the sky. Mark was sitting in his usual place on the couch. The TV was dark. The only light in the room was the city's light coming in through the sky wall, but it was enough to see several cans on the floor by Mark's feet.

After Mira moved her studio from the apartment, Mark always had something to say to her when we came home later than he did, and usually not in a kind way. But the stillness and darkness of the apartment that night raised the hair on the back of my neck.

Mira stopped at the end of the entrance hallway. Normally, she would have bent down and removed my leash and coat, but she simply stared across the room at the back of Mark's head. "What's wrong?" she asked.

Mark did not answer at first. I sat down at Mira's feet and looked up at her in confusion. The usual night sounds filtered in through the sky wall, but they did not comfort me. Something had changed about Mark, and I got up and whined and hoped Mira would follow me to the door. Mira ignored my tugging on the leash, so I sat down again with a heavy sigh.

"What's wrong?" Mira asked again.

"They fired me," Mark said finally. I could barely hear him speak.

Mira gasped. "Why?"

"I punched someone."

"You punched …Why?"

Mark breathed in deeply. "He said I was a lackey for a woman and a dog."

"Then he deserved to be punched," Mira said. She bent down and removed the leash. "You'll find another job. Why don't you come work with me at the studio? You know how to fix the computers."

I heard the crinkling of metal and the thud of another can falling to the floor. "And you'll pay me a salary?"

"Of course."

"And you'll be my boss?"

"We'll work together."

Mark stood up and turned toward us. His face was a dark oval in the middle of the sky wall. "No more," he said.

"No more what?" Mira asked.

"I am tired of living with that dog. I am tired of everything being about that dog. It's time you found it another home."

Though I still had my coat on, the air in the room seemed colder. Mira picked me up and held me tightly to her chest. I could feel fear inside her in the tightness of her muscles and the way her hands trembled.

"I can't do that," Mira said. "He's a good dog."

Mark's voice grew louder. "That dog means more to you than I do!"

"Don't be silly."

"You think I am being silly?" He kicked the cans laying at his feet like the balls the kids played with in the park and they went clattering all over room. "You dress up dogs like clowns and you think I am the one being silly?!"

Mira stood frozen in the entrance hall muffling the sounds of her distress in my fur. I felt the first warm drops from her eyes fall on the back of my head. When there were no more cans to kick, Mark strode toward us and Mira squeezed me more tightly.

"You spend all your time with it!" he shouted. "Even at home, you can't sit next to me without the dog in your lap. When we're out, people recognize you when you're with the dog, but me ... I might as well be invisible." He stretched out an open hand for Mira, but she took a step backward.

"It's your beer talking." Mira said. "Go sleep it off. I'm going over to Francesca's."

Mira turned toward the door, but Mark reached out, grabbed her shoulder and yanked her backward. Mira had me clutched to her chest facing over her shoulder. Mark's hand lay there in front of my nose stinking and squeezing and hurting Mira. I wanted him to stop. I just wanted him to stop, so I sunk my teeth into the back of his hand, just a quick strike to make him let go.

Mark let go. He screamed horrible names at Mira even though I was the one who bit him. And then his hand came back harder than before. I am sure the punch was meant for me, but Mira turned around the moment Mark swung his fist and it struck her square on the right side of her face. The blow sent her crashing into a wall. She dropped me and slid to the floor in a heap.

I'd like to say at that moment, freed from Mira's grasp, I had lunged at Mark and bit him again. I'd like to say I stood my ground and defended Mira who lay next to me on the floor, but I didn't. I ran. Whenever Mark lunged for me, he clutched only air. Dogs are faster and far more agile than humans, especially drunk ones. He chased me into the room with the table and chairs. I ran underneath the table and between his legs to enter the kitchen. He stumbled backward and fell.

In the kitchen, I ran inside the box with the door made of metal bars. It is where I had always taken shelter whenever Mark had been violent before. My whole body shivered uncontrollably as I listened to him shouting and swearing as he grabbed at the chairs to pull himself up. He came into the kitchen and kicked the box as hard as he kicked the cans sending it sliding across the kitchen floor. The box ended up with its door flung open facing Mark as he strode toward me.

The instinct of survival, I was to learn, is a stronger impulse than fear. It takes over when flight is no longer an option and a dog's only choices are to fight or die. I bared my teeth and made sounds I didn't know I was capable of. My breath foamed and flecked my saliva. Mark halted momentarily and crouched in the middle of the kitchen breathing heavily. His eyes were as wide as mine. I did not stop snarling and barking until I heard Mira scream.

"Get out!"

Mark stood up and looked in Mira's direction. His eyes which had flared with hatred as he stared at me inside the box moments earlier now seemed subdued.

"Get out!" Mira screamed again.

Mark held up one hand like he was waving goodbye. "Put the gun down, Mira," he said.

"Get out! I mean it!"

"You'd shoot me over a dog?" I heard a loud click. Then I saw Mark's knees start to wobble slightly and he wiped his brow with his forearm. "I'm sorry, okay? Let's talk this out."

"Get out before I call the cops!"

"Mira!" Mark had both hands raised now.

"No more! You said it yourself. No more!"

"So that's how it's going to be?" Mark lowered his arms slowly and stood trembling. "Okay. Okay, I'm leaving. But just remember, you made this choice. And you will regret it."

Mark disappeared into the entrance hallway. I heard the scuffling of his feet, and finally the slam of the door. But the apartment did not fall silent. Mira was sobbing. Mira was sobbing while I still shivered uncontrollably in my box. I wanted to go to her, but my legs would not obey me.

When my shivering finally subsided, I crept out of the box and stole quietly across the kitchen floor into the room with the sky wall. I found Mira lying on the couch. A shiny, black object with a small opening at one end and a dark, wooden handle at the other lay on the floor by her outstretched hand. I sniffed it and detected a faint smell of oil and smoke. I jumped up on the couch by Mira and curled up in the space between her stomach and her bent legs. She laid her hand over me and stroked my fur.

"I'm sorry, Pequeño," she said. She began to cry softly.

My heart hurt more that night than it had on the first night without my mother and my brothers and sisters. Mark and Mira had separated because of me. I suppose it should not have surprised me that Mark would return to the apartment later to separate me from Mira, too.

IV

In the weeks after Mark left the apartment, Mira spent more time in the studio than she ever had before. Mira hired a driver to pick us up in front of the apartment building in the morning and take us home every night. At night, he accompanied us to the apartment and did not leave until Mira closed the door behind us and set the latch in place. The apartment became little more than a place Mira and I slept at night. I think if the studio had a bed, we would have stayed there.

There was a hurt inside Mira now that had not been there before. She tried her best to conceal it, but she could not hide it from me. She did not speak as much to the other humans in the studio, and when she did, her voice had a different tone. In the apartment at night, I often heard her crying in the bedroom. I hopped up into the bed, curled up beside her in Mark's place, and did my best to comfort her. Even though Mark had made Mira cry more often than he made her laugh, the separation still caused her pain. Like dogs, humans choose to live in packs. Sometimes humans would rather be with someone who hurts them than live alone.

On a rare day we did not go into the studio, Mira slept late. When she finally stirred, I hopped out of the bed next to her and ran down the hall to the spongy mat to relieve myself. Sunlight already poured into the apartment through the sky wall.

Mira appeared in the kitchen still in her thin, white dress. She made herself a beverage she never offered me even though its aroma was moist and pungent like tree bark and gratifying to my nose. She sat on a stool at the half wall sipping her beverage from a large cup and slid her finger across the screen of a small computer she called a laptop. Like the computers in the studio, the laptop showed her pictures and it came with a board full of buttons Mira liked to push. The screen sometimes played sounds and voices just like a TV. But Mira could put the laptop in her bag and carry it with her.

"Pequeño," Mira called to me. I hopped out of my basket and trotted over to her. She turned the screen off and stood up. "I have to go out for a while this afternoon and I can't take you along. I'm meeting an investor in her big, fancy office. Wish me luck."

She bent over and lifted me up off the floor. I lay on my back in the crook of her left arm and grunted while she scratched my belly with her right hand. Later, when I was homeless, I would often go to sleep at night remembering the way Mira looked at that moment. Her gaze simply bathed me with affection and I felt so deeply loved.

"If I get the investment, Pequeño," she said, "I can hire more people, and then we can spend more time together like we used to."

I followed Mira to her bedroom and lay on the bed while she bathed. In front of her mirror, she combed her hair and swirled it into a bun on top of her head. She dressed in a skirt and a blouse and slipped on shoes that made her taller. I followed her out of the bedroom to the entrance hallway. She put on her leather jacket, grabbed the laptop off the half wall, and put it in the bag she always carried. She bent down and scratched my ears.

"We'll go for a walk when I get home," she said. "It is a nice day. *Hasta luego*, Pequeño."

Mira undid the latch. It was a rod that slid back and forth. She slid it one way when we went out and the other way when we came home. However, when she went out without me, there was no one to slide the latch. She opened the door and stepped out into the hall. The door closed behind her and she was gone. I would not see Mira again until I was much older.

I did not enjoy being in the apartment alone. In the studio, there were other humans to play with and things to do even when Mira was not there. In the apartment, my options were limited. I listened to sounds and tried to identify them. I played with my toys, but without Mira to tug the other end of the rope or throw my ball down the hallway, it wasn't much fun. Mostly, I curled up in my basket and napped although I was never fully asleep. I lifted my head at the slightest noise and moved my ears back and forward. The shush of the elevator doors.

Footsteps in the outside hallway approaching. The clicking of the round knob on the door as it turned. These were all sounds in sequence that signaled Mira's return.

Mira had not been gone long when I heard the elevator doors and footsteps in the hallway outside the apartment. They moved quickly and made a hard thump, not a soft patter like Mira's. I knew it was not Mira and did not get out of my basket even when the footsteps stopped by the apartment door. Other humans lived on our floor. Humans delivered packages to the humans who lived on our floor. Hard footsteps were not unusual. But I hopped out of my basket and ran to the entrance hallway when I heard the clicking of the doorknob.

I knew the human outside the apartment door did not have Mira's permission to come in. I began barking with as much alarm as I could muster. Sometimes my barking was enough to make a human go away. But the scraping and clicking in the door continued until it finally opened and Mark stepped in.

I barked more. I barked as loud as I possibly could, but there were no humans to hear or none who cared to intervene. Again, I would like to say I fought Mark and defended Mira's apartment, but I yielded ground as he walked down the entrance hallway. And when he lunged for me, I ran into my box in the kitchen. Although I kept barking, Mark did not try to pull me out or kick the box. He simply shut the door.

Mark walked around Mira's apartment breaking things and my barking did not stop him. When the sound of the crashing and breaking stopped, he walked into the kitchen. To my surprise, he picked up the box with me inside and shook it like I shook my toys. He shook the box until I felt dizzy and stopped barking. In between the metal bars of the door to my box, I saw broken glass and overturned furniture all because of me. I laid my head down and my ears back and whimpered. Perhaps it was just as well I should go.

Mark did not carry the box through the lobby and out the front doors of the apartment building. Instead, he took the elevator to the garage floor where the humans kept their cars. The garage was dimly lit and smelled of the fumes of cars. The smell of fumes made me feel worse. I closed my eyes and did not even notice the size or type of the vehicle Mark slid my box into. All I remember is the jostling, the thud of the car door closing, and the sound of the engine.

Dogs cannot tell time like humans in minutes and hours, but we have an inner clock. We are aware of time in the sense of short or long in comparison to the change of daylight and time based on the activities of our human companions. I could always tell when it was time for my walk. And I can tell the difference between a short drive in a car and a long one. The light was still bright in the sky when Mark took me from the apartment and was almost gone when the car engine finally stopped.

From inside my box, I could see the tops of leafy trees and a narrow swath of the darkening sky. For a moment, my heart raced with the hope that Mark had brought me back to the lady with the gray hair. Although my brothers and sisters would be full grown like me, I would still know them and my mother, and they would know me, by our scents. What a joyful reunion it would be!

The car door opened. Mark pulled my box out and set it on the ground. We were in a parking lot and there were trees all around, but I did not see houses or smell the scents of familiar dogs. Except for litter on the ground, there were no signs of humans at all. The sound of water came on a breeze, a steady quiet gurgling rather than the running of a faucet in Mira's bathroom or the spray of the spout in the city park's pond, but it was moving water nonetheless. My throat was dry. I hadn't had water to drink since earlier that day in the apartment and I barked hoping Mark would open the cage and let me go. Instead, he picked up my box, carried it to the middle of the parking lot, and set it down again.

Mark walked backed to the car. He opened a lid on the back of the car, pulled out a large can, and walked back to my box. I could smell the heavy odor from the can as soon as he lifted it out of the car, an odor of fumes that come from the back of cars and trucks when they are noisy, only much stronger and more irritating to my nose. He set the can down next to my box, bent down, and looked in through the metal bars.

I could not look Mark in his eyes. Instead, I showed him my teeth and snarled.

"*Diablo*," Mark said. "Go to Hell." He stood up, lifted the can, and poured a liquid over my box. The liquid made the fumes, and now that it was loose from the can, its odor was so strong it hurt to breathe it in. I would have breathed easier had I laid quietly inside the box with my paws over my nose, but fear compelled me to bark and scratch at the sides and run in circles.

Mark walked back to the car, placed the can inside, and closed the car lid. As he walked toward me, he took a white stick from his shirt pocket, put it in his mouth, and made it glow. He stood beside my box for a few moments breathing in on the white stick while I scratched and barked and choked on the fumes. When light suddenly swept over the parking lot, Mark dropped the white stick and ran. Another car had pulled in. I didn't see Mark get in his car and drive away because my box was engulfed in flames.

V

Every animal since Creation instinctively knows fire and fears it more than anything else. I heard it crackling and hissing and knew it wanted me. The heat inside my box built up quickly. In a coat of long hair, I should have laid still on the floor of the box with my nose in the blanket, and still I barked and scratched at the box and ran in circles. Only humans can make fire, and only humans can make it go away. If a human could not make it go away, I knew the fire would come for me. My box could only keep it away for so long.

I was not brave. I did not sit quietly and contemplate my death. Instead, I howled and scratched until my paws hurt and left blood smears on the walls. I howled more when I heard yelling and voices outside.

"There's a dog in there! Get the fire extinguisher!"

A few moments later, I heard a sound like the rush of air when a car window opens, and all I could see were white clouds. Clouds swirled inside my box, around the box, everywhere. I breathed in the clouds, too, and it nearly stopped me from breathing altogether. My eyes burned. I could neither smell nor see, though my ears still heard a jumble of sounds. The snapping of the dying flames. Heavy footsteps. Human voices.

"The sonofabitch tried to burn it alive."

"I'll call dispatch and give 'em a description of the vehicle."

I heard water again. Water splashed down all over the box. Then a hand jiggled the door with the metal bars.

"Ouch! Damn, the bars are still hot!"

Moments later, water splashed through the bars and wet my fur. When the door finally opened, I did not wait to see who it was or rejoice with jumps and tail wags to thank the humans who had saved my life. I burst through the open door and ran as fast as I could across the parking lot, into the woods, and toward the sound of running water. Unseen fingers ripped at my hair and slapped my face, but they did not slow me down. Fear is a powerful propellant. It drove me forward until I was up to my chest in wetness. I plunged my face into the water and drank deeply.

I had never seen a river before. Water stretched out ahead of me several times further than the width of the city park pond. There were lights from houses on the far bank that reflected in the water and offered the promise of shelter and food, but the water stretched out to my right and left as far as I could see.

For a long time, I simply stood in the cool river water as it swirled around me. The water took away the heat from my skin and the burning in my throat. My thirst had been quenched, but a gnawing hunger in my belly

The Meaning Of Home

remained. I thought of swimming toward the lights on the other side of the river, toward the world of humans and their comforts and safety. In the city, I had learned it was far better to live inside than outside. I had seen humans living outside, humans Mira called homeless who slept on park benches and on the sidewalks where steam came up from underneath the ground through metal bars. I did not want to live outside like them. Yet, I had not swam across anything but Mira's bathtub, and the river was so much wider. When the chill of the river water crept into my bones, I walked up on the bank and shook until my body warmth returned and my coat began to dry.

The open bank offered an easier path with mud to soothe my paws and no fingers to grab at my hair or slap my face. By now, the moon appeared above me in the sky. I saw one in the river, too. I kept one eye on the moons as I trotted off down the river bank and thought it was odd how they always seemed to stay in the same place no matter how far down the bank I had traveled.

There were no lights on my side of the river. Here and there along the river bank, humans had left things behind that smelled of fish or the food that had once been inside. I sniffed and licked, but not enough had been left behind to satisfy my stabbing hunger.

The river bank was a collection of new and wonderful smells, scent trails leading to and from the water, the droppings of creatures I had not known in the city, sweet mud, rotting wood, and human debris. Had I not still been scarred from my recent brush with death and in such need of food, curiosity would have compelled me to investigate each one closely and add what I learned to my knowledge. Instead, I hung by the edge of the woods slinking along tree to tree, ears up, nose down, eyes ahead.

I crossed a scent trail far stronger than the others, strong enough to make me stop and look to my left down to the water's edge. I saw the silhouette of a creature about my size sitting on its haunches in the water. And it was eating something!

The creature's hearing must not have been as keen as mine. I was nearly to the water before it whirled around and dropped whatever it was eating. It was not about to share. The creature rushed at me with sharp, white teeth bared and bathed in moonlight. It gnashed and clacked its teeth and made a sound like a woman screaming. I retreated to the tree line, but the creature did not pursue me. It was reluctant to stray far from the mound it had dropped in the mud that smelled of fish.

I sat on the riverbank and watched for a while hoping it would venture far enough away from the mound to give me a chance to swoop in with my speed, snatch it, and keep running. I could tell from the creature's movement it was not as fast as I was. It waddled when it walked. Its head was similar to mine with a long, narrow nose and whiskers, but its front legs were short. All its power was in its hind legs. And it had a tail as long as mine with dark rings.

Several times I crept toward it on my belly. Each time, it charged me with its snapping teeth and hideous screaming before I came close enough to attempt a steal.

When it had its fill, it ambled off into the woods with a last glaring look at me over its shoulder. All it left by the water's edge was a mound of bones and scaly skin with flecks of white flesh. I was so hungry, I crunched it down but promptly threw it up again. My stomach was not accustomed to fish carcasses.

I wandered on down the river bank in search of food. The sharp pangs in my stomach had diminished to a dull weariness that pervaded my entire body and my fatigue overpowered me. For a dog used to napping in a studio or apartment most of each day, the stress and exertion since I had left the apartment that morning had taken its toll.

I thought of Mira. I thought of her returning to the apartment and the broken glass and overturned furniture. She would call my name as she always did, but I would not answer. And when she walked into the kitchen, she would see my box was gone. I wondered what Mira was doing while I walked along the deserted river bank in the moonlight. Was she looking for me? I remembered the day I ran away from her in the city park and how upset and relieved she looked at the same time when the strange woman gave me back to her. *Don't do that again. If you ran away, I'd miss you so much my heart would break.* Now I was far away from the city park and I was not wearing my leash or the vest Mira had made to replace my collar. If I found another human, how would they know Mira was my companion?

I came to a fallen tree lying on the river bank. Where it once stood in the ground, its roots were raised up like the half wall in the apartment and underneath was a big hole that had filled in with leaves. I sniffed around the edge of the hole and cautiously crept in. I rooted amongst the leaves with my nose and paws to assure myself the hole was not already occupied before I curled up in my new bed. Beyond tired, hungry, and afraid, there was nothing else to do but sleep.

VI

The sound of cars aroused me. Across the river, cars were driving back and forth on a road further uphill from the river bank. The sky turned pretty colors again just like it did every morning outside the sky wall of the apartment and the sun soon brightened my bed of leaves just like it had my basket. It was the time of year when the air turned cooler and the leaves on the trees began to change colors and fall off.

I raised my head when I heard human voices. Soft. Faint. At first, I could not tell where the sound came from. I listened. They came again, this time loud enough to tell they were on my side of the river and back through the woods. The sharp pangs in my stomach had returned and reminded me humans were the best chance I had of finding food. Despite my lingering fears of what may await me on the other side, I started off through the woods.

The voices found me from time to time as I picked my way through the trees and brush. They were brash, sharp, and most likely male. I heard them more clearly the further I went, voices in conversation, not argument, responding to each other playfully and sometimes erupting in laughter.

Where the trees ended, I found myself at the edge of a wide clearing as big as the parking lot where Mark had left me, but this one was made of stones, not pavement. The smells were different. I did not see my box and the odor of car fumes, although present, was not as strong. At one end of the clearing, humans moved about among dwellings that, comparably for humans, did not look much bigger than my box. I saw several windowless box-shaped dwellings fashioned from wood and covered with plastic sheets. And there were round and square dwellings with fabric stretched between curved poles. Cuts in the fabric created windows and doors with flaps that were tied back to keep them open. Across the area occupied by the dwellings was another thin strip of woods. Through the trees, I saw cars moving back and forth, and beyond them, buildings.

Two men stood in front of one of the box-shaped dwellings with food in their hands, sandwiches with bread and turkey. My stomach twisted itself up in a knot and I licked my jaws. Theirs were the voices that had beckoned me. I had seen humans living in similar dwellings even in the city. They sprouted up occasionally in the city park until men in overalls came and tore them down. Mira had called the people who built the boxes "homeless," too, even though they had homes of a sort. From a dog's point of view, they simply weren't as big or as comfortable as Mira's apartment or the home I had been born in. In the city, the humans who were truly homeless slept on benches in the city park or on the sidewalk wrapped up in nothing more than blankets and coats and did not have food. I had not wanted to be like them, and yet there I stood, homeless, envying the humans' food and shelter.

The two men were still a distance away from me and unaware of my presence. Sticking to the tree line, I crept closer.

As I approached the nearest dwelling, the round kind, a small, gray-haired woman stepped out between two flaps of fabric and stood up. She wasn't much taller than her dwelling. Her face was marked with age. She had even more deep wrinkles and flaps of skin than the gray-haired woman who gave me to Mira, and her hair looked like the wild brush in the woods. She wore a gray coat that reached practically to her knees, a dark shirt, dark pants, and dirty sneakers. I gathered from her sunken cheeks and thin fingers she was not as round underneath as the gray-haired woman was in her clothes.

The old woman did not see me at first and walked over to a metal basket on wheels just like the ones Mira used at the store where she bought our food. Mira called it a shopping cart. The woman rummaged through the contents of the cart, an assortment of plastic bags and blankets, odds and ends, and eventually pulled a couple crusty rolls out of one of the bags. When I saw the rolls, my mouth began watering again. I watched her as she walked over to a small chair nearby, sat down, and began to eat.

It had been more than a day since I had eaten, and the rolls looked so much more pleasing than anything I had smelled along the river bank. Although I feared the woman would be unkind like the ring-tailed creature when it came to sharing her food, I was desperate. And seeking her kindness did not scare me as much as the thought of seeking kindness from men. I stepped out from the brush along the edge of the woods and sat down where she could see me, far enough from the dwelling I could easily run back into the woods at the first sign of trouble.

The old woman looked up from her roll. Her eyebrows rose, and she smiled. "Well, hello, Charlie. Where have you been?" Her teeth were discolored and there were gaps between some of them. She spoke in a melodious voice similar to Mira's although it, too, had been weathered by age. "I have been waiting for you."

I smiled. My mouth opened. My tongue hung forward just a little, but I wasn't panting. I held my head up with my ears perked and my eyes bright and questioning. And, of course, I wagged my tail. With my eyes fixed on the roll in her hand, I stood up, moved a little closer, and sat down again.

For anyone unaccustomed to my species who thinks we can't smile or frown or feel the emotions humans do, I assure you we can. Tail wags and bright faces are more than a simple instinctive response to a kind act or word from a human. As I sat in front of the old woman, I was truly happy to see a caring face as much as I was unhappy and anxious in Mark's presence. Happiness, sadness, fear, anger, contentment, loneliness and longing. If a human can feel it, so can a dog.

The woman broke off a piece of the roll and extended her hand. The smell of its sweet glaze tugged at my nose. I stepped up, took the offering from her hand gently, and backed away.

"They said you weren't coming back this time," the old woman said, "but I told them my Charlie would always come back when he was ready. You must be hungry." She held out the rest of the roll. I trotted forward and took it from her hand. This time, I lay at her feet and ate it.

The woman got up from her chair and went over to the shopping cart. I noticed she had a lighter step than when I had first seen her walk from her dwelling. She rummaged through her bags again and pulled out a plastic bag, a plastic jug and a metal bowl. When she came back to her chair, I could see she had more food inside the plastic bag. She opened it, removed half a sandwich, and laid it on the ground in front of me. I lost my manners and began to eat greedily complete with gulping noises and burps.

"The other half is for dinner," she said. Then she set the metal bowl in front of me. It was dull, dented and scratched, but still useful. She poured in water from the plastic jug, clear water still with the coolness of the night air. I stood up and lapped the water until there was nothing left in the bowl but the film of my saliva. With wet jaws and a full stomach, I lay down at her feet again feeling a measure of comfort and relief. She reached down. I rolled over on my back and allowed her to scratch my belly.

"You're a good boy, Charlie," she said.

I was no longer Pequeño, and I didn't much care what the old woman called me as long as she was willing to share her food.

The old woman put the bowl, the plastic jug and the half sandwich back in the shopping cart. As she did, she kept talking to someone although I did not see another human or dog nearby. "Jim, did you hear? Charlie's back. I told you he would come home. Just like I told you Billy will come home, too, when he's ready but you never listen to me. Billy will come home, and we'll have our boy back. You'll see."

My ears perked up at the sound of human voices approaching, the same ones I had heard through the woods that drew me to the clearing. The two men I had seen earlier were now walking toward the woods carrying long poles and small boxes. When they saw me, they stopped.

"Look at that, Al!" one said to the other. "Crazy Mary has company. Hey, Mary!" he said. "Who's your friend?"

Mary began grumbling and cursing. "Jim, I told you not to bring them around here!" she said. She did not look up at the men. "They're just lookin' to take me away again like they done the last time and I'm not goin'."

"Leave her alone, Bruce," the second man said. "She has enough torment."

"No one here has had it easy, Al," Bruce said. "She's the one who don't speak to no one unless it's to curse at them. She ain't right in the head."

"What happened to her affected her mind, no doubt," the man named Al said. "Only kindness may help her find her way back."

"Aw, c'mon Al," Bruce said. "You been lookin' out for her all this time and she curses you all the more. I don't know why you bother."

"It's not a bother," Al said.

Al turned and walked toward Mary's dwelling. He was a large man, taller than Bruce by a head, with dark skin, broad shoulders and muscular arms. Despite his strength, there were telltale signs of advanced age for a human, thinning gray hair and gray whiskers. He reminded me of the breed they call a bull dog. His face was square and rutted with wrinkles and his nose looked like the cap on a fire hydrant in between a pair of droopy eyes. I sat up and snarled and barked as he approached. I was having no parlay with men. My barking must have scared Mary because she covered her head with her arms and began screaming. "Stay away! Stay away! Help! Somebody! They're coming to take me away again! Stop! Stop!"

Al stopped and spoke in a low voice. "Mary, it's just me. Al. No one's going to take you away. The church bus comes around five this afternoon. How about coming with me, just this once?"

"Stay away! Stay away!" Mary yelled. The more she yelled, the more I barked. It was the least I could do in return for her kindness.

Bruce stood at a distance shaking his head. "I told you it's no use, Al," he said. "She can't be saved. Even by God."

Al turned and gave Bruce a sharp look before the two men walked off toward the river with their long poles and boxes. "God doesn't give up on anyone," Al said to Bruce, "Even you."

After the sound of their voices faded, Mary uncovered her head. She walked over, knelt beside me, and hugged me. "You kept them away," she said. "I knew you came back for a reason. You're a good dog, Charlie. You have always been a good dog."

VII

Mary stood up and pointed a long, bony finger at someone I could not see

"If it wasn't for Charlie, Jim, those men would have taken me away again. I'm not crazy, Jim, I swear it. Just because I don't believe my boy is dead? Just because I won't give up looking for him? What kind of mother gives up looking for her son? How come you gave up on him? How could you? Lockin' me up won't do me no good. I'm gonna look for him every day long as I'm breathing. I'm not goin' to quit til Billy comes home or I find him. One way or another. And now I have Charlie to help me."

Mary untied the flap on the door of her dwelling and let it close. She walked over to the shopping cart and pushed its handle. In the sparse grass and gravel around the dwelling, it did not move easily. The wheels left ruts in the dirt. But there was strength left in her withered frame, whether in her muscles or her will or a combination of both. She moved off several yards toward the thin strip of woods and the road beyond before she stopped and looked back at me.

"Well, Charlie? Are you coming?"

I was unrestrained by a collar and leash or even Mira's coat. Having eaten my fill, I could have run off into the woods to explore for the day and returned to the clearing when my stomach grumbled again. Yet, I chose to follow Mary like I chose to follow Mira around the studio. When I was hungry and scared, she fed me and showed me kindness. It seemed only fitting I should follow her. And so a new companionship began.

I trotted alongside the shopping cart as Mary followed a worn path across the clearing into the thin strip of woods on the far side. Other humans among the dwellings cast us dismissive glances and moved away. Since Mary moved slowly, I had plenty of opportunities for short side excursions to sniff human debris laying among the gravel and leave a new scent trail for myself.

When we reached the road, Mary pushed the cart along its paved edge where its wheels turned easily. I stayed off inside the woods away from the cars. They moved much faster here, and there weren't any sidewalks with corners for them to stop and give us a turn. We reached a place where there were colored lights on poles just like the ones in the city and the cars finally stopped and allowed us to cross.

Across the road, there were long buildings with tall glass windows, pictures, and signs with big words like "SALE." The buildings were surrounded by parking lots as wide as the city park pond and filled with cars. As Mary wheeled the shopping cart through the parking lots, other humans walked in between the buildings and their cars. They never came as close to us as humans walked next to each other in the city. In fact, it seemed the humans in the parking lots walked even further away from us after they saw us to avoid crossing our path. Mary paid them no attention.

"We'll go to the playground later, Charlie," Mary said. "You and Billy used to play there, remember? Before they built all these stores. Jim, remember how they used to play in these woods after school—all day on the weekends—come home all muddy?" Mary laughed. Her laughter still haunts me when I recall it. It had a bright tone like a birdsong and yet something about it also made me feel sad.

"Remember how he and Billy walked through these woods every day to school and come home until …" Mary's voice trailed off into a mumble. I heard only a few of her words. "Charlie—came home— I didn't remember." Then she moaned. "I forgot to let Charlie out to bring him home!"

Mary began sobbing right there in the middle of the parking lot. "Jim, they took our boy!" She bent over the handle of the shopping cart and let her tears fall into the bowl she used to give me a drink of water. "If I'd a let you out that day, Charlie, maybe Billy woulda come home. Oh, you looked everywhere for him. I know you did."

A young woman weaving through the cars with two children, a boy and a girl, stopped and stared, but then shooed them off in another direction. Mary recovered her composure and wiped her face on the sleeve of her gray coat. Glancing off toward something unseen, she put her hands back on the handle of the cart and pushed on.

The storefronts were shiny glass like the sky wall of Mira's apartment. Behind the glass were many curious and wonderful things. Tiny, sparkly stones and shiny rings. Pots and pans. TVs and laptops. Inside one store, humans were stuffing clothes into large white machines with small round doors. In another store, they sat down at tables and ate food. I wanted to linger there. The smells coming through the door when it opened and closed reminded me of stores along the sidewalks in the city where humans ate. Baked bread. Cooked meat. Varieties of cheese. Mary did not seem to notice the smells and walked on.

When we reached the last store at the end of the row, my heart began to beat like the wings of the city park geese. In the glass, I saw Mira's and my own reflection staring back at me. I remembered how Cindy had shown me the reflection in the city and said I was famous. I ran to the window and barked and jumped up and down and spun around in circles. Surely, someone would notice me and take me back to Mira. But no one did. The humans along the sidewalk in front of the stores ignored me just as they had Mary. When I tired and sat panting in front of the glass, I noticed my reflection had changed. I was much smaller. My long, cream colored hair was now dark and snarled with bits of brush and leaves. Even my white tail was more like the color of Mary's hair. And I was bare. No buttons. No bowtie. I no longer resembled myself.

"Charlie?" I heard Mary's voice behind me. "Charlie? I'm sorry. I have no money to buy you anything in there. But I'll find you a bone, Charlie. And we'll have food. Somehow, I always manage to find something to eat."

Mary looked at me, and at Mira and I in the glass, but said nothing more. She could not see I was the same dog. To her, I was Charlie and I would never be Pequeño.

We walked around behind the long building. At the rear, the parking lot was narrow and there were no cars parked there. There were no glass windows either, only doors and trash bins and piles of human debris. Mary poked through them for anything that caught her fancy. She found some forks and knives, the kind humans use and throw away, and she put them in a bag in her cart. She picked up a broom with a broken handle. Mary was especially pleased to find sheets of clear plastic bubbles inside cardboard boxes and she put them in the cart also.

I noticed movement around a trash bin a few doors away and recognized the tail of a cat extending from behind it. I had glimpsed cats in the city on my walks with Mira and was familiar with the strong odor of their urine. In my limited experience, cats were furtive creatures found in alleys, garages and other dark places and were more often smelled than seen. Unlike dogs, cats did not come forward with cheerful greetings and tail wags anxious to smell your scent. On the few occasions I came face to face with a cat in the city, it always hissed and spat at me and ran away.

I crept toward the trash bin with my eyes fixed on the cat's rust-colored tail. When a door suddenly opened nearby, an orange and white tabby darted out from behind the bin and headed for a tangled thicket of short trees and briars strewn with rubbish where the parking lot ended. The instinct to taste, to smell, to discover overcame me and the chase was on. In the open, it was a close race.

In my youth, I loved to run. I loved the wind in my face and the feel of warm blood surging through my body when I was moving at full speed. I loved the unrestricted feeling of running until my energy was spent. It may seem strange for anyone to miss any part of being homeless, but I sometimes miss that unfettered opportunity to run with all the vigor and delight of a young dog.

The cat's short hair, narrow body, and agile feet enabled it to slide more easily than I through the tangle of stalks and roots in the thicket. A few feet into the thicket, fingers of briars scratched at my face and pulled at my already knotted hair. When the cat's tail slid out of sight, I backed out of the thicket and promptly marked it to let the cat know it now lived in my territory.

I returned to find Mary standing at the open door of the building talking to a man wearing a white apron over a dark, short-sleeved shirt and dark pants. It was the first time I saw her have a conversation with someone I could see. He was a heavy man, large and round, but not muscular, and his face was flabby with a prominent double chin.

The smells coming through the open door were the same odors I had smelled in front of the building where the humans went inside to eat. Mary clutched a brown paper bag that smelled of rolls and meats. The man looked at me and laughed when I sat down panting at Mary's feet.

"There's a new sheriff in town!" the man said. I liked his smile and the deep, hearty sound of his laughter. He was almost as big as Al, and since I had never seen Mary this close to Al, he made Mary look even smaller in comparison. The man had no hair on top of his head. His beard, however, was black and thick and trimmed close around his mouth and the first of his two chins.

Mary was smiling. "Thank you for the sweet rolls," she said. "Billy loves them."

"Might as well have them," the man said. "You wouldn't believe the food I throw out every day from the day before. But let's keep this our secret, huh? I can't have the entire camp coming over here. If the health department knew I was feeding the homeless out of the back of my deli, they'd shut me down." Mary nodded, but did not answer. "How about something for your dog?"

The man stepped inside the building and came back a few minutes later with a handful of thinly sliced meat. He knelt down and held out his hand. I sniffed the meat cautiously, gently lifted it out of his hand, then trotted a few steps away to eat it as was my custom. "Better learn to eat faster," the man said to me. "There are bigger dogs around here who will steal your lunch."

"His name is Charlie," Mary said.

"How come I haven't seen him before?" the man asked.

"He's been gone for a while," she replied. "Went looking for Billy again, I suppose. He misses him."

The man smiled sadly and shook his head. I sensed he wanted to say something to Mary, but he shook his head again as though he dismissed the thought as a bad idea.

"You will tell me if you see him?" Mary asked. She looked up at the man with wide, sorrowful eyes. "He could be homeless, too."

"Of course, Mary," he said. "If I see him, I'll bring him right to you."

Mary's mouth curled upward ever so slightly. "Thank you," she said. She set the brown paper bag in the shopping cart. "I have to go now. The school will be letting out soon."

Mary pushed the shopping cart on down the parking lot behind the building. As I followed her, I looked back over my shoulder and saw the man still standing next to the open door shaking his head.

At the end of the parking lot where the thicket began, a worn footpath meandered around the thicket downhill toward a stream, though it was not much of a stream. More like a gully. It was choked with vegetation and more human debris and had only the tiniest trickle of water running through it.

Before we started downhill, Mary pushed the shopping cart into an open space in the thicket where it could be seen only by someone who happened to walk right past it. She glanced around. By now, the man in the apron had gone inside. Satisfied she had not been seen stashing her cart, Mary ambled down the footpath ahead of me.

About halfway to the stream, I picked up the trail of the orange and white tabby and veered off into the vegetation. Its scent was strong, and I could tell it was not far away. I heard Mary struggling to keep up with me after she followed me into the tall grass and briars.

"Did you find something, Charlie? Did he go that way?"

The cat's trail circled back across the footpath further down, then started back uphill. If I raced up the footpath, I was sure I could cut it off and lie in wait at the edge of the parking lot for the cat to appear.

"Charlie, where are you? Charlie?" Mary was behind me still wading through the vegetation. Her voice had the same frantic tone as Mira's the day I ran away from her in the city park. I abandoned my pursuit of the cat and trotted down the footpath toward Mary instead. When she saw me, she smiled a big, toothy smile. "Good boy, Charlie! You've always been a good dog." I suppose I had matured since my run at the city park geese. Or perhaps it was the heartbreak in her voice that bent my will to hers.

A couple boards had been laid over the gully at the bottom of the hill where the footpath met the stream. We crossed and started up the other side where the grass was not as tall. I zig-zagged back and forth in front of Mary looking for any scent trail that might interest me until the grass became as sparse as it was in the area around Mary's dwelling. I noticed several rusted metal objects rising from the ground ahead of me like monstrous insects. One looked like a large, metal dish big enough for humans to stand on and had U-shaped bars rising up along its edge. Another simply had a gray board with handles at either end across a rusty rail. One end of the board was up in the air and the other touched the ground. A third object looked like a giant metal spider large enough for a human to ride.

The rusted objects sat in back of a red brick building with boards where windows used to be and some windows higher up with broken glass. Chains were wrapped around the handles of the only doors I saw.

"School will be out soon," Mary said quietly. "Why don't we wait here a moment." She walked over to a small bench and sat down. I lay down at her feet happy to have a moment's rest. I was not accustomed to the exertion.

The moment turned into several, and then a quantity of moments I measured by the length of the shadows beginning to stretch across the schoolyard. Occasionally, people walked by on a sidewalk out in front of the school and cars passed by on the road beyond. No one paid any attention to an old woman sitting on a bench or the dog beside her. Every now and then, Mary would ask, "Do you see the boys and girls? Do you see Billy?" I lifted my head and perked my ears. I could not tell whether she was speaking to me or Jim and I did not see anyone but the passersby on the sidewalk.

Leaves drifted down from the two trees in the schoolyard and landed nearby. The shadows cast by the school building and the trees crept across the schoolyard and nearly touched us before Mary stood up. "I guess Billy went on ahead," she said. "Time to go home."

We started back the way we came, across the schoolyard and down the grass covered slope behind it, across the gully and up the footpath around the thicket to where Mary had hidden the shopping cart. As we walked through the parking lot, Mary moved slowly as though extra weight from the few objects she added to the basket now made it harder to push. She stopped several times and looked back in the direction of the school before we finally crossed the road at the colored lights and returned to the clearing with the round dwelling Mary called home.

When we reached the clearing, a big yellow bus had parked in the gravelly area with its engine running and men and women from the camp were getting on. I saw Al standing next to the open door. He waved.

"Mary," he yelled. "Come get some dinner and clean up. You can park your cart inside my shelter until we get back. No one will bother it." Al started to walk toward us, but Mary started screaming.

"Stay away! Stay away! Jim, I keep telling you don't you bring those men around here." With renewed strength, Mary pushed the shopping cart in the opposite direction and took the long way around the camp to her dwelling. When we arrived, she took some of the food the man with the apron gave us, ate it, and gave some to me. She set the metal bowl down and poured water into it. As I washed down my dinner, I heard the engine of the yellow bus grow louder and the crunch of gravel underneath heavy tires. I wondered where it was taking the humans from the camp and whether it would bring them back. I wondered if the yellow bus could take me back to Mira. Though I was free to leave Mary at any time, I did not have the slightest sense of how to get back to the city. I only knew it was far. Inside my box on the floor of Mark's car, full of his scent and the smell of white sticks, I had been deprived of sights or smells outside the car that may have given me a direction.

I slept that night inside Mary's dwelling in a space no bigger than the hole formed by the uprooted tree. I discovered Mary used the sheets of plastic bubbles to lay on the floor of her dwelling like the carpet in the apartment. She covered them with blankets and we lay on top. Mary took off her coat and climbed into a puffy blanket with a zipper I had seen some of the homeless people in the city wrap themselves in. I sniffed among the other blankets she had lying around the dwelling looking for one that pleased me.

Mary's dwelling contained but one piece of furniture, a tiny table too small for any human. On it, stood three faded photographs in wood frames. In the smaller frames were photographs of a young boy and a slightly taller, young girl. The boy had wavy, light-colored hair, bright eyes, and a big smile that showed his two front teeth sticking out a little further than the others. He wore a striped shirt. Because of the age of the photograph, it was difficult to tell the colors. Everything looked black or white or yellow, and only the boy's head and shoulders were visible.

The girl's hair was straight, the same light color, and shoulder length as far as I could see because that is where her picture ended, too. She wore a light-colored blouse and a necklace with a small cross hanging from it. Although she smiled, her lips were closed as though she hadn't wanted anyone to see her teeth.

The Meaning Of Home

In the larger frame, the same young boy and girl appeared in a photograph with a man and a woman. In this photograph the humans were standing, the man and woman behind the young boy and girl. I could see the similarities between the couple and their children. But what caught my attention was the dog in the photograph seated next to the boy. Although it may have been a little larger in size, it looked just like me.

I found a blanket with a musty odor of dirt and leaves I preferred to others smelling of cars or smoke from the white sticks and curled up in its folds. The air inside the dwelling turned much cooler than the air inside Mira's apartment at night, but I was warmer underneath the blanket than I had been the night before in my bed of leaves. Warmth is where a home begins.

The sounds inside Mary's dwelling at night were different, too. I had never heard a human snore before and was startled by the grunts and growls that came from Mary's mouth. Outside, the cars seemed much closer. I heard the tires on the road but not as many horns. And the creatures in the woods made strange night sounds, trills and chirps and croaks.

I lay in the folds of my blanket listening, guessing, and wondering about the sounds outside and tried not to be afraid. I made a game of trying to match the sounds to familiar things from my memory until I recognized the sound of the yellow bus engine followed by the crunch of gravel underneath its tires. A few moments later, human voices joined the chorus of night sounds. Some were singing. Some were talking. They spread out through the camp as the bus engine revved up again and the renewed crunching of gravel signaled its exit from the parking lot. I listened to the sound of human footsteps dispersing among the dwellings, but one set of footsteps grew more distinct. Someone was approaching.

I sat up and barked. At first, Mary continued snoring. The footsteps stopped right outside the tent. I barked again. Mary rolled over and grunted and coughed.

"Charlie? Who is it, Charlie? Is someone there?"

I got up and slipped out between the closed flaps and barked more. A tall figure stood by Mary's shopping cart with a large bag in his hand. I recognized Al's scent from earlier that day and began to growl. Al had not been unkind to me, but Mary did not want him, and I did not think he should be taking Mary's things. Al left the bag on the ground by Mary's cart and walked away before Mary stumbled through the flaps of her dwelling.

"Who is it, Charlie? Who is it, boy?" I continued barking and ran after Al a short distance. When I returned, Mary had walked over to her shopping cart and was inspecting the contents of the bag Al left on the ground. She pulled out a coat and blanket and held them up to her face. They held the fresh scent of washed clothes and it stirred a memory from Mira's apartment when I found her clothes neatly folded and stacked in a white basket. I remembered Mira's excited shout when she found me curled up among the clothes inside.

"Oye, Pequeño!" she had said. "This is not for you!" She gently lifted me out of the white basket and carried me to my own basket in the room with the sky wall.

"This is your basket." She sat me inside and walked away laughing. Mira had a way of making me feel wanted even when she corrected me.

Mary searched the pockets of the coat. She went through the contents of her shopping cart, bag by bag, to assure herself nothing had been taken, and then went back inside her dwelling with the new coat and blanket underneath one arm.

"Why won't they leave me alone, Charlie?" Mary asked as she pulled the puffy blanket over her. "Bad men took Billy away and they tried to take me away, too. Why won't they stop?"

I did not think Al was a bad man and I did not think he wanted to hurt Mary, but I did not know how to explain that to her.

VIII

Dogs have routines just like humans. Routines give structure to daily life and provide familiarity in times of uncertainty. Perhaps that is why I chose to make Mary's routine my own.

We arose with the daylight and sounds of increased human activity, walked off into the woods, and did on the leaves what I used to do on the spongy mat. We shared our morning meal in front of the dwelling she called her tent, often a roll or bread and, on occasion, deli meats and sweets from the man in the apron. Sometimes, Al left food in shiny metal wrapping in Mary's shopping cart. I noticed Al was a frequent visitor to Mary's tent, although Mary was hard of hearing and would not have heard anyone outside even if they stomped their feet. I could always tell the sound of Al's footsteps and his scent and I stopped barking and alarming Mary when I knew it was him.

Every day, Mary and I followed the trail around the camp and through the woods to the road and went across to the stores and parking lots. Every day, I'd sit and stare at the image of Mira and I in the window for a little while until, one day, the image disappeared. In its place was an image of a woman holding a cat. I did not know humans had any affection for cats or that a cat could be famous like me. The cats in the back of the store by the trash bins were the same variety as the city cats that hissed and spat at me and ran away.

And every day, Mary hid her shopping cart in the thicket and walked to the bench in the schoolyard where she sat down and waited for Billy. Only Billy never came. Often, Mary became angry with Jim as she sat on the bench and cursed him for giving up on Billy and bringing the men that took her away, but I never saw Jim in all the time I was Mary's companion.

The season passed to the time when the trees were mostly bare of leaves and white flakes of snow fell from the sky instead of rain. It was the time of year in the city Mira always had me wear a coat on our walks outside. The sun was not as long in the sky, the air grew much colder, and the wind seemed to peck at my haunches like the city park geese.

My hair grew even thicker and more matted than it had been in my first few weeks of homelessness. I was looking far more foxlike than Pomeranian. In Mary's tent, I was warm enough underneath the blankets on most nights, but on the nights when the water in my bowl froze solid, the cold was unrelenting. I remembered the homeless in the city sleeping on top of the metal bars in the sidewalk when the weather turned cold and the steam that came up from underneath, but the only source of heat inside Mary's tent besides Mary was me.

One night, I heard Mary tossing and turning inside her puffy blanket. She unzipped the zipper and then called to me. "Charlie? Here, boy." I slipped out from underneath my blanket, already shivering myself, and crept inside the puffy blanket with Mary. She pulled up the zipper while I nestled in between her body and the blanket with my nose poking out just far enough to breathe. Mary reached over and pulled my blankets on top of us. Although our shivering subsided, I could only dream of the warmth I remembered from the baskets in the home I had been born in and Mira's apartment.

There were mornings I did not want to get out from underneath the blankets. The cold chill in my nose when I breathed in was enough to deter me from venturing out on my own. But the cold did not deter Mary. When she threw off the blankets, my day began anyway. Some mornings were so cold, the wheels of her shopping cart had frozen in the ground and would not budge no matter how hard she pushed. On those days, she simply selected a bag from her cart and carried it with her.

Al never stopped trying to persuade Mary to get on the yellow bus and sleep the night in the church. From the tone of his voice, I could tell he was genuinely concerned. We returned from our walk one day to find a tall metal barrel with a fire inside standing near Mary's tent. A pile of wood lay next to it and an area like a circle around the barrel had been cleared of grass and sticks and covered with gravel. At first, the fire frightened me and the sound of the wood in the barrel crackling and snapping brought back memories of being inside my box with the fire engulfing it. I barked at Mary and backed away. I did not want her to go near the fire. Although I barked furiously, she walked forward slowly with her arms extended. After she stood by the barrel for a few moments, Mary did the strangest thing. She took off her coat.

"It's okay, Charlie," she said. "Come, stay warm." She picked up the little chair she sat on when she ate her meals and carried it closer to the barrel. She sat down and removed food from the bag the man in the apron had given us that day. "Come, Charlie," she said again. "Have something to eat."

I walked closer. I did not need to walk as close as Mary to feel the heat spreading outward from the barrel and ate my dinner at the edge of the gravel circle. The heat from the barrel even spread far enough to give a little warmth to the tent. Sometimes during the night, I heard Al's footsteps outside walking around on the gravel and the sound of wood clunking against metal and the hungry snapping and crackling of the fire as it devoured the wood. Mary slept through it all.

I had learned to trust Al. I knew far more of his comings and goings than Mary did and recognized he meant to help her. Perhaps because of his size, Al commanded the respect of the other residents of the camp. While he talked easily in conversation with others and had a deep, belly laugh like the man with the apron, he also barked human words as loud as the large dogs in the city had barked at me. On occasion, a human would bark back, but more often they slunk away with their heads down like a dog with its ears back and its tail between its legs.

On another cold day, Al stood within earshot of Mary's tent with another man I did not recognize. Al always stood a few tents away and pretended as if he paid us no mind at all. The man with Al was much younger. He wore a long, dark coat and kept his hands inside the pockets. From what I could see of his pants, they were a dark blue or black and tucked inside the tops of his ankle high black boots. The man wore a hat that looked like a silver cat curled up on top of his head.

While Mary napped in the tent, my curiosity got the best of me. I trotted closer toward the two men and listened.

"I can't get her on a bus to go to the shelter or the church for a shower or even a meal," Al said to the other man. "Some of them complain about the way she smells, although I doubt anyone has gotten close enough to her to get a really good whiff. She starts screaming bloody murder if anyone comes within ten feet. Thinks we're all out to commit her to a psychiatric hospital."

"Maybe it's the help she needs?" the other man said.

"Is it?" Al asked. "To be shackled and doped up til her mind is so washed she can't even talk? That isn't the kind of peace she needs."

"Do you think she'll speak to me?"

"I doubt it," Al said. "Many have tried. The local cops know her and told me her story once. They all have stories how they got here, but hers is worse than most."

"What happened?"

"She and her husband, Jim, lived near here in one of those neighborhoods that sprouted up around the steel mills after the war. They had a boy, Billy, and a girl. I never learned her name. Well, the little boy went to an elementary school just a mile or so from here. Close enough to home that he walked back and forth through these woods to school. Back then, these were all woods, I'm told. Acres and acres of them. The shopping center wasn't here, and the highway was just a two-lane river road. No one gave a thought to where their kids went to play, and everyone left their doors unlocked at night.

"In the mid-sixties, little boys playing in these woods began to disappear. Billy was one of them. The cops eventually caught the guy, and he told them where some of the bodies were, but they never found Billy's. Mary simply refused to believe Billy was dead. They say she walked all through these woods searching for him. People tried to get her help. She was in an institution, once, but they couldn't keep her there. Eventually, the husband moved away with the daughter and Mary began living on the streets. They say she was among the first of the homeless to live in these woods."

The other man shook his head.

"We leave her plenty of food and water and she has clothes and blankets. I keep the barrel going for her when the temperature drops below freezing, but I'm taking a risk, and everyone knows it."

"Has anyone said anything?"

"Not from the township. Not yet. But several residents think the fire will attract unwanted attention. They say let her freeze if she's too stubborn to get on the bus."

"Our work here is to save lives."

"Of course, Father. I have no intention of letting her freeze even if it means staying up nights to keep the fire going."

In my heart, I knew these were good men. There comes a time for dogs, like humans, to ignore the knots in your stomach and make new friends. I trotted out to greet them.

"Where'd he come from?" the man in the dark coat asked.

Al smiled. "That's Charlie, Mary's new friend," he said. "It's a good thing he's living with her now. It's like Heaven sent a guardian angel to see her through another winter."

My ears perked up when I heard my name. I knew they were speaking of me. I did not know what it meant to be a guardian angel, and if I had known, I would have told them I was not a very good one. In truth, Al was Mary's guardian angel and he might have saved her had he been there when she died.

IX

Mary died in the season humans call Spring when slender green stalks were poking up through the leaves in the woods and the air had changed from the dry, biting cold to a cool moistness. Little puffs of color were dotting the tree tops and new birds appeared in the clearing, little black ones with red bellies and orange beaks. I had seen a few in the city park when the warmer weather arrived, but they were more plentiful here. I'd lay outside Mary's tent and watch them hop and bend their heads. While they were a curiosity, I never had the urge to taste one.

Al had rolled the barrel away. The black circle it left behind in the gravel remained as a mark of his kindness. The yellow bus still rolled in and out of the gravel parking area regularly, and Al pleaded and cajoled and endured Mary's profane outbursts, but Mary never got on.

The morning of our last walk together, Mary seemed especially sad as though the day held a special meaning that set it apart from others. She began talking to Jim shortly after she stirred and threw off the blankets.

"Jim, it's Billy's birthday today. Did you remember?" She sat there amidst the blankets looking at her hands. "How old is he today? I'm his mother! I should know old he is!" She began to cry softly. "How old am I?" Mary's cry, like Mira's, elicited from me an almost instinctive response. I felt compelled to get up and curl up in her lap as if a force beyond my control lifted me up and put me there. I felt her hand in my fur, shaky, calloused, but loving.

Mary reached over and picked up the small photograph of the little boy in the wooden frame, clutched it to her chest, and began rocking back and forth. She rocked back and forth for quite a while. Her tears left tracks through the dirt on her cheeks. I carried my own grief, though I had only memories of Mira and my mother and brothers and sisters to hold onto. Few might see a similarity between an old woman and a young dog, but we took solace from each other.

She set the photograph next to the others on the tiny table and wiped her face with a corner of a blanket. "Charlie, I have to get Billy a present today," she said. Her resolve returned.

After our morning meal, we set off with the shopping cart on our usual route. I saw Al standing outside his big box home. He smiled and waved. Mary ignored him, but I took the opportunity to run over for a treat and a pat on the head. Al had begun dropping treats around the tent for me during the cold weather. I suppose he was trying to buy my silence which was fine with me, and after our formal introduction, I often went looking for him while Mary slept. If Mary was displeased by my friendship with Al, she never let it show.

Across the highway, Mary pushed her cart past the same row of stores with all the curious things in their windows. Some of the store windows were decorated with pictures of colorful bird eggs and large, white rabbits. In the window of the last store in the row, there was a new image of Mira where she and I had once been. When I saw it, I felt a horrible, empty, sick feeling in my stomach and pain in my chest. Humans call it heartbreak. Mira's reflection gazed out from the window happily, but she was holding another dog, a small dog with long white hair, bright pink bows behind its ears, and a pink collar studded with sparkly stones around its neck, no doubt of Mira's design. I did not know it was possible to feel worse than I did the night Mark took me from Mira's apartment, but the sight of Mira holding another dog crushed my hope of one day being reunited with her.

I suppose I had expected Mira to look for me, like Mary did for Billy. I suppose I thought if I stayed in one place long enough, not far from where Mark left me, Mira would find me, or someone would notice me and tell her where I was. I never dreamed Mira would replace me. But then again, I should not have assumed I meant as much to Mira as a human child, like Billy, means to his mother and perhaps I set myself up for heartbreak by expecting too much.

My thoughts were in a jumble. I imagined the little white dog trotting around Mira's apartment and sleeping in my basket or next to her on the bed. It would be the center of attention in the studio. I barely noticed Mary's excited cackle when she found a ball with black and white squares in a pile of debris behind the stores. It did not matter to her that the ball was not perfectly round.

The orange and white tabby appeared from behind a trash bin, and I ignored it. It sat at the edge of the parking area licking its paws, perplexed by my inaction, and probably suspected a trick. I lay on the ground near Mary with my head between my front paws and moved only when she did. The man in the apron did not come out of the back door when Mary knocked so she moved on down to the end of the parking lot and hid her shopping cart in its usual hiding place inside the thicket.

Instead of wandering off into the vegetation searching for interesting scents, I followed Mary down the footpath close by her heels. I lay underneath the bench while Mary waited for Billy perhaps for the first time with some understanding of the depth of her sorrow and the grief that comes from having been given up on. I fell asleep dreaming of the feel of Mira's arms, her scent, and the sound of her voice.

"Charlie? Charlie, let's go home."

When my eyes opened, however, I was still underneath the playground bench with Mary. Mary still wanted me. As we walked back along the path toward the parking lot, I thought of dogs I had seen in the city without any human companion. Their bones showed through their skin and their eyes were dull and cold. In the camp with

Mary, I still had a bed, shelter, food, and companionship. I had a place to go home to even if it was not a home like Mira's. I suppose home can be just a matter of how you look at it.

When we reached the top of the footpath by the thicket, Mary screamed and became highly agitated. Her shopping cart was gone.

"Jim! Jim! Damn you! Damn those men! You bring back my things! You bring back Billy's birthday present! Damn you! I told you not to bring them around here!"

Mary stormed out of the thicket into the parking lot still screaming. She spied her shopping cart about the same time I did, further down behind the stores, and the three men standing by it.

"Stop! Police! Police!" she yelled and rushed toward them as fast as her spindly legs would carry her. "They took my boy!"

I ran toward the men. With my speed, I reached them well before Mary and wanted to stop them from stealing her things. I ran in a circle around them and barked. Yet, I felt the hair on my neck bristling and the troubling sense of danger as if someone was telling me I should run the other way.

"It's the crazy bitch from the camp," I heard one of the men say as Mary came closer.

"Let's split," another said. "She might recognize us."

"No, let's have some fun with her," said the third man wearing a black, hooded sweatshirt. He took the ball Mary found for Billy and threw it at her. "Here. Catch!" It hit Mary's head and stunned her.

When I saw the ball hit Mary's head, I forgot my fear and felt a surge of anger, the same warm, uncontrollable sensation that had seized me when I saw Mark grab Mira's shoulder. I jumped up on the man in the black, hooded sweatshirt and bit his leg through the fabric Mira called denim. The man screamed in pain and cursed. He whirled around and kicked me hard with his boot. The force of the blow sent me tumbling in the parking lot and I felt a shooting pain in my hind quarters far worse than the bites from the geese. The man came toward me again. I tried to limp away on three legs, but the pain stole my speed. He would have surely kicked me again, no doubt to death, if Mary had not stopped him. She pounded her fists on his back and swore at him worse than I had ever heard her swear at Al.

And she kept shouting. "You took my boy!"

The man pulled something shiny from the pocket of his black hooded sweatshirt. He spun around and thrust his hand into Mary's stomach. Mary stopped yelling and groaned. When he stepped back, she fell to her knees in front of him clutching her stomach. A dark liquid began seeping through her fingers.

The other men still stood by the cart. When they saw Mary fall, their faces turned pale and their eyes were big and round.

"What did you do?" the one man asked as he stared at Mary.

"I shut her up," said the man who kicked me.

A door slammed open behind me. The man with the apron stepped out waving a small gun like the one

Mira pointed at Mark in the apartment. When the three men saw it, they ran off down the parking lot into the thicket.

The man with the apron rushed over and knelt next to Mary. He held her head in his lap and pressed his hands against her stomach. Soon, his hands were covered in the dark liquid, too.

I tried to hobble back to Mary, but the man in the apron pushed me away. His fingers left drops of the sticky, dark liquid rich with Mary's scent in my fur. The air filled with the sound of sirens from the cars and trucks with the flashing lights, a black and white car first, then another, and then a red and white truck. The man with the apron slipped his gun into a pocket of the apron and stepped back as other men and women crowded around Mary. Two men ripped off her coat and shirt and pressed white bandages against her stomach while the woman stuck something in her arm. They laid her on a bed with wheels and rolled her into the back of the red and white truck. In less time than it took the orange tabby to run across the parking lot, the truck had raced off toward the highway with its siren wailing.

The man with the apron stood motionless while I sat at his feet. My hind quarters were throbbing. A man in a blue uniform with yellow stripes on the sides of his pants walked over to the man in the apron.

"Whose dog?"

"He followed her around," the man in the apron said. "I'll take care of him."

"We'll need your help to identify the men who did this."

"Whatever you need," the man in the apron said. "Mary was troubled, but she didn't deserve this."

"Do you know her?" the man in the striped pants asked.

"She's from the homeless camp across the highway," the man in the apron said. "Most days, she walks by here on her way to the old elementary school and then goes back to the camp later on."

"Crazy Mary," the man in the striped pants said.

The man in the apron nodded. "I've heard some call her that. I prefer to say troubled."

"We tried to help her," the man in the striped pants said and walked away. All the lights stopped flashing and the cars drove off leaving me alone with the man in the apron. He reached down to lift me up. I yelped in pain and hobbled a few steps away.

"Oh, you're hurt, too?" He knelt beside me. "You're a good dog, Charlie. I know you tried to help her. Maybe she'll pull through. Let me go find something to carry you in."

I knew he meant well, but as soon as he stepped inside the store, I hobbled off into the parking lot out of sight. I had to find Al.

X

I hadn't witnessed a human dying before, but from Mary's stillness as she lay on the ground and the smell of the dark liquid that stained my fur, I understood her life was in danger. Strange thoughts troubled me as I limped across the parking lot toward the highway. What would happen to Mary's shopping cart? Was I allowed to sleep in Mary's tent if Mary was not in it? The constant, shooting pain in my hind legs made the parking lot that once seemed no bigger than the city park pond now seem wider than the river. I had to stop and rest every few minutes until the pain subsided. But I never rested for long. Only Al could answer my questions.

At the colored lights, I started across the highway. Normally, I crossed ahead of Mary in plenty of time before the cars started moving again, but with the hindrance of the pain in my hind legs I was only halfway across when the color of the lights changed. The sound of revving car engines paralyzed me. Seconds later, the whoosh of car tires in front of and behind me blew my hair like the hair dryer Mira used after she gave me a bath. The tires kicked up little pebbles from the road that stung like bees.

A car finally stopped, and a man got out. He stood in the middle of the road, held up his hand, and kept the other cars from moving until I was safely across. When the cars started moving again, the man pulled his car off to the side of the road and came walking down into the woods looking for me. I hid underneath the brush until he left. I'm sure he meant well, but I simply had to find Al.

Al's shelter stood in the center of the camp closer to the road than Mary's tent. It was much larger than the other shelters and tents and had a wood frame covered on all sides with sheets of hard plastic and insulated with heavy blankets. Al had sheets stretched over the top of his shelter, too, and slanted so the rain would run off. A little metal pipe poked out of a hole in the roof. Al's scent was all over the camp and it was easy to follow his trail right to the door.

Al's door was a heavy sheet of a smooth, hard material on hinges. I sat outside and barked and scratched until he poked his head out. When he saw I was alone, he frowned.

"Charlie, where's Mary?" I barked and tried to run, but limped badly instead. "What happened to you, boy?" He stepped outside and looked down at me, and then off in the direction of the shopping center. His dark, bushy eyebrows lowered until they almost came together. "Where you both hit by a car? Is that what all those sirens were about? She walks so slowly, and it only takes one person who's not paying attention." He stepped back inside the shelter and held the door open for me. "Come on inside, Charlie. I have to call someone."

The inside of Al's shelter was almost as big as the room with the sky wall in Mira's apartment, although there were no windows and the ceiling was not as high. And he had lots of things, so many things they could not have all fit in one shopping cart.

Al had plenty of furniture. A bed stood next to one wall. At the foot of the bed were small boxes stacked like shelves and stuffed with books. On the wall over the bed hung a large, black sheet with a strange picture of the shadow of a man's head on a white circle and the letters

POW MIA.

Across the room from the bed, Al had a long table like the ones in Mira's studio with more books and a light and even a laptop! In Mary's tent, the light left when the sun went down and did not come back until morning. Above the table, Al had hung an American flag. I had often seen the flag flying from poles on the tops of buildings in the city and a tall pole in the middle of the city park. Mira told me what it was. Underneath Al's table were black metal boxes with green lights and cardboard boxes filled with tools.

At the far end of the shelter across the room from the door stood a large, gray metal box. It gave off heat and the dull metal pipe that went up through the roof started there. The air was so warm in Al's shelter, he did not need to wear a blanket or a coat.

Al picked up a shiny metal object on the table, poked it with his finger a few times, and then held it up to his ear. He had a phone like Mira's!

"Father Paul, please." Al paused and waited. "Father, it's Al. I think there's a problem with Mary. She may have been hit by a car." He paused again. "Charlie came back from their walk just now without her. He's limping, too. And there were a bunch of emergency vehicles at the shopping center not long ago. Would they take her to St. Francis?"

Another pause. I lay down on a rug by the bed. My hind legs were still throbbing.

"Can you find out if she's there? I'd like to see her." Al drummed his fingers on the table. "I see. Please call me as soon as you know. Thank you, Father."

Al lifted his coat off a chair by the table and slipped the phone into a pocket. "Charlie, I have to go look for Mary," he said. "I can't take you with me. You seem pretty banged up anyway." He walked over to a metal box with a door and a handle underneath the table and opened it. The smell of food spilled out, specifically cold French fries and leftover burger.

Al broke the food up into bite size pieces, dropped them on the rug in front of me, and poured a little water into a cup. "Sorry, I wasn't expecting company," he said. "Stay here until I get back."

He didn't have to tell me twice. I ate the food without moving from the rug and had no intention of leaving the warmth and comfort of his shelter until I heard Al outside speaking to someone. The voice sounded familiar.

And the tone of Al's voice had changed from concern to sorrow. "Oh, no! Oh, no!" Al repeated several times. Despite the throbbing in my legs, I hobbled over to the door and squeezed through.

Al had his back to me. The man in the striped pants I had seen behind the deli stood in front of him. "Can you show me where she lived?" he asked. "Perhaps something she left there may help us contact her next of kin." Al nodded, wiped his eyes with a cloth he pulled from his coat pocket, and blew his nose in it. When I hobbled up, the man in the striped pants saw me and said, "How'd you get here?"

"That's her dog," Al said.

"He was out in back of the store with her when it happened. He probably saw everything. I left him with the deli owner."

"He limped in here about fifteen minutes ago. Charlie knows his way around the area quite well."

"He may have gotten into a scuffle himself with one of the assailants," the man in the striped pants said. "If he bit one, I'll bet he'll have the DNA in his mouth."

Al scratched his head. "So, what are you saying? He's evidence?"

"Could be," said the man in the striped pants. "I should take him to a vet soon before we lose the DNA if it's there. He should have his back legs looked at, too." The man in the striped pants bent down to pick me up, but I growled and backed away. "Umm, if he knows you, perhaps he'll let you carry him. You can ride with him in the back of my squad car if you like."

"If it will help catch Mary's killer," Al replied.

Al went into his shelter and came out with the rug. He laid it on the ground.

"Here, Charlie."

I hobbled over and lay down on the rug because I was tired, and my back legs hurt, but I would have rather laid down on the rug inside the shelter. It was brown and shaggy and dirty like me and held a collection of scents from food to cars to traces of smells from other camp residents. To my surprise, Al bent over and picked up both ends of the rug and lifted me up in a makeshift sling. I was uneasy at first, but Al rolled up the ends of the rug until I was wrapped up tight. He held me underneath with his log of an arm.

Al and the man in striped pants walked through the camp toward the gravel area where the yellow bus came every week. There was a black and white car parked there. The man in the striped pants opened a door so Al could get in. I began to squirm and bark and cry when Al obliged. Nothing good had ever come from a car ride.

"Charlie, you have to see a doctor," Al said.

Inside the car, I whined and cried more and began to drool on Al's pants. He didn't seem to notice. The man in striped pants sat in the front seat and drove.

"It's a shame she had to go this way," he said to Al. "Can't say I'm surprised though. Some of the gangs in the area will kill you just for being in the wrong place at the wrong time. Probably what happened to her. She was just in the wrong place at the wrong time."

Al held me tightly on the car seat. Wrapped up in the rug, I could not see anything but the back of the seat ahead of me. The seat had a strange fence on top that went all the way to the roof. I could see only the back of the man in the striped pants' head through the crisscrossed bars\

When the car stopped, and Al got out, we were in a parking lot behind another red brick building with a dark color roof and large, outdoor fences attached to it. The area inside the fences was empty, but still smelled heavily of the scent of other dogs I did not recognize. By now, the sky was dark and lights on the building bathed the parking lot brightly enough to see. Al carried me under his arm and followed the man in the striped pants around a sidewalk to the front of the building. In the yard by the street stood a brightly lit sign with the words "RIVERDALE VETERINARY HOSPITAL," and a picture of a big dog and a small cat sitting beside it. I did not think it was possible for a dog and a cat to sit so close together.

Inside the building, a young woman wearing a blue shirt and blue pants led us into a small room with a shiny silver table. Al set me on the table and unwrapped the rug allowing its ends to fall over the table's edges. I laid there shaking, too scared to move. Al kept his hand on my back, I suppose to calm me, and it gave me some comfort. The man in the striped pants stood in a corner of the room with his arms crossed.

When the door to the room opened again, a woman wearing a white coat walked in. She had dark brown hair and wore it in a bun on top of her head. Her dark brown eyes sparkled cheerfully behind silver rimmed eyeglasses. Although she was shorter and heavier, and clearly older than Mira, her skin was still smooth and unblemished. She smelled faintly of the scent of other dogs mixed with a sharp smell of soap. The young woman in blue walked in behind her.

"Hello, Sergeant," the woman in the white coat said to the man in the striped pants. "Who's this little fella?" I liked the sound of her voice. I have always found women's voices more comforting than men's.

"His name's Charlie," Al said.

"Hi, Charlie!" the woman said to me. "I heard you had a bad day?" She walked up to the table and extended her hand for me to sniff. It smelled of soap and I wrinkled my nose.

"I'm Doctor Karen Deaver," she said to Al extending her other hand. "Do you know Charlie well?"

"We're good friends," Al said.

"Normally, I'd give him a treat to calm him," Doctor Deaver said, "but we have to collect the DNA evidence first. He's not going to like it so please hold him tightly."

Al wrapped me in the rug again and pinned me to the table. Not a good sign. I began to wiggle and whine.

"Charlie, has anyone checked your teeth before?" Doctor Deaver asked as she pulled on stretchy gloves. She placed on her head the funniest hat I had ever seen. It had a band that went around her head and thick glass she pulled down in front of her eyes that made them look like the giant eggs in the store windows.

The Meaning Of Home

"This isn't going to hurt, Charlie," she said, "although you may find it annoying." She placed one hand behind my head and tilted it back, then raised up my jowls and looked at my teeth and gums. I didn't like her fingers poking in my gums and told her so.

"Alright, Charlie. I understand completely," she said. "He has some fabric caught between two molars. Jen, hand me a pair of forceps, please."

The woman named Jen handed Doctor Deaver a long, shiny metal object that reminded me of the object the man in the hooded sweatshirt had used to hurt Mary. I whined and shook my head and tried to move, but Al held me still. He saw the shiny object, too. Apparently, it did not frighten him.

"Hold still, Charlie," Al said. "She's not going to hurt you. This is to help Mary."

Doctor Deaver repeated my name in a cheerful voice and told me I was a good dog while she lifted my lip and touched my teeth with the forceps. When she held it up to the light, I saw a tiny piece of thread in the tip. Jen opened a bottle and the doctor dropped the piece of thread inside.

"Okay, Charlie, now I just have to swab your gums and teeth and this part will be over." Doctor Deaver took a stick with a fuzzy, white bud on the end and rubbed it along my teeth and over my tongue. It tickled. She did this several times with several sticks and placed each stick in its own clear bag.

"Now that wasn't so bad, was it?" Doctor Deaver said. She took off the funny hat and walked over to a jar on a counter. When she lifted the lid, I smelled the wonderful scent of bacon. My ears perked, and I struggled to sit up even though my back legs hurt more. Al unwrapped the rug and allowed me to sit up on the table.

"I thought you'd like these," Doctor Deaver said as she handed me a moist, bacon scented treat. I took it from her gently and ate it sitting up on the table since there was nowhere else to go. "Would you like another?" she asked. I wagged my tail. It was the first time I had a reason to wag my tail since that morning.

"He's hurt in his hind legs, Doctor," Al said. "He may have been kicked."

"Let's take a look," Doctor Deaver said. She switched places with Al, put her hand underneath my belly, and made me stand up. She started moving my right leg slowly. I felt a sharp pain go from my right leg into my back and yelped. "I can't tell whether it's a small fracture or just a bad bruise without an x-ray," Dr. Deaver said. "Jen, can you take Charlie in for an x-ray? We'll be back in just a little while, gentlemen."

Jen placed her arms underneath my belly, lifted me up, and carried me down a long hallway into another room with a big, white machine. She sat me on a metal tabletop on the machine underneath what looked like a big lamp. Jen and Dr. Deaver put on thick aprons and gloves. Whenever Dr. Deaver pushed buttons on the machine, it clicked and hummed, but I did not feel anything. Then Jen carried me back to the room where Al and the man in the striped pants were still waiting.

Dr. Deaver came into the room a few moments later looking at a black and white picture. "Charlie has a hairline fracture of the right femur," she said. "A vicious kick would explain it." She looked up at Al. "Unfortunately, the best thing for Charlie is to simply keep him quiet and give the fracture time to heal on its own. It is not bad enough to require surgery, but if he doesn't stay put until it heals, it could get worse."

Al ran his fingers through his hair. "How long will it take to heal?" he asked.

"Four to six weeks," Dr. Deaver said.

Al sighed. He stood at the side of the table petting me. I sensed he was troubled and I smiled and wagged my tail to make him feel better. I hoped he would take me back to the camp soon.

"Well, he's not my dog to begin with," Al said. "What happens if he stays here?"

"We'll keep him several days for observation," Dr. Deaver said. "But then we'll have to send him to a shelter until they can find a home for him. We'll also put his picture up on our bulletin board and website to see if anyone recognizes him. Handsome little guy and well-behaved. Someone should want him."

Al pet me some more, but the more I smiled and wagged my tail, the more deeply troubled he seemed. "Charlie," he said finally, "I'll miss having you in camp, but you're better off here. They can find you a home." When he said that, his eyes watered a little and he quickly wiped it away with the sleeve of his coat. "No one should be homeless." With that, Al walked out of the room.

I barked for Al and kept barking despite Jen's attempt to comfort me. Dr. Deaver and the Sergeant looked at each other. "Thank you, doctor," the Sergeant said. "Send your bill to the Chief." The Sergeant left the room and I heard Doctor Deaver sigh. "Find Charlie a cage, Jen," she said.

Jen picked me up again and carried me in her arms down another hallway to a set of stairs. I barked more and winced in pain. As she started down the stairs, I heard other dogs barking, a few at first, and then more and more as we reached the bottom step. High yaps. Refined, tenor barks like mine. And the deep woofs of the big fellas. At the bottom of the stairs, we entered a room with metal cages stacked all along the walls, big ones on the bottom and smaller ones up top. The dogs I had heard were all trapped inside the cages behind doors with metal bars and I recognized many of their scents from the fenced-in area outside. They barked even louder when we entered the room. Jen began talking to them.

"Hey, guys, this is Charlie! He'll be staying with us a little while." A big black and tan dog in a bottom cage began growling and tearing up the paper on the cage floor. "Hey, Clarence, cut it out!" Jen said. "I just cleaned you up an hour ago."

Jen opened the door of an upper cage and sat me inside on clean white paper. "I'll get you some food and water, Charlie," she said. When she closed the door, I joined the chorus of captives. I wanted to go back to the camp. I much preferred freedom of movement and even the sparse comforts of Mary's tent to steel walls and metal bars. Al had called me homeless, but didn't he understand the camp had become my home?

Jen returned with bowls of food and water and placed them in my cage. I drank because my barking had made me thirsty, but only enough to cool my throat and bark some more. "See you in the morning, Charlie," Jen said.

When Jen left the room, the light left with her. The other dogs gave up barking one by one. I was the last. The rest of them had already realized it was no use.

XI

Al had answered one of my questions. I would not be staying in Mary's tent without her. Our partnership had ended and life in the camp would move on. If Mira had replaced me in her heart with a little white dog, how much easier would it be for the camp residents to forget Mary and me?

Inside the metal cage, I lost track of time as dogs tell it. There was no sun-up or sundown, no shadows of different lengths, no way to tell time from the sounds of human activity like the rush of cars on the road during the day. Jen and another young woman came in every now and then to give us food and water and we vied for their attention. Some dogs were treated to the privilege of being taken outside to the fenced-in area for a while, but not me. I was confined to my cage.

Once each day, Jen or the other woman took me upstairs to see Dr. Deaver. They brought me to the same room with the silver table where Al left me, and Dr. Deaver made me stand up while she moved my back legs.

Sometimes when she moved my right leg it still hurt, and I told her so.

"Okay, Charlie," Dr. Deaver said. "It's going to take a little while before it feels better."

"The homeless man was here today asking about Charlie," Jen said to Dr. Deaver.

"I know," Dr. Deaver replied.

"He'd like to have Charlie back," Jen said.

"I know," Dr. Deaver repeated. She pressed her fingers along my back while Jen held my head and scratched behind my ears.

"Well? Are you going to let him have Charlie?"

Charlie, Charlie, Charlie. Of course, Jen was talking about me, but I sensed it didn't concern my leg.

Dr. Deaver sighed. "What kind of veterinarian would I be if I put a homeless dog back on the streets? Charlie needs to find a good home."

There was that word again.

"If he had taken Charlie with him that night, would you have stopped him?" Jen asked. "He obviously cares very much about him."

"Wanting the dog and being able to care for him properly are two different things."

"He said he would see Charlie has everything he needs. He has shelter with heat and enough food and water ... he invited us to stop by and have a look. Even the homeless need companionship, Doctor."

Dr. Deaver took a strange object out of a pocket of her white coat. It had buds she put in her ears and a shiny object attached to it like Mira's phone, but it was small and circular instead of a large square and she held it against my chest instead of her ear when she listened.

"Your heart's just fine, Charlie," Dr. Deaver said. "You have strong lungs, too."

"He'll take good care of Charlie," Jen said.

"There are laws," Dr. Deaver said. "Dogs are supposed to be licensed. Dogs are supposed to be kept leashed when they are off the owner's property."

"And how many dogs have we seen kept on a chain on the owner's property that have been terribly neglected? The law doesn't assure a dog's well-being. A caring heart does."

"Did you check his stools?" Dr. Deaver asked.

"Yes," Jen said. "He tested positive for round worms."

"I'm not surprised," Dr. Deaver said, "with all the garbage he has probably eaten. See that he gets dosed."

"He's already had the first one," Jen said.

"And we might as well vaccinate him and see that he's neutered before he goes to the… shelter," Dr. Deaver said. "And give him a gentle dry bath."

"What if Charlie stayed with the homeless man until we found him a permanent home? Is he really better off in a cage?"

Dr. Deaver stared at Jen and did not say anything for a few moments. Then she began petting me. I smiled and wagged my tail. "Did you put his picture on our bulletin board?" Dr. Deaver asked.

"Yes," Jen replied.

"He's such a well-behaved even-tempered dog," Dr. Deaver said. "He certainly wasn't born on the streets. It's too bad no one ever thought to put a chip in his ear."

"I can post his picture on the lost dog website," Jen said. "If someone is looking for him, that would be the place."

Dr. Deaver nodded. "He'll need to stay here several more days to be certain the fracture heals," she said and winked at Jen. "Let's see what happens."

The next time Jen brought me upstairs, Dr. Deaver stuck me in my front leg with an object that looked somewhat like the pins Mira stuck in the humans without faces. I don't remember what happened after that. When I awoke, I was inside my cage lying on my side with a plastic collar around my neck. The collar was hard and wide and uncomfortable, and I'm sure it was not one of Mira's. My groin itched, but the collar prevented me from licking back there. I was very thirsty and drank all the water in my bowl.

I could not understand why Dr. Deaver had treated me this way. Human behavior perplexed me and, lying on my side in the cage, I had little else to do but dwell upon it. What made Mark so angry that he took me away from Mira and tried to set me on fire? Why did Mira forget me and make clothes for another dog? What made Mary so profoundly sad and why did that man have to hurt her? And I thought Al was my friend. When would I have a home again? For better or for worse, it is the lot of dogs to be subject to the will of humans and being helpless to alter my circumstances hurt worst of all.

There were several more trips upstairs to see Dr. Deaver. Eventually, the itching stopped, and the collar came off. My right leg did not hurt anymore when she moved it. Jen cut my hair very short and gave me a bath which I did not like very much. And she finally let me go outside in the area enclosed by fences. Jen called it "the runs," even though it was not big enough to run in. The runs had a roof and a hard, slippery floor. Through the fences, I could see the sky and trees and the parking lot where the man in striped pants had parked the evening I had arrived, but I was not free to roam.

One day, Jen walked into the downstairs room with a collar and leash and opened my cage. She smiled and said in her high, excited tone of voice, "Hey Charlie, you're finally getting out of here! And, boy, do I have a surprise for you!" The other dogs started barking and their tails banged against the insides of their cages adding to the racket. I allowed Jen to place the collar around my neck and fasten the leash. When she set me on the floor, I raced for the door until the leash snapped my head back and choked me.

"Hold on, Charlie. Don't hurt yourself," Jen said.

She picked me up at the bottom of the stairs and carried me down a hallway and through another door that led to the parking lot. Outside, Jen set me down again and I jumped and pranced and barked and leaped, unable to control my joy to be outside and going anywhere. Yet, my excitement was short-lived. Jen walked up to a white vehicle that was bigger than a car but not quite big enough to be called a truck. It had white sides with the same picture of the dog and cat I saw on the sign out in front of the building. Jen opened the back door of the mini-truck. Inside, there were small metal cages. I crouched down and did not want to get in.

"Don't be afraid, Charlie," Jen said. "I hate to put you back in a cage, but I can't let you ride in the front seat of the van. Hospital rules. It won't be a long ride though."

My wiggling and writhing did not stop Jen from putting me in a cage and closing the door. When she shut the back door of the van, it frightened me more. I howled and barked as loud as I did the first night in Mira's apartment, but I doubt Jen could hear me above the noise of the engine.

I kept howling and barking until I heard the sound of gravel crunching underneath the van's wheels and it reminded me of the sound the yellow bus made at the camp. When the back door of the van opened, light flooded in. Someone was standing there making a big shadow. Although my eyes took a moment to adjust to the light, I recognized the man's scent instantly. It was Al.

"Look who's here, Charlie!" Jen stepped in front of Al and opened the door to my cage. I burst through into her arms. "Okay, okay. Hold still!" She turned around and handed me to Al who bundled me up in his big arms. I licked his face with my tongue and did not care how rough it felt.

"Forgive me, Charlie," Al said. "I don't have much of a home, but you're welcome to share it."

What good does it do to live in a mansion if you are not wanted there? I knew Al wanted me, so I was content to be his companion now that Mary was gone. What I did not know was there were other people who did not want us, any of us in the camp, and were already plotting to take away the little shelter we had.

XII

Dogs often benefit, or suffer as the case may be, from the characteristics of their human companions. While I was Mary's companion, people ignored me because people ignored Mary and avoided her. I knew little more of the residents of the camp than I could deduce from their scents. Now that I lived with Al, my status in the camp had changed completely. I was "Al's dog." I was the center of attention, anxious to meet guests, generous with my tail wags, and always willing to be hugged.

So many people came to visit Al: residents of the camp, Father Paul and people from his church, Jen from the place with the sign of the dog and cat. Even the man in the striped pants stopped by. He congratulated me for helping them catch Mary's killer.

"The DNA and the pant fiber from Charlie's mouth placed him at the scene," he told Al. "And we found the knife in some brush by the creek. He'll be going away for a long time."

The Meaning Of Home

The man in the striped pants bent down and reached out his hand to pet me, but I ran underneath Al's table.

"He remembers what happened the last time you were here," Al said.

Jen stopped by in the mornings and, for the first few visits, exercised my back legs. I stood on Al's table while she pulled and rotated each leg in different directions.

"He walks funny now," Al said, "almost sideways like the blow knocked his spine a few clicks off center."

"He's pain free with good range of motion," Jen replied. She picked me up and set me on the floor. "Where's the chewy toy I bought him?" she asked Al. He pointed underneath the table.

Jen bent over and picked up my only worldly possession, aside from the collar I wore, a long, fuzzy, hot dog roll shaped thing with a tail. It looked like one of the squirrels that clambered in the tree tops around the camp and gorged themselves on our trash. Jen threw it toward the door. I promptly ran over, picked it up, and then ran back and forth between Jen and the door growling and shaking my head. I wanted her and Al to come and play outside.

"His movement looks good. Let me know if he starts to limp or favor the right leg again."

Al shrugged. "Maybe I just didn't notice it before."

"Keep him leashed, will ya?" Jen said glaring at Al. "And crate him when you're not here. I stuck my neck out for you."

Al kept the box Jen brought for me at the foot of his bed with the metal bar door open. I never went inside.

113

It looked too much like the one in Mira's kitchen. Al did try to coax me inside on my first night back in his shelter. I lay on the shaggy rug beside his bed with my head down, pretending not to hear, and disobeyed him. Even though I trusted Al, my fear of what might happen if the door closed was too strong. Al did not bother after that.

One afternoon, Jen stopped by unexpectedly while Al was away from the camp with Father Paul. I was down in the woods below the gravel area cavorting with the squirrels when I saw the white van with the sign of the dog and cat pull in. I waited until I saw Jen get out of the van and then trotted out of the woods to greet her.

"Hey, Charlie!" she said. "How are you, buddy?" My tail wags accelerated, and I jumped and shimmied and barked. But then Jen's tone of voice changed. "Where's Al? And what are you doing off your leash?" She reached down, scooped me up, and carried me off to Al's shelter.

Jen stood outside the closed door and knocked on the hard surface. "Hello, Al? It's Jen. May I have a word with you?" When Al did not answer, Jen began talking to me. "Maybe I should have found you a better home. You weren't meant to be an outside dog." The muscles in her arm tensed. From the scowl on her face, I sensed Al and I were both in trouble.

A resident of the camp I knew as Bruce stepped outside his shelter down the row a little way from Al's. He and Al were close friends. They talked often ever since that first day I happened upon the camp. "Hi Charlie," he said and flashed a toothy smile, but it quickly disappeared when he shifted his attention to Jen. "May I help you, ma'am?"

"Do you know where Al is?"

"Who's askin'?" Bruce wore a red and white checkered shirt, denim jeans and his work boots. He was an older man, near Al's age, with a full head of wavy gray hair, sunken cheeks and a sharp, beak-like nose. His eyes were always red like they were tired and had seen too much. In the camp, Bruce kept to himself much like Mary did, but he did not scream at other people or talk to people who weren't there, and Al said he was good at fixing things.

"I'm Jen … from the veterinary hospital." She glanced around nervously to see whether anyone else was nearby. "I came to check on Charlie."

"Oh, sure, sure. I remember you now," Bruce said. "Charlie looks just fine to me. You're fine, ain'tcha Charlie?" He grinned, and I wagged my tail. "I'll tell Al you was askin."

Jen shifted her weight on her feet, gathered up her assertiveness, and stared at Bruce. She kept me cradled in her arms. "Tell Al Charlie's not supposed to be running loose."

"No harm's come to him, ma'am," Bruce said. "We all look out for each other around here."

"He had a broken femur," Jen snapped.

"The way I heard it, he got hurt defendin' Miss Mary."

"Well, he shouldn't be out walking in parking lots and across highways. He could get hit by a car. I told Al he had to put Charlie in a crate when he wasn't around."

Bruce reached into his jeans pocket and pulled out a small, round tin. He opened it, took a pinch of its dark, brown contents, and stuck it between his cheek and gums. "Ma'am, have you ever been put in a cage?" he asked.

Jen gasped. "No. Of course, not."

"Al has," Bruce said. "A bamboo one." He shoved the tobacco tin back in his jeans pocket and moved his jaw slowly. "It wasn't big enough to stand up in, so he had to sit or crouch with his knees up to his chin. Imagine a man Al's size wedged in a cage the size of a dishwasher. Sometimes, the cage was in the river with just enough room to keep his head above water. They'd keep him there for hours."

A look of horror disfigured Jen's face. "Who'd do something like that? That's torture!" She studied Bruce' expression trying to decide whether he was telling a fib.

"Yes, ma'am, it was," Bruce said. "Happened in Vietnam years ago. You prob'ly weren't even born."

"Al was a prisoner of war?"

"Yes, ma'am. For almost five years."

"I mean I saw the flag inside, but I didn't know it was … he was…"

"They tried to break him. They tried to get American POWs to give fake confessions and put down their country for propaganda purposes, you know. Al don't like to speak about it and he won't be happy if he learns I told you. Still, I'm tellin' you so you understand. Al don't want to put Charlie in a box he doesn't want to go in. He just can't bring himself to do it."

"I don't want anything to happen to Charlie," Jen said.

Bruce nodded. "Ma'am, you're young and you look like you come from good folk and a safe home, but life is a risk, plain and simple. It don't matter whether you're walkin' through a jungle or drivin' down that road over there as long as you choose to do it. I bet if you asked Charlie, he'd say he'd rather rely on his own good sense than be caged up and told it was for his own good."

From the tone of the conversation, I sensed Bruce was trying to persuade Jen to change her mind and my freedom hung in the balance. I looked into her eyes, gave her the most reassuring look I could muster, and barked to be let go.

Jen hugged me so hard I almost stopped breathing. She scratched my head, then put me down on the ground. When I looked up at her, I saw her wipe tears from her eyes. "Be careful, Charlie," she said and walked away. I followed her a little way to the edge of the gravel area and watched until she climbed into the white van and drove away. I did not understand why she was sad, but I was relieved she had not taken me with her.

Al tried to help people. And being Al's dog made me a companion to many instead of a companion to one. When Al counseled a resident in his shelter, I sat in the resident's lap and listened. It was my new role within our extended pack. Al said I was a good listener and helped him draw out the resident's story. Dogs keep many secrets. No one felt awkward sharing a confidence in my presence.

Everyone had a story, but as I came to know the camp residents, I noticed some tried to write their own story while others let the story write them. I had high hopes for a young man named Jeremy. He worked at the table in Al's shelter with the laptop for hours looking for jobs and learning. Al said he was going to school! People from Father Paul's church sometimes stopped by with nice clothes and Al gave a suit and tie to Jeremy. He tried it on in Al's shelter.

"I feel like I'm back in uniform," Jeremy said.

"Wear it proudly," Al replied.

"Do you ever miss it?" Jeremy asked.

"Miss what?"

"The Corps. I mean I never wanted to make it a career, but you had a place. You were always part of something bigger than yourself. After my discharge, I felt lost."

Al sat down on a chair with a deep sigh. "I miss the men I never brought back," he said.

I trotted over and inspected the cuffs of Jeremy's pants. They had already picked up some of the odors of Al's shelter, including my own. In Mira's studio, I had little to do other than model her clothes, but in Al's shelter, I touched human souls.

"What do you think, Charlie? Do you think they'll give me the job?" I wagged my tail and barked. "I hope so," Jeremy said. Wearing the suit instilled confidence in him, or perhaps I should say it brought out more of what he already had on the inside. If only he and Al could have seen how good I looked in one of Mira's suits.

"You'll make a fine assistant store manager, Jeremy," Al said.

"Thank you, sir." Jeremy said. He turned to leave Al's shelter, but then Jeremy turned around and stood stiffer than I ever saw anyone stand before. He snapped his hand to his forehead and stared straight ahead at some unknown spot on the wall of Al's shelter. I had never observed this strange human behavior before, but I sensed it meant something to Al. He stood up and raised his hand to his forehead in the same fashion. Jeremy dropped his hand to his side stiffly, then turned and left the shelter without saying another word.

For as many peoples' stories as Al and I listened to, there were some endings we did not foresee. If I could have rewritten just one, it would have been Daniel's.

He arrived at the camp in the warm months humans call summer after Mary's death. No one stayed at the camp without meeting Al first, and Al sensed as I could the humans who could be trusted from the ones who could not. When we first met Daniel in Al's shelter, we both took a liking to him.

Daniel looked older than his years as many homeless people do. A harsh life ages humans more quickly. Still, he was a young man. He stood as tall as Al's shoulders which meant he was average height for a human male. He had long, scraggly brown hair and scruffy whiskers, but he had a kind face. Daniel's blue eyes were expressive and inquisitive. That told me he was willing to listen. People who sat across from Al with a scowl and their arms crossed moved on.

There were rules to be followed if one wished to stay in the camp and Al made no bones about telling a homeless person he could go elsewhere if he did not want to follow them. Daniel listened intently as Al recited them.

"No drugs, no alcohol, no weapons, no violence, no sex between unmarried persons. You will keep your own campsite clean and you will do the camp chores assigned to you. You will be respectful to everyone in this camp and they will respect you. In return, you will never go hungry, you will have basic shelter, and you will have others looking out for you."

"I want to get clean," Daniel said. I sat in his lap as he faced Al. The two men sat on folding chairs in Al's shelter with their knees just inches apart.

Al leaned forward. "We can get you help," he said. "I've been where you are."

They sat in silence for several moments. Al always left it up to his guest to decide when to speak. Daniel began to scratch my belly and run his fingers through my fur.

"I played soccer in college," Daniel began. He looked at me when he spoke. Humans found talking to me less intimidating, so they often told me their stories as if Al wasn't in the room.

"I was a good student. Never so much as smoked a joint. The school had given me a scholarship and I wasn't about to blow it for some cheap high. Everything changed when I tore my ACL." Daniel stopped scratching my belly, sat back in his chair, and ran his fingers through his gnarled hair instead.

"I took the pills the doctor prescribed for my pain," he said. "When the doctor wouldn't prescribe anymore, I still had to have them. Oxycontin. It wasn't like any pill I had taken before for a headache or a stomach virus. I just couldn't stop. It was easy enough to find them, too. I just asked around my fraternity.

The Meaning Of Home

"I tried to wean myself off. I kept telling myself after each high it would be the last one. Then I was busted on campus for possession, lost my scholarship, and my whole world caved in."

Daniel leaned forward and burrowed his head in his hands. I was pinned in between his elbows. "Maybe I'm too far gone," he mumbled. His face was inches away from mine, so I licked his nose. It made him laugh. As Al would say later, it was exactly the medicine he needed at that moment. "Charlie, your breath stinks!"

Since Daniel did not have a job, he was around the camp much of the time Al was not, and he often came looking for me. Although I still kept up my guard around men in general, something about the way Daniel held me and spoke to me in Al's shelter the day we met told me he had loved a dog.

"Hey Charlie, whassup?" he shouted whenever he found me. "Let's go for a walk."

I began to spend more time with Daniel than I did with Al. Daniel liked to roughhouse. He got down on the ground and wrestled me. We rolled around and growled and nipped like puppies and played tug-of-war with one of his socks. He even held it between his teeth and shook his head. I had never seen a human act so much like a dog.

Daniel and I went for long walks along the river. He threw sticks for me to fetch, although I refused to go in the water after them, and sometimes we sat on a log for hours and watched things float by.

"Charlie, sometimes I feel like my life keeps flowing by me like the river and I'm just standing on the bank watching it." I sensed a heavy regret in Daniel's voice and laid my head in his lap. In such a moment, I have always found a gentle touch more meaningful than a bark or a tail wag.

"You're alright for a furball," Daniel said and placed his arm over me. "My Caesar's head was as big as you." Daniel smiled. "He laid his head in my lap, too. I miss that dog."

When Al and Daniel were in camp, I felt a tug between competing desires to be with them at the same time. And when they left the camp together, I sat outside Al's shelter and sulked until they returned. Al said he was pleased with Daniel's progress. He had cut his hair, shaved, and with clothes donated by the folks at Father Paul's church, he was ready to start interviewing for jobs. Daniel had shown all the outward signs of positive change until he grew tired of a beta role in our pack and decided to challenge Al.

Al held a meeting of the residents to announce a group called Habitat for Humanity had picked Jeremy to own his own home as long as he helped build it. And Jeremy had been given the assistant store manager position. He was as excited as Mira the day all the photographers came to her studio. Jeremy talked endlessly about building the home and how he would invite everyone in the camp to come visit once it was finished.

While Al saw this as motivation, a glimpse for Daniel and the other residents of what was possible with hard work and determination, I sensed a different response from several residents, a response not unlike

Mark's reaction to Mira's success. Behind polite words of congratulation was a tone of resentment.

Al and Daniel began to argue. I trotted along with Al when he made his rounds to inspect the camp much like I did when I accompanied Mary on her walks to the shopping center across the street and the old school. He took notes in a little book and then he went looking for anyone who hadn't done their chores.

"You haven't been showing up for the sanitary detail lately," Al said when he found Daniel seated on a folding chair by his tent. "I went looking for you this morning and you were nowhere to be found. Where were you?"

"I've been getting up early and going for a walk down along the river," Daniel replied. "We're still free to come and go around here, aren't we?"

"Camp chores are a requirement if you want to stay here," Al reminded him. "They're not optional."

"Aren't they?" Daniel asked. "Some in this camp say you play favorites. They said you let a crazy lady stay here and never made her do chores."

Al's jaw shifted back and forth, and his face turned a darker brown. "Her name was Mary. Did they also tell you she was living in these woods by herself before any of us?" Daniel nodded. "She was an old woman when I came," Al continued. "She deserved her peace. I took it upon myself to do her share."

Daniel rolled his eyes. "Some also think it's not a coincidence that a fellow Marine is going to be the first one from this camp to own his own home."

Al stepped closer to Daniel and now towered over him. Daniel did not move and looked straight ahead past Al's legs with an air of indifference.

"Jeremy is the first one from this camp to have a chance to own a home because he was the first one to bust his ass and make the most of his opportunities," Al snarled. "I didn't give him his job nor sit for the interview for his home application."

"You think you're better than all of us, don't you?" Daniel replied. "You can't be the boss anywhere else, but you can be the boss here. Who made you the dictator? This camp isn't a dictatorship. It's supposed to be a democracy. I think maybe it's time we elected ourselves a new leader. That's what I think."

By now, the lines on Al's neck had grown very large and I heard him grinding his teeth. Yet, his anger was not strong enough to overcome him like it did Mark and the man in the black hooded sweatshirt. Al fought hard to control it. He breathed deeply and let his anger dissipate through his mouth and nose.

"Then start a campaign," Al said. "Let's see if you can convince anyone other than yourself that you have what it takes to be a leader." Al stormed off toward his shelter. For a moment, I hesitated. I stood in front of Daniel, watched him brood, and wondered what I could do to relieve the tension between the two men. I ran into his tent and came out with his sock in my mouth.

"Go on, Charlie," Daniel said and waved his hand. "Leave me alone." My heart troubled me. I didn't want my walks and roughhousing with Daniel to come to an end. But I knew when I was unwanted. I dropped the sock and ran after Al.

To everyone's surprise, Daniel took up Al's challenge to campaign against him for camp leader. I think Al silently admired him for it and hoped it would help Daniel recover the drive that once motivated him on the soccer field. For a few weeks, Al held meetings in his shelter and offered Daniel the opportunity to speak about how he'd run things differently. Daniel also made his rounds among the tents and shelters in the days leading up to the vote talking to anyone who would listen to him.

But most of the camp residents were fond of Al and content with his leadership. He had helped too many people. Daniel lost the election badly.

In the weeks after the vote, Daniel did his chores, but kept to himself. One evening, he came to Al's shelter and told Al he would be leaving the camp soon. Al invited him to sit down and talk, but Daniel declined. After the vote, Daniel rebuffed my friendship also. I visited him every day hoping he'd change his mind and go for a walk with me. I'd playfully growl, go into his tent, and bring out a sock.

"Go away, Charlie," Dan said again one afternoon as I sat next to him with the sock in my mouth. "This is Al's camp and you're Al's dog. You can't have two masters." He got up, went inside his tent, and zippered it closed.

I wanted to tell him I could have many friends. Like a human, a dog has an infinite capacity to love. It's a tough lesson to learn you can't help a human who doesn't want to be helped, and tougher still to watch them walk away.

The air had turned cooler and the leaves were beginning to change color when Al and I walked past Daniel's tent one morning. The flap was open, but I did not hear him moving around inside. His belongings were still scattered about. Al walked over and peeked in.

"Dan?"

He had not left. He lay inside the tent on a mattress, but Al could not rouse him out of his sleep.

"Dan, get up!"

Al ran back to his shelter while I barked and pawed at Daniel trying to wake him. I noticed a thin tube lying next to Daniel with a pin at the top like the one Dr. Deaver had used to stick me. Al burst into the tent and nearly stepped on me. He had a small plastic object in his hand and shoved it in Daniel's nose and squeezed, but that did not wake Daniel either. Al looked up and screamed.

"Lord, why? Why?" Al just kept shouting, "Why?"

The truck with the flashing lights came and took Daniel away just like it had Mary. The man in the striped pants showed up, too. He sat down with Al inside Al's shelter after the truck had left.

"You've had a run of bad luck this year," the man in the striped pants said. Al did not answer. He sat by the table leaning on his elbows and staring at the rug on the floor. I scratched at his pant leg until he picked me up. I wanted Al to tell the man in the striped pants to leave us alone, but he said nothing. Although it is good to share grief, the man in the striped pants hadn't come to share ours.

"I know you're trying to do good things here," the man in the striped pants continued. "The Chief knows, too.

But there were rumblings after the old woman's death. This is illegal housing after all. A second death is only going to make things worse. You may want to start thinking about an exit strategy."

"And what would that be, Mike?" Al sat up and asked. Al called the man in the striped pants by a different name when they were alone. "Where are all the residents here going to go? The county doesn't have enough beds for them, and even if it did, many will not go to the temporary shelters. Do you think crime doesn't occur there?"

"I don't have the answers," the man in the striped pants said. "I just know pretty soon I'm going to be told to do something I'd rather not have to do." He stood up, walked over to Al, and placed a hand on his shoulder. "You've held your ground here longer than anyone expected."

Al looked up. "It's not over. Tell the Chief it's not over. I'm not leaving until I know every one of my residents has been taken care of. I'll be the last one to leave the field."

XIII

The battle over the campground began in the time when the leaves on the trees were at the height of their color and the woods along the river were a canopy of brilliant red and gold. There were occasions standing amongst the tents and shelters looking up through the trees at a blue sky one might even say it was beautiful. I loved the woods. I loved living in the company of so many humans who wanted me despite the difficult circumstances we found ourselves in. The camp, with all its problems and petulence, had become my home.

Sergeant Mike, the man in the striped pants, showed up one day and began handing out slips of paper to residents of the camp. I was laying on the rug in Al's shelter napping in the warmth of the space heater. Al was at the table working on his laptop when Bruce came in.

"Trouble," Bruce said. I lifted one eyebrow and saw Bruce hand Al a yellow slip of paper.

"What's this?" Al asked.

"Read it," Bruce said.

Al took the slip from Bruce's hand. His eyes had barely crossed the paper when a wave of anger flashed across his face and he crumpled the paper in his hand. "Where is he?" Al asked. I opened both eyes and sat up.

"Not far," Bruce said.

Al stormed out of the shelter and I followed close at his heels.

Outside in bright sunshine and only a few tents away, Sergeant Mike was writing on a pad he held in his hand. One of the newer residents of the camp, a wide-eyed young woman named Claire, stood next to him on the verge of tears. Other residents nearby were reading the yellow slips.

"Sergeant, you could have given me some warning!" Al growled.

"I did," Sergeant Mike said. "I told you when they took that boy out of here in a body bag a few weeks ago I was going to be told to do something I didn't want to do and sooner rather than later. That time has come."

"But thirty days? You can't be serious? Where are they going to find a place to live after Thanksgiving and before Christmas? You know as well as I do it's the worst time of year to find housing. There's going to be no room anywhere!"

"Al, I also told you I didn't have the answers. All I do is write the tickets."

"That's not good enough, Sergeant," Al said. "If the heart underneath that badge is telling you something different, maybe you ought to listen."

As Al spoke, Sergeant Mike ripped a slip of paper out of the pad, but he hesitated before he handed it to Claire.

His hand was suspended in the air for a moment and the slip bent in the breeze. Claire, a short, excessively thin woman with purple-dyed hair and olive skin, stood rigid and mute glancing back and forth between the two men. With a deep sigh, Sergeant Mike extended his hand toward Claire, but Al stepped forward and snatched the slip away. "If you have any more to write," he said, "give them to me."

"I don't like this any more than you do, Al," Sergeant Mike said. "When I'm off duty, I'll make some phone calls. I'll see what I can do to help you get these people housed."

"I'm going to hold you to that, Sergeant," Al said.

"But I cannot do anything in my official capacity. I'm just following orders. If you have a beef, take it up with the Chief or the Township supervisors."

After the Sergeant left, the mood of the residents turned as gray and somber as the weather sure to come. The sky was still blue, yet I felt unsettled as though I had heard the distant rumble of thunder from an approaching storm. The weather was changing. The friction between Al and Sergeant Mike had not been there before and it was a bad omen.

As I wandered among the tents trying to lift spirits, residents greeted me with blank stares and furrowed brows instead of the usual, "Hey, Charlie! Whatcha doin?" Even my smiles and tail wags did not elicit smiles and belly scratches in return. As I passed by Claire's tent, the muffled sound of crying from inside grabbed me as if a hand had reached out and taken hold of my collar. Even though I did not know her well, I couldn't ignore it.

When I poked my nose under the flap of her tent and pushed my way in, Claire looked up. She sat with her knees up against her chest. She must have been crying into her pant legs because they left red impressions on her cheeks.

"Hi Charlie," Claire said. She wiped her nose on the sleeve of her shirt.

I walked over, upbeat, wagging my tail and sat down next to her. Claire reached out and began scratching my head and I promptly rolled over and offered her my belly, too. She leaned over, gathered me in her arms, and held me the way humans often hold their infants. I lay in her arms looking up at her tear-stained face, close enough to lick them away.

"Nobody wants us, Charlie," Claire said. "Even my parents don't want me." She hugged me tightly. "I'm just white trash swept up here like the garbage along the river bank."

She laid her cheek against me. The warmth and wetness seeped into my skin like a summer rain.

"The people with homes and jobs don't want us here. You know why? Because we scare them. We're a reminder they're just one disaster away from being here, too. Better us than them.

"What are you doing here, Charlie? You're so cute. How did you end up in a place like this?"

Suddenly Claire started laughing. It was an abrasive sound infused with anger and bitterness. "Can you believe Al told me I'm a child of God?" Her tone of voice turned somber. "Where's God now, Charlie?" She looked at me as though I knew, but I could only offer her the softness of my fur to run her hands through. Dogs don't have many answers. We just listen. Sometimes that's all a human needs.

"Al said I'd be safe here until I found someplace better. He promised to help me get my GED and even look for a job!" She laughed again. "I would have settled for a place to sleep where I didn't have to wonder if I'd be woken up and raped in the middle of the night."

A human's voice is an echo of the heart. In Claire's, I heard the sound of a heart that had been bludgeoned and beaten, but still beat defiantly. I wiggled and waggled in her arms and licked her face. I knew instinctively to offer my love and companionship, and always hope, even when I didn't feel it myself.

"Charlie?" Al called. "Charlie, where did you disappear to?"

"I wish you could stay longer," Claire said. "You won't tell him what I said, will you?" I smiled and wagged my tail. "Cross your heart?"

"Charlie?" Al called again.

"Go," Claire said. "Before he finds out I've been crying."

That night, Al held a meeting in his shelter. I love company, and, for me, camp meetings meant lots of attention. Al could fit nearly all the camp residents inside if they sat on the floor which meant I ended up in someone's lap. But, that night, the camp residents brought with them inside the shelter the same tense mood I had sensed earlier that day. It permeated the air like the smoke sometimes did if Al's roof pipe was clogged.

Father Paul sat next to Al on a folding chair dressed in his usual black shirt, black pants and black shoes. He did not attend meetings often and his presence on the same day Sergeant Mike had handed out the slips was the second omen. First the clouds and then the wind.

Al stood up. "This is not my first camp," he said. There were surprised looks from some of the newer residents, including Claire, who did not know Al well. "I've been through this before. And I will not leave you to your own devices. Nor will Father Paul or his church.

"Unfortunately, there will have to be some changes. In the next few weeks, I will not have much time to spend helping you find jobs or education. I will be looking for permanent housing options and doing what I can to delay the day we all have to move for as long as possible."

"So, they're actually going to kick us out?" someone asked.

"Why now after four years?" another said.

"That kid and his dope," someone else said.

"Anything goes wrong around here, and they blame it on us just because we're homeless."

"Where do they think we'll go?" another man shouted. "We don't just disappear."

Shouts of indignation and murmurs of discontent spread throughout the room. I had squeezed into the space underneath Al's chair and gazed out upon a sea of unhappy faces. It wasn't the first contentious meeting ever held in Al's shelter, but it was the first meeting in which I sensed a shared anger mixed with the fear of an uncertain future among all the camp's residents.

Al held up his hands. "You're right," he said. "No one disappears." The shouts and grumbling diminished. "We will stay here as long as we can. We will make it unpleasant for the Township. We will be visible and there will be people in the community, including the people from Father Paul's church, who will make their voices heard. We can buy time to explore other options, but the simple fact is this is not our property. For whatever reason, someone has made the decision to remove us and we'll have to find another location where no one will bother us for a while."

"So, what do we do?" someone asked.

"Same thing you've been doing," Al said. "Keep the camp clean. Stay out of trouble. And don't give up hope."

Father Paul stayed with Al in the shelter after the meeting. Al made him a cup of the pungent, dark beverage Mira enjoyed, but never offered me. Al did not put any in my bowl either. He sat down on the edge of his bed underneath the white letters on the black POW MIA flag.

I occupied my usual spot on the rug and gnawed on my chewy while I listened to the men talk. Anyone who saw me laying there with the chewy between my paws may have assumed I was untroubled by the day's events, even blissfully ignorant. What cares could a dog have? But they would have been wrong. Gnawing on the chewy massaged my gums and relieved my anxiety.

"What will it be, Al? Your sixth move?" Father Paul asked. "You're not a young man anymore."

"I still have fight left in me," Al replied.

Father Paul was a collie to Al's bulldog, sleek of face with graceful lines, well-groomed dark hair with a touch of gray, and gentle, kindness-filled eyes. Father Paul listened more often than he spoke, and I never heard him raise his voice. If I had to guess, I'd say Father Paul, though much younger than Al, was his mentor.

"How many residents do you have in the camp?" Father Paul asked.

"Thirty-two," Al answered.

"We've housed more than that for Code Blue," Father Paul said.

"But only overnight," Al replied. "And only on nights the temperature dropped below freezing. How many was that?"

"We can manage to house them longer."

"Father, it's only a temporary solution," Al said. "Sleeping on a cot, without privacy, and with all their worldly belongings stashed underneath in a garbage bag is not home. Some won't do it. As strange as it may seem, these tents, these shelters are at least a space they have in this world they can call their own. I need more time. Time to figure out where to organize another camp."

"Perhaps you should look for someone else to handle it this time," Father Paul said.

"You brought me to this work," Al said. "Now you would have me leave? When the camp is facing a crisis?"

"I am not suggesting you abandon them. I am suggesting you look at this move as an opportunity to involve someone else and groom another for leadership. We are temporary. God's work is not."

Al sighed and hung his head. For a moment, the only sound inside the shelter was a buzzing from one of the metal boxes underneath Al's table.

"What's bothering you, Al?"

Al didn't answer. Father Paul sipped his beverage silently and gazed at the flag above Al's head for several moments. "Daniel's death is not your fault," he said. "The edict from the Township to shut down this camp is not your fault. I worry about the weight you have placed upon your heart unnecessarily."

Al clenched his fists. "I shouldn't have challenged him to campaign against me. I could have shared some authority, given him some responsibility, but it was my pride."

"Perhaps," Father Paul said. "But perhaps he would have led others astray. You shouldn't blame yourself for testing him. Didn't you tell me once officers who second-guessed themselves risked men's lives and bred uncertainty in their leadership?"

Al nodded.

"You're on a battlefield in a different war," Father Paul said. "You have one more battle to fight, my friend. Don't start second-guessing yourself now."

Father Paul set his cup down on the table. When he stood up, he placed his hands on Al's head and began speaking with his eyes closed, but he wasn't speaking to Al. He spoke to someone called God, although God wasn't anywhere to be seen—just like Mary's Jim. Father Paul asked God to give Al strength, peace, and the wisdom to know what to do in the coming weeks. When he finished speaking, Father Paul bent over and kissed Al on the top of his head.

"If God is with us, who can stand against us?" Father Paul said as he put on his coat. "Thanks for the coffee."

XIV

The camp hummed like a beehive as the days counted down toward the deadline the Township had established for everyone to move. Father Paul's parishioners and the camp residents made red, white and blue signs that read "CAST OUT POLITICIANS. NOT THE HOMELESS" and "WE'RE AMERICANS TOO!" They carried them as they walked back and forth along the highway by the shopping center, singing and chanting, while men in striped pants watched from black and white cars parked nearby. I thought it was great fun to walk with them and add my voice to the chorus, except it was one of the very few times Al ever kept me on a leash.

Sometimes, cars passing by would honk their horns and the people inside waved, but a few times people in the cars shouted angry, hurt-filled words at us the way Mark had yelled at Mira. I simply cannot understand some aspects of human behavior. We did nothing to provoke them.

In the evenings, there were frequent meetings in Al's shelter. Father Paul brought along a new guest, a young woman named Sonia Ramirez who told everyone she was a lawyer for the Interfaith Council on Poverty and Homelessness.

Sonia could have been Claire's sister. She had the same small stature, shoulder length black hair (without the purple dye), oval face, dark eyes, and olive skin. Yet, there the similarities ended. Where Claire was timid and shrank from public exposure, Sonia was assertive and showed no hesitation to speak in a crowded room of mostly older, disheveled men. Where she moved, the men parted and allowed her to pass. If she caught a man's gaze in the snare of her amber eyes, he looked away.

"I have asked the court to grant us a stay," she said. "What that means is the court may prevent the Township from taking steps to forcibly remove you from the camp for a period of time."

"How long?" someone asked.

"Since it is already December, I hope until at least April," Sonia said. "The County and the Township are not going to be able to prove there is adequate shelter available elsewhere for everyone. I think the court may let you stay here over the winter. You have lived here with the property owner's knowledge for a long time and your right to safe shelter during the winter is greater than the property owner's or the Township's right to have the property cleared at this moment."

"What happens in the Spring?" another man asked.

Sonia frowned. "Unfortunately, when the warmer weather arrives, there will be nothing more I can do. In the past, we have sued governments on occasion to make more funding available for housing projects, but those can take years."

"So, there's no hope?" the same man asked.

"There's always hope," Al interjected. "It was never our goal for you to remain here the rest of your lives, but to eventually find you a proper home. If we must, we'll simply continue the mission somewhere else."

When the meeting ended, and the residents began to disperse, Claire shuffled toward the door with her head down avoiding eye contact with anyone. I weaved in between legs and found Claire at the same time Sonia did. She walked up and tapped Claire on her shoulder.

"Sixteen years ago, I was homeless," Sonia said. "I was living in a camp like this one in the D.C. area and Al was running it." Claire simply stared at her wide-eyed and open mouthed. She ignored me when I scratched at her leg. Sonia reached into a bag like the one Mira had carried, pulled out a small piece of paper, and handed it to Claire. "Here's my card," she said. "Al challenged me once to make a difference, so now I'm challenging you. You'll need help. Call me." Sonia smiled, but Claire turned and pushed her way out the door leaving me at Sonia's feet puzzled by her behavior.

I went looking for Claire and found her in her tent. She lay inside in the dark covered in blankets, but looked up when I pushed my way in.

"Is that you, Charlie?

I crawled under the blankets and scooched my way forward until I lay by her chest and nuzzled my nose against her cheek. It tasted salty.

"What's going to happen to us? In a week, I may be panhandling again. And where will you go?"

As I lay next to Claire, I remembered the nights I lay next to Mira—the first night Mark made us leave their bedroom, the last night Mira made him leave the apartment and so many in between—just the two of us to comfort each other. I understand I am not human, but I felt closest to being human when I lay next to her.

When the day of the Township's deadline arrived, Al woke up early. He sat on the edge of the bed in his night clothes for several minutes speaking softly to someone I could not see. Like Father Paul, Al said he spoke to God. He repeated this odd human behavior as often as Mary did, except he did not yell or call God names the way Mary had with Jim. And instead of irritating him, Al's conversations with God always seemed to bring him peace.

While Al talked, I often wondered whether God would speak to me. I listened carefully for his voice, and not hearing it puzzled me. My hearing was much better than Al's. Inside the shelter, I could hear footsteps out in the gravel parking lot. Al couldn't hear himself sing. It must be a unique attribute of being human that humans can talk to and hear other humans who aren't there.

When Al and God finished speaking, Al got down on the rug and pulled a large box out from underneath his bed. Inside was a uniform I had never seen him wear complete with striped pants. The pants were a lighter blue than the color of Sergeant Mike's pants and the stripes were red instead of yellow. The coat was a dark blue with one row of shiny gold buttons down the front, colored ribbons on the left chest, and stars on each shoulder. Al lifted the coat and pants out of the box and laid them on his bed. He reached under his bed and pulled out a second box that contained black shoes, a white belt with a dull buckle, and a faded white hat.

The uniform did not fit him well. Al could not button each button on the coat or the top button on his pants. Yet, he stood solemnly and stiffly before the doorway of the shelter and took a last look around. He held my leash in his hand.

"Come here, Charlie," he said. At first, I stayed by his bed wagging my tail until he gave me an order. "I said come." He attached the leash to my collar and we left the shelter.

Many of the camp residents were already standing in the parking area wearing jackets and hats and milling about to keep warm. The morning air had a sharp edge to its coldness. As the sky lightened, cars entered the parking lot and parked in a line in front of the first row of tents and shelters along the gravel area instead of off to the side as they usually did. Father Paul stepped out of the first car as car doors opened and people spilled out. Many were carrying the signs they carried earlier along the highway. Father Paul walked up to Al and they shook hands. Father Paul wore the long, dark coat that covered him from his neck down to below his knees and the hat that looked like a silver cat curled up on top of his head.

"Captain."

"It promises to be a beautiful day, Father," Al said looking up at a sky the color of his pants.

"Indeed," Father Paul said.

A few moments later, the van from the veterinary hospital arrived and parked at the other end of the gravel area away from the camp. Jen and Dr. Deaver had come dressed warmly in puffy jackets and long pants, and wore hats, gloves and thick scarves. I sat at Al's feet and felt a knot forming in my stomach as I watched them approach.

"Thank you for coming, doctor," Al said. He reached out and shook her hand.

"I'm still hoping for a miracle," Dr. Deaver replied.

"So are we," Al said. He looked down at me and I sensed in him the same emotions he had the night he left me behind at the veterinary hospital. Al handed my leash to Dr. Deaver. "If I'm arrested, take Charlie with you."

I scratched at Al's pants and barked. Why would he give me away again when I had done nothing wrong? I told Al in no uncertain terms I did not want to go back to the veterinary hospital, but he misunderstood my concern.

"I'll be fine, Charlie," he said. He tried to bend down to pet me, but his uniform was too tight. "Hopefully, neither one of us will end up in a cage today."

Dr. Deaver handed the leash to Jen. "Go on, Jen. You heard Al," Dr. Deaver said. "Take Charlie."

"Dr. Deaver?"

"You can come pick me up at the Township building later on, that is if the Chief lets me out after I give him a piece of my mind."

"Come on, Charlie," Jen said.

I barked, shook my head, and tugged fiercely against the leash. My toenails left lines in the hard soil as Jen tried to pull me away from Al and Dr. Deaver. The people around us frowned, shook their heads, and murmured their disappointment. Jen was about to pick me up and walk away when Bruce stepped forward.

"It ain't right, Al," Bruce said quietly. "He's your dog and I mean no disrespect, but Charlie's been with us this far. He means a lot to these folks. It ain't right to take him out of the fight now."

Al looked at me and then at Dr. Deaver and Jen. Dr. Deaver shrugged her shoulders.

"Keep him here for now, Jen," Al said, "but if they arrest me, you know what to do."

The residents of the camp and Father Paul's parishioners had spread out behind the parked vehicles in a line that stretched from the woods on the river side of the camp to the woods along the highway. When they saw Jen and I take our place in line, a loud cheer erupted, and several birds took flight from nearby trees. Al, Father Paul and Dr. Deaver stood at the center of the line. They made an interesting trio with Al in his uniform towering over Dr. Deaver wearing her puffy coat and hat, and Father Paul next to her with the silver cat on his head.

The next vehicle to enter the gravel parking area looked like the van from the veterinary hospital except it had a big number 6 on each side and a tall pole attached to the roof with a dish balanced on top. A young man and woman got out of the van and began unloading equipment from the back. The man lifted a box with a bright light to his shoulder and walked toward us while the woman carried a black stick. She walked up to Al, pointed the stick at him, and began asking Al questions.

The young woman heard me barking while she was speaking with Al. She walked over to Jen afterward.

"He's adorable," she said. "but isn't this an unusual event to bring a dog along?"

"Oh, he's not mine," Jen said.

Someone shouted "That's Charlie! He's our mascot!" He began chanting "Charlie! Charlie!" until soon everyone in line, including Al, Father Paul and Dr. Deaver were chanting my name. The young woman motioned to the man with the box and he turned the bright light on me. She began speaking into the black stick.

"Here at the homeless camp in Riverdale, a small dog has inspired the less fortunate in their fight against a government order to drive them off this ground. His name is Charlie. This little guy is determined to speak his mind."

The young woman pointed her black stick at me. I squinted and barked at the man with the box because the light hurt my eyes. At that moment, the first black and white cars arrived with their lights flashing. The young woman turned back to the man holding the box.

"There you have it. A line has been drawn. Riverdale's finest will soon find out whether Charlie's bark is worse than his bite," she said. "Back to you, Jim."

Sergeant Mike got out of the first black and white car and walked up to Al. I lunged toward the Sergeant barking—I no longer trusted him—but Jen restrained me.

The two men spoke. Their faces were hard and lacked the sparkling eyes and easy grins of their earlier conversations in the shelter.

"You have to move these cars, Al," the Sergeant said.

Al simply shook his head.

Sergeant Mike spoke into a tiny box attached to the shoulder of his heavy leather jacket and then turned and walked back toward other men wearing striped pants that had emerged from the black and white cars.

A big tow truck with yellow flashing lights pulled into the parking lot, turned, and backed up toward the line of cars. The people in the line began to sing "We shall overcome" mixed with shouts of "Hell, no. We won't go!" Jen held onto my leash with both hands. My collar dug into my windpipe as I pressed forward and barked at the truck with every fiber of my being.

When the truck stopped, a fat man in overalls jumped out. He began moving sticks on the side of the truck and the truck's flatbed began to rise. Two more tow trucks with their lights flashing entered the gravel parking area, and behind them, a large garbage truck.

When the fat man from the first tow truck began dragging a large hook on a long cable toward a car in the middle of the row, a man from Father Paul's church went up to the car and laid across its hood. Men in striped pants swarmed around him. They lifted him off the hood, placed him on the ground on his stomach, and then put silver rings around his hands. They dragged him toward one of the black and white cars.

A woman in a hooded sweatshirt and dark pants left the line and jumped on the hood of the car, but she did not lay down. She stood up facing the men in striped pants and raised her fist in the air.

"Claire, get back in line!" Al shouted, but she did not listen. As the men in striped pants tried to grab her legs, she swore and kicked and screamed at them—"Get your hands off me!"—until a man in striped pants caught her from behind and lifted her off. Several camp residents cheered Claire on. She struggled and fought and yelled all the way to the black and white car and scuffled with the men in striped pants as they tried to push her inside.

The sound of a honking horn broke through the din of all the shouting and singing, my barking, and the beeping and clanking of the tow trucks as they hauled the first cars onto the flatbeds. A small car that reminded me of Mira's entered the gravel parking area with its headlights on, its horn blaring, and kicking up gravel and dust. It stopped in front of the first tow truck in another shower of stone and dust and Sonia jumped out.

"I've got it!" she yelled waving a piece of paper in her hand. "I've got the injunction!" When she spied Sergeant Mike, she ran over and handed it to him. "You have to stop," she said.

Sonia was breathing heavily and brushed her hair back from her face. The man from the news truck walked closer shining the bright light from the box on Sonia and Sergeant Mike. Al, Father Paul and Dr. Deaver remained rooted in the center of the line like the tall trees along the river bank.

Sergeant Mike seemed relieved when he read the paper. He waved it in the air. "We're done here," he shouted. Cheering broke out up and down the line. Parishioners hugged the camp residents while others got in their cars and honked the horns. Jen was about to walk up to Al and hand him my leash when she saw Sergeant Mike approaching. She stopped, and I sat by her feet panting.

Sergeant Mike handed Al the piece of paper Sonia gave him. "I hope I'm still welcome to stop by," he said.

"Are you going to release the man and the girl you've got in the back of the squad cars?" Al asked.

Sergeant Mike turned and looked in the direction of the cars. "I'll tell them to let the man go, but the girl took a swing at one of my men, Al," he said. "I can't have that."

"Then take me in her place," Al said. He held out his hands. "Put me under arrest."

Sergeant Mike looked at Al with a bewildered expression. "Why would I do that, Al? What is she going to learn from having you stand in front of the judge and pay the fine for assaulting a police officer?"

"That there is someone in this world who cares about her," Al said.

Sergeant Mike's look of bewilderment persisted, but he turned and motioned to another man in striped pants. "Frank, tell 'em to release both."

When they let Claire out of the black and white car and removed the silver rings, she ran toward the camp. She stopped suddenly when she saw Sonia standing with

Al, Father Paul and Dr. Deaver. For a moment, Claire stood frozen, simply staring at us, neither moving toward us or the camp. Then she was engulfed in a swarm of camp residents. Two men raised her to their shoulders and carried her triumphantly toward the camp while people around them shouted "Claire! Claire!" Claire turned and looked back over her shoulder at us and my heart swelled. It was the first time I saw her smile.

XV

After the reprieve for the camp, residents greeted me with cheers and "paw fives," a trick Al taught me. When someone knelt and held out a hand with the palm open and fingers spread, I'd swat the hand with my paw. It earned me thunderous accolades and treats. Humans are amused by the simplest things.

Al had put his uniform away and slid the boxes underneath his bed. In the evening, he pulled out two more boxes stuffed with shiny colored balls, strings of old popcorn, and crumpled tree branches. I got up from my rug to inspect. The underneath of Al's bed seemed to be a never-ending source of unexplored smells and curiosities.

The popcorn had a sharp, unpleasant aroma, not the buttery smell I expected, so I left it alone. Although the tree branches looked like they came from the short, prickly green trees in the woods, I could tell by the scent they were fake. To my surprise, Al unfolded the tree branches to form a small tree he set on the table. Al sang to music coming from his laptop as he hung the shiny colored balls on the tree branches with hooks. But unlike Mira's, Al's singing was not particularly pleasant to listen to.

Al's tree decorating signaled the beginning of the season called Christmas when humans I usually found in a good mood were in even better moods, and those I often found in a bad mood felt even worse. Mira had a tree in her apartment, a much larger tree than Al's with many decorations—glittery stars and icicles, flowers, ribbons and bows. But if Christmas was meant to be a time of celebration, Mira kept hers subdued. In the time I shared with Mira, I never understood the significance of the tree, or the time of year, other than it gave her pleasure. The tree went back in a closet a few weeks later.

When Claire noticed the tree in Al's shelter, she stopped coming by and skipped the bus for a special dinner at Father Paul's church Al called Advent. Afterwards, Al went looking for her and brought her food from the dinner in a shiny, metal pan. It was still warm and smelled oh, so good. I hadn't been invited to any dinners at the church, although Al always brought home leftovers. When Al walked past the shelter with what I believed was my dinner, I had to see where it was going.

"I brought a take-home box for you," Al said when he found Claire smoking a white stick outside her tent.

"Thanks," Claire said, "but I'm not hungry."

Al lifted the cover on the pan and breathed in the tantalizing aromas. "Too bad," Al said. "Turkey with gravy, stuffing, ham, candied sweet potatoes with a marshmallow glaze…" He glanced at Claire who pretended not to be interested. "The marshmallow glaze is exceptional."

I sat in between them shaking. My tongue was flapping back and forth trying to keep up with my saliva production. I have always disapproved of the way some large dogs let saliva hang down from their jowls like icicles and then shower everyone with a shake of their heads.

"Do you mind if I have seconds?" Al asked.

Claire looked at Al and then at the food before she put the white stick in her mouth and breathed in again. She exhaled a cloud of smoke. "Help yourself."

Al picked a piece of turkey out of the pan with his fingers and stuffed it in his mouth. "Um, ummm." When he reached for another piece, I began to whimper to remind Al the leftovers were supposed to be mine.

"Oh, I'm sorry, Charlie. Here you go." He bent down and handed me a thick piece of turkey. I took it from his hand politely and trotted off a few steps to eat it as was my custom. Al lifted another piece out of the pan that looked as if it was coming my way, so I ate faster.

"You're giving it all to him?" Claire asked.

"You said you didn't want any," Al reminded her. "Charlie has to eat, too."

"I'll try some," Claire said. She threw the white stick on the ground and stepped on it.

"Why don't we go back to my shelter and eat at the table," Al said. "I've been meaning to talk to you about the move anyway."

"I'll just take it inside my tent," Claire said.

Al handed me the second piece of turkey. "You know, I forgot to bring utensils," he said patting the pockets of his coat. "Come on. Come sit at my table and hear me out."

"Only if you put the tree away."

Al frowned. "What have you got against my tree?"

"It's not the tree. It's what it reminds me of."

"I'll throw a sheet over it."

Claire sighed and rolled her eyes, but she accompanied Al and me to the shelter and sat down at the table.

Al pulled the pillow case off a pillow and slid it over his Christmas tree. It was a short tree. The tree's roots stood on the table top and the treetop was no higher than I could stand on my hind legs. The pillow case covered the entire tree and it looked like Al had made the pillow balance on one end.

Al put the tray of food in front of Claire and gave her plastic utensils like the ones Mary had collected from the back of the deli. Claire began to eat noisily. I sat at her feet and watched as she ate with her face hovering over the tray. She shoveled in one mouthful after another in rapid, sloppy succession with barely a breath in between. I was appalled. The big dogs at the veterinary hospital ate with better manners.

"I could use your help," Al said.

"Doing what?" Claire asked in between bites.

"Organizing the move," Al said. "We have a lot to do."

Claire never stopped eating. "We?" she asked with her mouth full. I whimpered, but the pan was fully hers now, and my charm was not having its desired effect.

"The entire camp," Al replied. "Father Paul will find us a truck, but when it comes time to move, everyone will have to pack up his or her own belongings. They'll have to be marked before they're loaded on the truck, so we know what belongs to whom. Someone will have to be at the new site to oversee the unloading and make sure no one helps themselves to something that does not belong to them. I want someone there I can trust and who the other residents respect."

Claire stopped eating and looked up at Al. I could not tell whether she was angry or trying not to laugh. "Since when has anyone given me respect?"

"Since you stood up on the hood of that car. Have you forgotten they carried you from the parking lot on their shoulders? If anyone did not respect you before, they do now."

Claire poked at the remaining candied yams with her fork as she considered Al's words. "Why me? Why not someone like Bruce?"

"Bruce is a good man," Al replied. "He's always willing to lend a hand, but he's not a leader."

Claire's look of bemused anger returned. "What makes you think I'm a leader?" she asked. "I haven't led anything except a miserable life."

Al did not answer her at first. He bore into her with searching eyes. Whenever he looked at me that way with his eyebrows lowered and his jaw tightened, I laid back my ears and exposed my belly.

"When Father Paul first brought you here," he said, "I saw a young woman who respected herself enough to stay away from dope. If you have the strength to stay clean in this environment, you have the strength to lead. I saw a leader standing on the hood of that car."

Tears welled up in Claire's eyes, but she quickly wiped them away and finished eating the candied yams.

She wiped her mouth on her sleeve, burped, and then looked up at Al. "I'll help you," she said. "Where else am I going anyway?"

"Good," Al said. "I'll tell the others. I want you to sit in on the meetings with Father Paul to look for new ground and plan the move, but not much will happen now until after Christmas." Claire simply nodded. "You know, Father Paul's congregation hosts a Christmas dinner for us, too," Al said. "There's more where that came from." He pointed at the empty silver tray.

I grumbled and lay down on my rug.

"Bring me another take-home dinner," Claire said.

"I could," Al said, "but I can't bring you the company. Christmas is a lousy time to be alone."

A look of pain flashed across Claire's face. "I'm used to it," she said.

"Don't be," Al replied. "Why punish yourself? Whatever happened in your past, Claire, does not destine you to repeat it for the rest of your life."

Claire sat back in her chair and stared at Al. "Why do you care?" she asked. "What difference does it make if I get on that lousy bus and go to a stupid dinner at the church?" She meant the words to hurt, but Al didn't flinch.

"Because I want to help you avoid half the pain I've endured," Al replied.

"It's too late for that," Claire snapped. She stood up to leave, but Al motioned her to sit down. He stood up himself and went over to the bookshelf by his bed, removed a small box, and brought it back to the table.

When Claire sat down, I jumped into her lap and stretched my neck toward the silver tray. The smells were still there. I held out hope that a morsel of yam or shard of turkey might be also. Claire tipped the tray toward us.

"Here, Charlie."

No morsels or shards remained, but there was plenty of sauce. I licked the pan until it gleamed. When I turned and faced Claire, she laughed at the sight of me licking the gravy that dripped from my whiskers. It made my heart glad to give her a reason to smile.

Al sat down at the table, opened the box, and removed a few black and white photographs. He spread them in front of Claire. "I haven't shared these with anyone else here except Bruce and Father Paul." He pointed to one. "That's me in Vietnam," Al said. "1967."

Claire hesitated. Even though a curiosity burned in her eyes, she feigned boredom. Humans often try to conceal their emotions in conversation, but some are better at it than others. Underneath Claire's attitude of indifference and detachment lay strong emotions of sadness, grief, and anger, but also longing. The smell was simply too strong to disguise. Al had her scent, too. I could tell from his body language.

Claire leaned forward and glanced at the photograph by Al's finger. "Wow," she said. "You were thin."

"And young," Al replied. "I had a lot more hair back then ... and good looks."

Claire laughed, but quickly put her hand over her mouth as though she had embarrassed herself.

"How old were you?" she asked.

"Nineteen," Al said.

Claire studied the photograph. "You were younger than I am now." She pushed the photograph back to Al and sat back in the chair with her arms crossed. "Who are the other men?"

Al picked up the photograph and looked at it closely. I sensed his mood shift to one of intense grief, not on the surface of his emotions but deeply submerged. The wrinkles on Al's face grew more pronounced.

"Men in my company. Eddie Geller and Frank Hibbs. My friends. We had just gotten off the transport plane at the Tan Son Nhut airfield near Saigon. None of us had ever been outside our home states and there we were, in Asia, in a war."

Al laid the photograph down and slid another across the tabletop to Claire. "This one was taken at the fire base near Khe Sanh not long before our last patrol. We were filling sand bags to fortify the rifle pits."

"Wow, you guys were ripped," Claire said. Her voice grew more animated. "Look at your six-packs!"

"Basic training got us in shape," Al said, "but building a perimeter defense is like chain gang labor. And Nam was hotter than Texas in summer and more humid." Al sighed. "I sent this photograph in a letter to my mother. I didn't know it would be the last letter I'd write home from the war."

Al paused and studied the photograph as he did the first one. Claire looked up at Al the same way I looked up at him when he was eating.

"Okay, are you going to make me ask you why it was the last letter you wrote home?"

It took a moment for Al's mind to return from wherever it had been. Al sighed once more.

"The fire base at Khe Sanh was surrounded by NVA regulars, North Vietnamese Army. My unit wasn't in country very long before they sent us up there as reinforcements. So much for easing my way into the war.

"Not long after this photograph was taken, the CO ordered my platoon out on a patrol to see how close the enemy had moved toward our lines and, if possible, to capture a prisoner and bring him back for interrogation. They were closer than we thought."

Al's wrinkles were now as deep as canyons. His eyes were inside the photograph as if he could still feel the chill of fear even while sweat ran down his back. I looked at the image of the young Al and the men with him. Behind them were tents and what looked like low shelters dug in the ground. I wondered if it was a photograph from Al's first homeless camp and lamented he had been homeless so long.

"The first shell killed Eddie. Just a huge explosion of earth, and Eddie ... he was right in the middle of it. Then a machine gun opened up. I remember the sounds of the bullets hitting Frank's chest and then one hit me in the left shoulder and knocked me down. It happened so fast I never fired a round. Eventually, I lost consciousness because of all the pain and blood loss."

"How did you get back?"

"I didn't. I passed out and it was dark when I regained consciousness. Someone was rifling through my clothes. At first, I thought it was one of our medics thinking I was dead and looking for my dog tags. Then I saw his eyes. NVA. I don't know which one of us was more scared. We both reached for our knives, but he had his to my neck first, so I let go of mine. I don't know why he let me live. I spent the next five years as a prisoner of war."

Claire gazed past Al to the strange black and white flag that hung above his bed. She said nothing, but I could feel her emotions shifting, too. Her shield of detachment and indifference was weakening. Al and I had both met humans who simply did not care, who were incapable of empathizing with another human's suffering, or even a dog's. When a human lacks empathy, it's as obvious as a dog without a tail. Claire, however, had a big heart for humans and dogs, only hers had taken such a beating in her young life she was afraid to let it show.

"There were times I thought about dying," Al continued. "Many times. But I didn't want to let them win. They were trying to crush my spirit, to make me inhuman. Since I was black, they offered me privileges if I'd make racist statements about America sending the black man to kill the yellow man. When I refused, they put me in a bamboo cage in the river for hours. I came out covered with leeches.

"I remembered a song I had heard back home that was popular in the civil rights movement. 'We shall overcome.' And I sang that song over and over again. At first, I sang it out loud, loud enough for other prisoners to hear. Some of them began to sing along so the guards beat me and put me in solitary confinement. Later on, I hummed it or tapped out the rhythm on the wall of my cell."

Al slid a third picture across the table to Claire. Now she was leaning forward in her chair savoring Al's every word. "That's a photograph a newspaperman took of me hugging my mother when I arrived back in the States at Dover airbase. For five years, my mother thought I was dead. The Corps had me officially listed as missing in action, but the NVA never passed along my name as captured for whatever reason and the Corps told my mother they had little reason to believe I survived the firefight.

"After I had been gone over two years, my mother had a funeral for me and even placed a gravestone with my name on it next to my grandparents.' She said she had reached the point where she had to let go and say goodbye or her grief would have ruined her."

Claire's eyes widened. "You already have a gravestone with your name on it?"

"In the cemetery of the Mansfield Baptist Church. Mom said she'd have the gravestone removed if I wanted, but I told her to leave it there. No sense wasting the money. I'll use it someday."

"That's awful!"

Al shrugged his shoulders. "The son my mother knew never returned from Vietnam, so perhaps it was fitting."

Claire ran a finger over the faded newsprint. "Five years later. So you were twenty-four when this was taken. That's how old I am now."

"Two weeks shy of my twenty-fifth birthday. I'll never forget that birthday cake." Al smiled. "The candles, the taste of my mother's buttercream icing. Best cake ever."

"But you didn't find a girl, get married, and live happily ever after."

"No, I did not."

"Why?"

"Sometimes you can leave the war, but the war doesn't leave you." Al said. "I stayed with the Corps for a while. I became a recruiter, but at the end of the Vietnam war, it wasn't a popular job. I visited Frank's and Eddie's folks and told them about our last day because I thought they ought to know. Frank had a young bride who wanted to know why he died and I didn't. It was a question I'd been asking myself every day since. Was it just dumb luck? I certainly hadn't done anything in my life up to that point to earn a day more than Frank or Eddie."

"Sometimes it's better to be lucky," Claire said.

Al picked up the first photograph again. "I let the question eat away at me a little each day," he said. "It was clear from her tone of voice that she wasn't particularly fond of colored people and wished Frank and I had traded places. When my Mom died, I lost the only person who had put any positive thoughts in my head. I had turned to drinking already, but when she passed, I began to live inside a bottle. I gave up all responsibility for myself. I simply wanted to disappear, and so I did. I lost my job. I lost Mom's home. I became homeless, and I built for myself a prison far worse than anything the NVA ever kept me in."

Al laid the photograph down on the table. "Right now, Claire, you don't realize it but you're building the same sort of prison for yourself. You think you are building it to keep the pain out, but instead you're actually sealing it in. When you finish, there'll be no one there but you and your pain."

Claire's mood swung closed like the door on one of the metal cages at the veterinary hospital. She looked like she had been caught in the cone of a flashlight while, all around her, faces in the darkness were staring at her. Her fear, her anger, her grief were all looking for places to hide.

"Let it go, Claire," Al said softly.

Her stoic façade began to show signs of stress, a quivering lip, a facial twitch, until the emotions were too raw and too strong to hold back any longer. Claire began to cry like she did in her tent when I was the only one there to see.

Al allowed Claire to cry, saying nothing. While Claire buried her face in my fur, Al and I looked at each other across the table as we had on many occasions when a person's pain spilled out in front of him. Al's bulldog face seemed to gain more wrinkles with each one as if he absorbed it all. He smiled at me. I took it as a 'thank you' for comforting Claire, but I didn't need to be thanked. Being wanted, by Al, by Claire, by the camp, was reward enough.

Eventually, Claire sat up and wiped her face with her shirt sleeve. Her emotions shifted again, coming back like scattered birds to roost in the same tree. She looked up at Al with neither defiance nor surrender, just an air of hardness.

"My stepfather raped me for the first time when I was fourteen," Claire said. "I left home to put an end to that.

But then it was a man in a homeless shelter. This guy, Jerry, who said he'd watch out for me, see that I was safe, you know. Gained my trust and got me alone in an office.

"The worst one was the cop. He busted me for shoplifting some groceries then told me he'd drop the charges if I'd have sex with him. So he parked out in back of an industrial park and took me in the back seat. Then he just left me there. By the time I was nineteen, I learned I was wanted for only one reason, so I figured I might as well get something for it." The tears welled up through the cracks in her hard exterior. "I'm ashamed," she whispered.

Al reached into the box still sitting on the table and pulled out a small, red ribbon divided by a blue stripe with a bronze star hanging from it. He undid the clasp on the back and leaned toward Claire. "May I?"

"What's that?" she asked.

"A reminder," Al said. "Each of us possesses the ability to do extraordinary things and endure extraordinary things." He pinned the bronze star on Claire's shirt. "The greatest danger we face is when we allow our fear to prevent us from doing either one. I hope this helps you overcome yours."

XVI

The camp was nearly deserted after the bus left for the Christmas dinner at Father Paul's church. I lay on the rug in Al's shelter listening to the night sounds, the whine of the cars on the highway, occasional strains of music coming from the shopping center. The time called Christmas is a busy time for humans, even after dark.

There was a chill in the air inside Al's shelter. He did not leave the space heater on when he was not inside. The shaggy rug was as warm as any basket I ever had, and Al always left plenty of food and water for me in bowls underneath the table.

I was napping when the sound of excited voices aroused me. The crunch of gravel underneath bus tires usually signaled the residents' return to the camp. I raised my head to listen, but I did not hear the growl of the bus's engine. Now the voices were shouting, human voices full of urgency and alarm that raised the hair on the back of my neck. Instinctively, I began to bark and echo the alarm as my ancestors have done for man since the beginning of time. I got up and went outside to see what all the commotion was about and nearly ran into Bruce in front of Al's shelter. He was talking to someone on a phone.

"Al, the camp's on fire!"

I smelled the odor of smoke drifting through the camp. It did not smell like the smoke of burning wood inside a barrel, but was tainted with car fumes instead. I followed Bruce down the path in between the tents trying to get his attention until I felt the heat of the flames and saw their orange tongues leaping up and snapping at the treetops overhead. Bruce kept walking toward them. Memories of Mark and the heat and smoke inside my box sent me running off toward the river even as the sound of the sirens and horns of the trucks with the flashing lights filled the air.

I do not remember running or even the feel of the brush as I ran through the woods. Instinct tends not to record what happens between the impulse of fright and safety. Instinct is already ingrained in us and has no need to remember. Inside the woods, out of the heat and the reach of the flames when I stopped to catch my breath, curiosity compelled me to turn around and look back at the burning camp. Red and blue lights flitted among the trees like small birds until bright lights from the trucks turned on and chased away the darkness. The forest was aflame in a white brilliance and the darkness cowered behind tree trunks and in pools on the forest floor behind rocks and stumps. Even the stars overhead vanished in the glare.

Within the bright light, I saw black silhouettes of humans in heavy coats and hats moving from the trucks toward the fire. They pulled long ropes, ropes so heavy sometimes two or three humans had to carry them, and they pointed the ends of the ropes at the fire and drenched it with water. When the water struck some of the tents and shelters, they collapsed and blew away like leaves in a strong wind.

As I watched, I felt a biting chill. It came not from the cold, but from a sense of loss. The residents who owned the tents or shelters the fire and water had destroyed were truly homeless once more, and I wondered what had become of Al's shelter and my rug. A feeling of helplessness rooted me in the forest floor and prevented me from running further away or back toward the camp.

More water flowed from the long ropes. The orange flames spat and hissed at the humans like angry cats and grew smaller and smaller until they disappeared in the spray and the mist. The humans in the heavy coats and hats were still spraying water around the camp when the yellow bus pulled into the gravel parking area. It stopped beside a truck with flashing lights and the door opened, but only three people stepped off. One of them was Al. There was no mistaking Al. And he was calling me.

"Charlie!? Charlie, where are you?! Charlie, c'mon, boy!"

His voice boomed in short bursts, and in between I heard Claire shriek. "Charlieeeeeee! ... Charlieeeeeee!"

I ran through the woods toward the gravel parking area once again feeling the tug and the snap of brush and the sting of thorns. I ran faster when I reached the gravel and it was only a matter of seconds later until Al scooped me up in his arms. He nearly crushed me against his chest in a hug. My feet were still moving, my whole body shaking, and I licked his rugged, whisker strewn chin noticing a trace of turkey and stuffing still there from his interrupted meal.

Claire stood next to Al stroking my fur until Al passed me to her with a final squeeze. Her face was streaked with tears, and I licked them, too. Pressed against her chest, I felt her heart pounding and heard the rush of air inside her as she breathed in. I sensed in Claire a tremendous lightness and relief. She even laughed as I licked her face.

"Charlie, I was so worried about you!" As I made myself a little nest inside the open zipper of her jacket, I felt her heartbeat and her breathing subside, but as she gazed out over the ruined camp, her muscles began to harden.

Father Paul had been the third person off the bus. He stood several feet away with Bruce and Sergeant Mike, who always seemed to show up when bad things happened at the camp. Al walked over to them.

"How did the fire start?" he asked.

"Seems like it was deliberately set," Bruce said.

"We shouldn't make presumptions until we know all the facts," Father Paul said.

Bruce spat on the ground. "Beggin' your pardon, Father, Pete and Jake were the only ones here besides me," Bruce said. "Carla's tent went up first and she's right next to the woods. She don't have anything in there that would spark a fire like that. And the fire department was here real quick. Like someone planned to call them. The fire took only several tents and a shelter or two. Most of the damage is water damage."

"So what are you saying, Bruce?" Sergeant Mike asked.

Claire glared at Sergeant Mike. "He's saying you couldn't get us out legally, so you found another way."

Sergeant Mike opened his mouth to say something to Claire but thought better of it and turned to Al instead. "I swear, Al, if it was deliberate, we'll catch who did it."

"Sure," Claire snapped. "Right after you find us a new place to live."

"Claire, that's enough," Father Paul said quietly but firmly. "Sergeant McConnell is not the enemy."

Claire was not cowed. She turned to Father Paul. "If God loves us as you say, why would he allow this to happen? Why would he allow what little we have to be burnt and soaked while we're eating dinner in your church?" With anger spilling out of her eyes, she carried me onto the bus, past the solemn-faced driver, and sank into a seat.

The driver was a small man with less hair than Al and ears that stuck out from his head like mine. Once Claire sat down, I could not see him over the seat ahead of me, but I heard him say "I'm glad your dog was not hurt." Claire did not answer him. Instead, she whispered in my ear. "We're just trash to them, Charlie," she said. "They want to burn us like trash."

Al climbed onboard the bus a few moments later and sat down in the seat across the aisle from Claire. "Everyone will sleep in the church tonight," he said. "Tomorrow, we'll come back and see what we can salvage."

"I'm not coming back," Claire snapped. "Ever. I wish I never came here in the first place."

"Oh?" Al said. "Life sucks so I quit. Is that it?" Claire did not answer. "So what are you going to do tomorrow? Are you going to curl up on a cot all day feeling sorry for yourself?"

"Maybe."

Al sat quietly with his arms crossed for several moments. I could tell he was angry even though I could not see his face very well in the darkened bus. He sat across the aisle from Claire as he often did across the table in the shelter waiting for her to speak. But Claire said nothing and stared out the window. To my dismay, Al began to sing in his low, raspy voice.

"We shall overcome. We shall overcome. We shall overcome someday. Deep in my heart I do believe we shall overcome someday." The bus driver joined in and the two of them sang it again.

I barked and whined and buried my head in Claire's jacket. Claire chuckled and stared at Al. "Has anyone ever told you how bad you sound?" she asked.

"Make a joyful noise to the Lord," Al said. "You try it."

"Me?" Claire gasped. "No, I can't sing."

"Anyone can sing," Al said. "It doesn't matter how it sounds. Just sing."

"You can't be serious?"

"I am serious," Al said. "Sing! No one here's going to beat you."

Claire grinned. "I'm beginning to think the guards weren't beating you because of the words."

Now Al laughed. As he laughed, Claire started singing, although softly at first. *We shall overcome...* Her voice had a light, airy sound like Mira's that floated through the hollow bus with a pleasing tone.

"Who said you can't sing?" Al said. "You sound like an angel!"

Claire smiled and began again—*We shall overcome*—this time a little louder. When Father Paul climbed on board, he added his tenor voice to Claire's and, together, they almost overcame Al's and the bus driver's dour tones.

The bus driver started the engine. Outside the bus, in the bright lights of the firetrucks, smoke and steam still rose from the smoldering camp. Claire and Al and Father Paul paid no attention. They were singing along with the bus driver at the tops of their voices, over and over. *We shall overcome.* The bus lurched, and then slowly rolled forward past the trucks, past men in bright yellow coats rolling up the ropes and Sergeant Mike and his men in striped pants. Although I was still partially nestled inside Claire's jacket cocooned in a pocket of warmth created by our body heat, I was shivering. I was going for another ride to somewhere unknown without the assurance of a new rug or basket or even my next meal.

XVII

My anxiety comes from uncertainty, the not knowing what lies ahead and fearing the worst. It is a cold chill that is not of temperature, but fear, and cannot be extinguished with warm blankets and a basket. The chill is rooted in the heart, but creeps like a vine until it reaches all my extremities and, there, causes me to tremble. It is a voice in my ears that whispers of bad things and tells me I am unwanted.

As the bus rumbled on in the darkness past stores and houses adorned with multi-color lights and collections of brightly lit animals guided by a man as big as Al dressed in red, all I could think of was the fire and Al's shelter, my rug, and my basket in the room with the sky wall. A warm place, a safe place, one that comforts and protects. Isn't that what a home is? It is as important for a dog's sense of well-being as it is for a human.

Although I had spent most of my nights in relative warmth and safety in the company of humans, I remembered most vividly the one I spent slinking down a riverbank alone until I made my bed in leaves. Already in my short life, I had made my bed in five different places. I had no reason to believe Al did not want me anymore, but I had come to understand dogs were secondary to humans when it came to their own needs. Al had left me behind once before.

The bus pulled into the parking area of a large building with a tall, pointed roof and brightly colored windows filled with light. Several of the camp's residents stood on the sidewalk in front of the building bundled in hats, coats and scarves. Some waved at the bus. Others had their hands buried in the pockets of their coats and stomped their feet.

Behind them, bathed in light from big, round bulbs stuck in the ground, stood what looked to me like a shelter except it had only three walls. Large animals I had never seen before stood around it. A man and woman inside the shelter knelt by a wooden basket, and in the basket lay an infant wrapped only in white cloth. It seemed strange that neither the man nor woman, nor the infant, needed a hat and coat like the camp residents, and no one standing on the sidewalk paid them any attention.

As Claire carried me off the bus, some of the camp's residents came up to us with relieved faces and began to pet me. Others asked questions.

"How bad is it, Claire?"

"We won't be going back there for a while," Claire answered. "Maybe ever."

A woman began to cry. "Now I have less than nothing."

Claire sighed. "Listen," she said. "Don't give up. Al and I will go over there tomorrow and see what we can save. They're not going to get rid of us that easily."

Father Paul began ushering everyone into the church. As I passed the brightly lit outside shelter, the man and woman and the infant had not moved, nor had any of the animals around them. Stranger still, they all had the same, faint artificial smell. I wiggled in Claire's arms and barked at them.

"Stupid dog," Claire said. "They're not real."

Inside the church, the ceiling seemed as high overhead as the sky. The walls were covered with paintings, and silent figures of elderly humans in robes stood everywhere. A few of the residents still spoke loudly and angrily about the fire until someone said, "Shhhh. We're in God's house."

My ears perked. I began to look closely at everyone in the building I did not recognize and wondered which one God was. I wanted to meet God since Al spoke to him so often and ask him why he wouldn't speak to me. And I wondered why God had such a large house with room for so many people while others had none.

Down a long hallway, I smelled the wondrous smell of human foods, smells reminiscent of the food in the silver pan Al had brought Claire a few weeks earlier and the traces of food in Al's whiskers earlier that evening. Turkey, stuffing, gravy, potatoes. The smells grew stronger the further we walked along. We passed through a pair of doors into a brightly lit room larger than any room I could recall being in before. Much like Mira's studio, it had a shiny hardwood floor and only metal chairs and tables for furniture. At one end of the room, a long table stood against the wall covered with trays of all the food that had been beckoning me. The rest of the camp's residents were sitting at tables eating and drinking with people I recognized from the marches who had carried signs and stood with us the morning Sergeant Mike and his men tried to make us leave the camp.

At the other end of the room, humans were setting up rows of small beds, just green cloth stretched between wooden poles with legs. Nearby, a tall tree towered over the beds. It seemed to have as many shiny balls and lights as there were stars in the sky and a human with wings perched at the top watched over everyone in the room. Brightly colored packages lay underneath its lowest branches. Apparently, God celebrated Christmas, too, and had the biggest tree of all.

Still nestled in Claire's jacket, I stuck my head out further as she approached the table with the food. Two women stood behind it, an older woman with gray hair and a young woman with blonde hair. Both wore white aprons over their clothes and each held a large spoon in one hand.

The young woman's face beamed when she saw me. "Are you Charlie?" she asked. "I think I saw you on the news!"

"He is," Claire answered.

"We've heard so much about you."

"I don't think we've ever had a dog inside the church before," the older woman said. "Would you like me to make a plate for you?" she asked Claire.

"Yeah," she said and set me down on the floor at her feet. "I'm sure the first one is cold by now."

The older woman nodded and smiled. "We'll do the best we can to make you feel welcome here." She spooned food from the steaming trays onto a paper plate and handed it to Claire while I whistled and whimpered at Claire's feet.

"I'll bet Charlie would like something to eat, too," the young woman said. She spooned food onto another plate, carried it to a corner of the room away from the tables, and set the plate on the floor. I thanked her politely with tail wags and a smile and remembered my manners as I ate. I carried each piece of turkey a few steps away, as was my custom, to eat it off the polished wood floor, before returning for another. When I finished, I licked the floor until it shined and the plate until it was white enough it could have been returned to the pile of plates unused.

After I had eaten, I walked around the tables and received pets and scratches from several of the camp's residents and the people from Father Paul's church seated there. I sniffed and licked outstretched hands and jumped up in laps when invited. It was my way of making sure everyone from the camp was accounted for.

Father Paul's parishioners began to hand out the brightly colored packages stacked around the bottom of the tree to the camp's residents. As the sound of ripping paper mixed with human conversation, I slipped away quietly to explore, out an open doorway, up a dimly lit hallway past darkened rooms and more silent robed figures standing in hollow areas in the walls.

I came to a room even larger than the brightly lit one with the polished wood floor. Overhead, I recognized the lighted windows I had seen from the bus when I arrived. A soft glow drifted down from the windows and illuminated rows and rows of wooden benches covered with cushions, enough for an entire city of homeless people to sleep on. I walked noiselessly down a carpeted path in between the rows of benches but did not find anyone asleep there. The room was empty.

The floor sloped downward toward a large stone table draped in a white cloth at the front of the room. Three gold chairs stood behind the table each with a red cushion seat, and behind them, a stone wall with beautiful white and silver swirls shimmered in the windows' glow like the river in moonlight. On the wall high above the chairs, a single light shone on the figure of a man with his arms outstretched against a long, wooden beam. He was thin and gaunt, dressed in only a white cloth wrapped around his waist and wore a hat that looked like branches from the thickets in the woods. His face looked up toward the colored windows and his eyes and open mouth expressed an intense sorrow and pain. Like the humans in the shelter outside the church, he neither moved nor spoke.

I sat quietly looking up at him and wondered why a human would hang from a wooden beam on a wall. I wanted to comfort him as any dog would seeing a human in such a condition, until I remembered what Claire had said outside. *Stupid dog. They're not real.*

"Charlie, what are you doing here?" Father Paul's voice startled me. I had not heard him approach. I ran under one of the benches and peeked out with my ears laid back and my tail curled under my hind legs. "Charlie?" Father Paul said again. His voice had the same tone of surprise and dismay I had heard in Mira's when she found me in her basket of folded clothes.

I always found tail wags and a smile effective at softening the effects of human disapproval. I trotted out from underneath the bench and went to Father Paul. When he bent down, I lowered my head expecting to be lifted by the scruff of my neck and carried out of the room like a bad-smelling blanket, but he gathered me into his arms instead. He stood up and held me close to his chest like Al and Claire had and scratched my belly with one hand.

We gazed up at the sorrowful man on the wall together for several moments and Father Paul smiled. "I don't suppose he'd mind you seeking refuge here," he said. "He was homeless, too."

XVIII

Not long after the fire, Al and I returned to the camp along with several other residents whose shelters or tents were not seriously damaged. Al's shelter still stood where it always had and my rug and his belongings all seemed none the worse for the wear. But where there had once been many tents and shelters surrounding Al's, there were now few. Elsewhere, the ground lay bare.

After the fire, I sensed a change in Al, a subtle fatigue. His breathing was such that I noticed it when I had never given it a thought before. Each breath was audible and required effort. His steps seemed heavier. Perhaps the effects of time had been accumulating and only after the fire added to Al's already substantial burden did the weight begin to show. Still, the length of his day had not diminished. He began his day on his knees before the sun was up and finished it the same way long after dark.

Claire stopped by the camp often, although she no longer slept there, and I missed seeing her every day. She drove a car, a small one like Mira's with barely enough room inside for two humans and a dog. It was dark blue, rather dull, and made a funny rattle. Claire said someone from Father Paul's church had donated it to help the mission.

Whenever I heard the rattle, I knew Claire had come to see Al and ran out to the parking lot to greet her. On a pleasant afternoon not long after the day humans call the New Year, Claire arrived at the camp in such a good mood, it caught me by surprise. Instead of her usual stoic expression, Claire hopped out of the car wearing a big smile and jumped up and down and wiggled more than I did.

"Hi, Charlie! Guess what?" she bubbled. "I have good news for a change. Wait til I tell Al!"

When we reached the shelter, Claire burst in without knocking. Al looked up upon our noisy entrance.

"Guess what?" Claire asked. She hung her jacket on the back of a folding chair and sat down at the table across from Al. She could barely contain her enthusiasm. "Everything we lost in the fire has already been replaced, and it has only been three weeks! Dick's Sporting Goods pledged to give us all the tents we need."

Al smiled broadly. "That's great news!"

"Clothing, bedding, blankets, toiletries. People are dropping off bags of it at the church. Father Paul said it's more than we need and he's sending some of it over to the county shelter."

"Perhaps you'll believe me now when I tell you the Lord answers prayer?"

Claire rolled her eyes. "Have you told anyone where we're moving to?"

Al shook his head. "Only you, Father Paul and the property owner know at this point. Better we keep it a secret as long as we can. Even though it's in an industrial area in the lower county, we don't want to attract any attention that might spook the property owner."

"I'll be relieved when the new camp is finally set up and all the residents have moved in."

"Not more than I," Al said with a grin.

Claire looked down at me. "What about Charlie?" she asked.

At the mention of my name, I sat up and wagged my tail vigorously. Al reached down and scratched my head. "I've spoken to Dr. Deaver," he said. "She'll take Charlie for a few days when the time comes." I wagged my tail again even though Al had used my name and Dr. Deaver's in the same breath. I scratched at his pant leg to be picked up. He bent over, but grimaced as he lifted me onto his lap.

"You okay?" Claire asked.

"Yeah, I'm fine," Al said. "I think Charlie's put on weight." He gave me a playful tussle.

"Claire, I spoke to Sonia Ramirez yesterday," Al said.

"You mean the lady lawyer who got us the stay?" Claire asked. "Lotta good it did," she added under her breath.

"The same," Al said. "She's now the executive director of the entire Interfaith Counsel."

"Good for her."

"She makes all the hiring decisions."

"Good for her."

"She wants you to come work for her."

Claire gave Al the same look she gave him when he first asked for her help with the move. "Why?"

"Because she needs help," Al said. "And it is a paying position. Executive assistant. Fifteen dollars an hour to start plus benefits."

Claire's eyes widened. "You mean a real job?" Al nodded. "But I've never done that type of work! All I've ever done is bag groceries."

"Sonia's confident you can learn."

"I don't have any office clothes!"

"Father Paul's parishioners will find you some."

"How will I work for Sonia and help you with the move?"

"Sonia says you can start after the move. I want you that long. Then you'll move into the city with her."

"Move?"

Al leaned over the table and stared into Claire's eyes. "Yes, move," he said. "Living in a tent camp is not supposed to be a permanent housing option, nor should running one be a career goal for a young woman like you."

The tone of the conversation had changed. I sensed Claire's mood shift, and my anxiety returned along with it like a troublesome tick. Although I did not understand all the words, the tension in Claire's voice signaled Al's words left her with a difficult choice. The air held the scent of uncertainty.

"But where will I live in the city?" Claire asked. "I can't afford an apartment there on fifteen dollars an hour."

"You'll live with Sonia. Together, the two of you can afford a nicer apartment than the one she has now. And if she gets the grant she applied for, there will be money to send you to school, too."

"School?" Tears welled up in Claire's eyes.

"Your GED first and then community college," Al said. "This is your path, Claire. God has plans for you. It is a new year and an opportunity for a new life. Take it."

"What about you?" Claire asked. "Why don't you get to move into an apartment somewhere with Charlie? You shouldn't live like this the rest of your life either."

Al sighed, sat back again, and locked his hands behind his head. "You know, when I was in Vietnam, the soldiers I admired most were the medics," he said. "While the enemy was shooting at us, they were trying to save lives."

"What's that got to do with you being homeless?" Claire asked.

"I'm saving lives," Al replied. Claire gave Al an odd look. "Besides, Claire," he said. "I don't consider myself homeless. Before Father Paul found me, I was homeless. I was lifeless. Not now. This is my purpose. I have all I need. When I see Frank and Eddie again, I want to tell them I made good use of the time they didn't get."

"Will I still see you?" she asked Al.

Al reached across the table and took Claire's small hands in his gnarled and scarred Great Dane sized paws. "I don't know," he said, "But even if you don't, I'll always be with you." He touched the bronze star pinned on her hoodie.

Claire fought back tears and wiped away with her sleeve the ones that came anyway. She stood up, leaned over the table, and wrapped her arms around Al's neck.

"Thank you," she whispered. "Thank you for what you've done for me. I'll make you proud."

"I already am," Al replied.

I went outside with Claire to say goodbye and remained in the parking area until the rattling sound of Claire's car faded away. After a foray into the woods I returned to Al's shelter and accompanied him on his evening round of the diminished campground. Every now and then, it seemed he stopped to catch his breath. After a visit with Bruce, we returned to the shelter for the night.

Al followed his usual bedtime routine and I followed mine. I lay on the rug with my chewy while Al made himself a cup of the delightfully strong-smelling beverage he never shared with me. After he read from a book, he turned off the light and got down on his knees by the bed. I gave up my rug for him to kneel on.

When Al climbed in bed, I jumped up on the bed beside him. I always preferred sleeping next to someone when the opportunity presented itself. I lay awake listening to the night sounds which now included the raspy sound of Al's breathing. Every now and then, it stopped, sometimes for several moments, and I held my breath while I waited for his breathing to start again.

XIX

Sometime during the night, I had dozed off, for how long I don't know. I only remember something startled me as though Al had got up and left the shelter. I sat up, perked my ears and listened. Stillness has its own sound so different from the nighttime hum of a vibrant city, a hollowness as though every living creature around had suddenly disappeared. No car noises on the highway. No wind rattling empty tree branches overhead. No raspy breathing or the sound of Al clearing his throat.

But Al hadn't gone anywhere. He lay still in the bed beside me. I knew instinctively his life had left him as soon as I pressed my nose against his skin. It was cold, and his body was as stiff as the blanket that covered him.

My body felt numb as though I was outside of it looking down on Al. I whimpered and nuzzled Al's ear and licked his face. Although my mind presented me with the facts, my heart simply refused to accept them. Not Al. Not him. All I had to do was awaken him before a truck with flashing lights showed up to take him away. I licked his face more and pawed at his chest, gently at first, but then as forcefully as if I'd been digging a hole underneath a fence.

The blanket fell away. Al remained still. I curled up on his chest with my fur brushing up against his face and willed the heat of my body into his. I had laid on Al's chest before, as I had laid on Mira's as a pup, and felt it rise and fall with each breath, the simple rhythm of human life. Now Al's chest was flat and cold and still, and yet my heart would not acknowledge it would never hear his voice again, not his sharp commands, nor his playful teasing or his lousy singing. His footsteps would never fall upon the paths of the camp again and I would not tag along behind them. And I would never again share from his plate the food we shared as friends.

Grief cannot be stilled. Do not think for a moment a dog is incapable of grief, nor feels it any less than a human. As I lay on Al's chest, waiting for it to rise and fall again but knowing it would not, the pain was more intense than anything I had felt before. I lifted my head and allowed it to spill out in a loud howl.

Aahhhrooooooooo! Aahh-Aaahhhroooooooooooooooooo!

I repeated my howl a few more times before Bruce burst into the shelter. He knocked me off Al's chest, shook him, and then held Al's nose while he breathed into Al's mouth. He pounded on Al's chest and then tried breathing into his mouth again. Two other men from the camp entered Al's shelter and began poking at shiny phones as soon as they saw what Bruce was doing. They held them up to their ears and spoke many words at the same time.

Hello, 9-1-1, we need an ambulance! Father Paul, please! River Road across from the shopping center! It's an emergency! *It's an emergency! It's Al. I think he's dead.*

Soon, the familiar sound of a siren grew louder as the truck with flashing lights entered the camp. I heard the crunch of ice and gravel under heavy tires and the rapid thump of boots running towards Al's shelter. Two men dressed in blue overalls and red jackets with white crosses were the next ones inside. Bruce backed away from Al's bed while they knelt beside it, ripped open his flannel shirt, and shoved a tube in his mouth. At the other end of the tube was a large plastic bag. One of the men squeezed it and I saw Al's chest rise. I began barking and stepped out from underneath the table. I saw his chest rise!

"What is that dog doing in here?" asked one of the men in the blue overalls. "Get him out!"

"It's Al's dog," Bruce growled. He grabbed me and held me tightly in his arms. "He ain't goin' nowhere."

The first man in blue overalls kept squeezing the plastic bag while the other stuck a sharp object into Al's arm. The second man opened a small box on the floor and pulled out two objects I can only describe as round with handles and wires attached. He held them to Al's bare chest.

"Clear!" he said. He pressed something on the handles and it made Al's whole body jump. The man looked down at lights in the small box and shook his head. "Again… Clear!" Al's body jumped in the bed a second time. After a few more tries, the second man in blue overalls turned to Bruce. "I'm sorry," he said, "but he's not coming back." He said to the first man in blue overalls, "I'm calling it. Time of death 6:03 a.m."

Bruce sat on my rug and held me in his arms while his grief spilled into my fur. A man from the camp stood behind him with his hands on Bruce's shoulders while the men in blue overalls brought a bed on wheels into Al's shelter. It took the two men in blue overalls and one of the camp residents to lift Al from his bed and lay him on the one with wheels. They covered Al's body in a white sheet all the way up over his face and rolled the bed outside. I leapt from Bruce's arms and followed them. I barked and lunged at their feet until Bruce scooped me up again.

"Let 'im go, Charlie," Bruce said. "We got to let 'im go."

In the parking area, past the truck with the flashing lights, I saw Sergeant Mike once again standing next to his black and white car. Its lights were flashing, too. The yellow bus from the church had pulled in behind Sergeant Mike's car. Father Paul, Claire, and several other residents from the camp were standing near Sergeant Mike, and Claire and the other residents were hugging in one big group. I could hear their grief across the parking area, as fresh and raw as my own, and I ran to Claire as fast as I could.

"Charlieeeee! Oh, Charlieeeeee!" Claire was inconsolable. "How can he be gone? I just spoke to him yesterday. You were there."

In her arms, I burrowed into her jacket and tried to remember the last warm days I had spent in camp with Al as if I could wish them back. Just a few weeks earlier, I had agonized over losing the shelter, but I would have gladly given up the shelter, my rug, and my chewy to stay with Al even if it meant sleeping with him on a park bench.

Snow began to fall and collect on hats and coats and my fur. Overhead, the morning sky was a forlorn gray.

Father Paul and Sergeant Mike spoke quietly and stood as stiffly as Al had in his uniform. Father Paul wore his usual black coat with the white collar, but he also wore a long, purple scarf I had not seen before. He held a book and a small, silver bottle. When he stepped forward to the side of the bed Al lay on, a man in blue overalls pulled the white sheet down far enough to reveal Al's face. Claire saw it and collapsed to the ground still holding onto me.

Father Paul opened the book and began to speak. I could not hear what he was saying nor understand why he sprinkled Al's body with water from the silver bottle. Nobody had sprinkled water on Mary or Daniel. Al was dead. Claire lay overtop me. And, strangely, all I pondered was the meaning of the water and why Mary and Daniel hadn't gotten any.

Father Paul bent over and kissed Al on his forehead before the man in blue overalls pulled the white sheet over Al's face again. He walked toward Claire slowly as if he was carrying Al's weight on his shoulders and knelt by her side. There were tears in his eyes also.

"It is right for us to grieve Al's loss," Father Paul told Claire. "We will miss him. But we should not begrudge him the rest and reward he so richly deserves."

I did not understand Father Paul's words and Claire said nothing more. As the truck with flashing lights pulled out of the parking area onto the highway, all I understood was I had lost my best friend.

XX

Dogs deal with loss differently just as humans do. Some can move on and bond with their next human companion as easily as the first. I thought I was able to do so until I lost Al. Perhaps it was because Mira was still alive and there was always the chance I might see her again that I did not feel her loss as deeply. And with Mary, our bond was affectionate but reserved, more like a partnership in which she compensated me for my watchfulness with food and a place to sleep. I always knew I was standing in for another dog. Al was my best friend. Al lived larger than life. His absence left an emptiness it seemed impossible to fill.

In the days after Al's death, I was confined to the brightly lit room with the polished wood floor in Father Paul's church. I heard someone call it a gym. The tree and the packages were gone. The rows of beds and the tables and chairs were still there. A woman from the church brought me my own wicker basket with a plaid cushion, a kindness that motivated my first tail wags since I had returned to the church. But it was not my rug in the shelter next to Al's bed. I think back on it now and wish they had brought me the rug instead because it had Al's scent on it.

I lay in my basket napping most of the time, getting up only to eat or when Claire or another resident from the camp took me outside for a walk and the opportunity to relieve myself. I was on their schedule now and wore a halter and leash any time I left the gym. I missed the freedom to come and go where I pleased when I pleased. I missed the smells of the woods and the camp, the sound of the cars on the highway and the occasional trip to the deli where the man in the apron still gave me food. But most of all, I missed Al.

Claire came into the gym one morning with the halter and leash. If it wasn't for her unique scent and the streaks of purple in her hair, I would not have known it was her. She had gained weight in her time at the church and was now slender instead of emaciated.

She wore a black dress that traced the curves of her body and shoes that made her taller. She had her hair spun up in a roll instead of hanging loose around her shoulders, glittery purple streaks highlighted her eyes, and her face looked like she had been out in the sun. Her lips were a bright red. I was awestruck and wondered what Al would have thought if he had seen Claire at that moment.

"Hi Charlie," she said softly. She looked into my eyes and must have read my thoughts. "Don't look at me that way. I have to dress like this for Al's funeral."

She fastened the halter around my chest and snapped on the leash. "They weren't going to allow you to come to the funeral," she said, "but I made a scene. You have the right to say goodbye. Let's hurry up, okay? We don't have much time."

Claire put on a long, dark coat with a fresh scent instead of the puffy jacket she used to wear with the stuffing coming out and smelling of smoke. We went out a door at one end of the gym. A long sidewalk skirted the edge of a wide parking lot with as many cars, it seemed, as the shopping center, and more entering. We walked along the sidewalk around a corner of the building to the front of the church. A line of people in hats and long coats were already waiting there. Claire walked past them and gathered me in her arms when we reached the front steps.

"Excuse me," Claire said as she entered the open doors of the church and tried to make her way toward another set of doors with colored windows. People stepped aside, some indignant, others surprised, and a murmur passed through the gathering like the rush of a breeze through the trees in the woods. I heard someone say, "That's Al's dog." I wanted to ask Claire why only well-dressed people had come to God's house that morning. If it was up to Al, he would have invited the homeless.

As soon as Claire carried me through the next set of doors, I recognized the room. The sorrowful man dressed in the white cloth still hung on the wall with his arms outstretched just as I had witnessed him before. The room, however, was now brightly lit and filled with people sitting on its benches all the way to the end of each row. I recognized Bruce and other residents of the camp seated in a row close to the stone table and barked a greeting, but Claire did not walk down the path between the rows of benches to join them. Instead, she walked along a path behind the benches until she found a seat on a bench by another door. After I barked, everyone in the room turned to look at us.

A sad music filled the room. It matched the expression on the sorrowful man's face, and I looked at the faces of other humans in the room to see if they were as bewildered as I was. In my time with Al, many people came to visit him in his shelter, but there were so many more people in the room I did not recognize, men wearing uniforms with shiny buttons and colored pins like Al's, other men in striped pants like Sergeant Mike, men in dark suits and women in black dresses. Sergeant Mike and Jeremy and even the man with the apron were there, although he did not have his apron on, and Dr. Deaver sat with Jen and other women I recognized from the veterinary hospital.

When the music grew louder, everyone in the room stood up. A young man in a long white robe carrying a tall pole entered the room through the doors with the colored windows. Behind him, six men in uniforms like Al's stood next to a long box covered with an American flag, three on either side. The box sat on a metal table with wheels the men rolled along the path in between the benches.

When Claire saw the flag-covered box enter the room, she wept. I shook as her body did and my fur, once again, absorbed her tears. I did not know Al lay inside the box. I did not know all the people in the room had filed past his body earlier to say their last goodbyes. If I had, I would have been upset that no one had asked me if I wanted to see Al one more time.

Father Paul and two other men in long white and gold robes walked behind the men with the box and followed them down to the stone table at the front of the room. Father Paul and the two robed men walked behind the stone table and sat down in the gold chairs while the men in the uniforms sat down on the first bench beside the flag draped box. After Father Paul sat down, everyone in the room sat down, too.

One by one, several people made their way to an odd piece of furniture in the front of the room to climb its stairs and stand inside. Some read from a book. Some sang. Others told stories of Al and made everyone laugh. The behavior of the humans in the room and the many facets of their emotions perplexed me as they sometimes will even to this day. I know of no other animal that can laugh in times of great sadness and cry with tears of joy.

Father Paul spoke last. His emotions were the most difficult to discern, his own grief carefully concealed behind words meant to soothe and comfort and give hope. I wondered if the humans in the room were able to detect the slight quiver in his voice or noticed the tremble of his hand when he lifted it from the book:

> "I first met Al in a soup kitchen in Washington, D.C. back in 1985. I was a young seminarian. He was homeless and suffering from several illnesses the root of which was his alcoholism. Al did not talk much at first. From the soup kitchen staff and

the other vets who knew him, I learned he was a prisoner of war and decorated Vietnam veteran. I tried to reach Al and the other homeless men and women the way I had been trained in seminary, but I could tell Al did not think much of the hope I had to offer.

"When I did not see Al in the soup kitchen for a couple weeks, I went out looking for him. My search introduced me to several other vets sleeping on the streets or under the highway overpasses of our nation's capital, men and women in destitute circumstances who had fought for our country, suffered the physical and mental trauma of their service, and now appeared to have been abandoned. I wondered how this could be?

"I found Al in a VA hospital. He wasn't going to die although he wanted to. My words of encouragement and my prayers meant nothing to him. In fact, he sat up in his bed in anger and told me if I had nothing more than prayer to offer, he wanted me to leave.

"I asked him how it was he survived five years as a prisoner of war when he could easily have died and now wanted to die when he could easily live. Al said 'I had a purpose then, to help keep us all alive. I didn't want to let them win.' I said, 'Al, think about it. There are plenty of people strewn around the DC area right now who need help to keep them alive, who are all prisoners of something—alcoholism, drug addiction, poverty. Some of them are your brothers in arms, but others are runaway teens, prostitutes, even former businessmen. If you want a purpose, I think I found one for you.' It was a life-changing moment for both of us, the beginning of a friendship and a partnership that would last for over twenty years.

"Al used to say he admired the medics in his unit the most because they saved lives on the battlefield. Well, Al was a medic among the homeless. He saved some of your lives … but he touched all of our lives. And we will miss him."

What happened after Father Paul spoke puzzled me more. Many people in the room stood up and walked down to the stone table at the front of the room where Father Paul and the other robed men gave them something to eat, but many, including Claire, did not. I assumed they weren't hungry but, once again, no one asked me.

When music played, everyone in the room stood up again. The young man in the white robe with the tall pole led the men in uniforms with the flag-covered box up the path between the benches and Father Paul and the other two men followed them just as they had walked in. During the procession, Claire sobbed, and others' eyes moistened with tears simply from looking at her. I felt exhausted and heavy with the weight of all the grief in the room. My body simply could not absorb it all.

By the time Claire had put on her long coat and carried me outside, cars were leaving the parking area. I saw the flag-covered box inside a long, silver car parked in front of the church. Father Paul, Jen, Dr. Deaver, Bruce and several other camp residents were standing nearby. Claire walked up to Father Paul and Dr. Deaver slowly and began to sob again.

"We'll take good care of Charlie," Dr. Deaver said to Claire.

Claire thrust me into Dr. Deaver's arms. Her face with all its color from earlier that morning appeared to have melted. "Goodbye, Charlie," she said. "I'll miss you as much as I already miss Al." She turned and ran up the steps of the church so fast she nearly tripped.

I barked and wriggled in Dr. Deaver's arms. I barked for Claire to come back. Claire was my one source of comfort I still had left, the only human who could spare me from loneliness now that Al was gone. My anxiety returned, and I began to howl. The humans in the parking lot stared at me, but Claire did not return.

"Charlie, it's a long ride to Mansfield," Dr. Deaver said. "You wouldn't like it." She gave me to Jen.

"Hey, Charlie, you're going to hang out with us for a little while!" Jen said in her best happy voice. "You'll make lots of new friends!"

"Thank you, Dr. Deaver," Father Paul said.

As Jen carried me across the parking lot behind Dr. Deaver, I spied the white van with the sign of the dog and cat. I barked and wriggled and twisted as best I could to escape Jen's arms, but she held me tightly against her chest.

"I'll give him a sedative as soon as we get to the office," Dr. Deaver said. "I knew having him here at the funeral was not a good idea."

Dr. Deaver opened the rear doors of the white van and then the door of one of the cages. Jen pushed me inside still barking and wriggling, still trying to run back to Claire. But Jen shut the door made of metal bars and fastened the latch.

"I'm so sorry, Charlie," Jen said. "I wish you could ride up front with me. Hospital rules, you know."

The back doors of the van closed. I was in darkness. Once more, I had been taken away from a life I had chosen and a person I loved.

XXI

When we arrived at the veterinary hospital, Jen carried me into the room where Dr. Deaver had examined me on my first visit. Dr. Deaver held in her hand another sharp pin. I wriggled as best I could, but a dog my size simply cannot out-muscle a human. I resisted the impulse to bite. I liked Jen. I simply wanted to get away.

After the sting of the pin, my body relaxed. I did not fall asleep but felt very drowsy. Jen placed me in a cage upstairs. Inside was the wicker basket from the church and it still held Claire's scent. As I breathed in and imagined her face and Al's, I thought of the shelter and the three of us together there. How quickly human lives change and a dog's life with them.

Jen stopped in the room often to see me and tried to brighten my mood. I wanted to ask her why she had taken me from Claire and placed me in a room with cats. Across the room, when Jen was not there, I saw green eyes fixed on me. They glowed like the buttons on the metal boxes underneath Al's table. From elsewhere in the room, I heard for the first time the purring sound of a contented cat and the rattle of the cage door as it brushed up against it. The cat's name was "Precious." Jen took her out of the cage and introduced us. Precious hung limply in Jen's arms unperturbed by my bark and sported a smug look of special treatment because she was in Jen's arms and I was not. "*Set us both on the floor,*" I said in my thoughts to Precious, "*and we'll see how smug you look then.*"

Grinch, the cat with the green eyes, never emerged from the shadows. Whenever I barked, or Jen approached his cage, I heard instead the siren-like yeow and the hissing and spatting I was more accustomed to hearing from cats. I did not wish to be left alone on the floor with Grinch. There are some cats a dog is better to stay away from.

I learned the room I was in was the "Quiet Room" for cats and smaller, timid dogs or dogs who had surgery. My stay in the "Quiet Room" was short-lived. Once the drowsiness wore off, I was quite vocal about being kept in a room with cats for company, so Jen moved me downstairs into a room she called the kennel.

My days in the veterinary hospital were dominated by boredom interrupted only by Jen's appearances and a brief spell in the runs outside morning and evening. The cold weather had not relented. Snow drifted into the runs through the fencing, melted, and then often refroze making my footing on the runs surface challenging. More than once, my legs went out from underneath me and I went down hard on my belly and banged my jaw.

My diet was now the hospital's dry kibble soaked in warm water to create a weak gravy. No more human leftovers, no crusts from pizza or buttered English muffins, no bits of chicken or beef, no cold cuts from the man in the apron or French fries and burger from the white bag Al had often brought back with him from his trips away from the camp.

With the hours inside my cage flowing along like the river, I often occupied my mind with a myriad of questions presented by my circumstances. I wondered what had become of Al's shelter and all his things, and my things, inside. Had Sergeant Mike and other men in striped pants carried them away? Had his books and flags been burned like trash? Where do humans go when the truck with the flashing lights takes them away? And why didn't anyone ask me what I wanted?

I dreamed of one day going upstairs to find Mira or Claire waiting for me. Or maybe Bruce even though he kept to himself like Mary did. Instead, I watched other dogs come and go and wondered how their families found them.

A new dog's entrance always created a ruckus. Each of us inside the kennel wanted Jen's or the new dog's attention first and their scents threw us into a frenzy, especially a female in heat. A dog's departure almost always created the same ruckus, whooped up into a greater frenzy by Jen's upbeat antics and her shouts of "You're going home! You're going home!" until the noise in the downstairs kennel from all the barking and banging and shouting was louder than the highway traffic at Christmas time.

One time, though, Jen entered the room with moist eyes. Although she held a halter and leash in her hands, she stood just inside the doorway for a few moments as if she did not want us to know which dog was going home. She walked slowly across the room to a large, floor level cage along the far wall, knelt beside it, and spoke in a soft voice.

"Hi, Katie. How are you feelin', ol' girl?"

Katie was a chocolate colored Labrador Retriever who I noticed had never got up and banged her tail against the inside of her cage or tore up any paper for the other dogs' comings or goings. Come to think of it, I had never heard her bark. When Jen spoke, Katie gave no more than two or three thumps of her tail and lay still. And when Jen opened the door of her cage, Katie made no effort to stand. Jen had to help her to her feet while she fastened the halter around her chest.

Katie moved slowly and stiffly out of her cage as if every step was painful. Her eyes were gray, her muzzle also. Except for an occasional whine or yawn, the rest of us sat quietly while Jen patiently led Katie across the room toward the door.

It is not so long a journey from the exuberance of a puppy to the solemn, feeble steps Katie took. I suppose each of us saw ourselves in Katie one day and wondered what lay in store at the end of her walk.

A few days after Katie left, measured by trips outside to the runs and warmer temperatures and nights with the lights out in the downstairs kennel, Jen burst into the room bouncing like a dog let out of its cage and headed straight for me.

"Hey, Charlie! Great news! We found a foster family for you! She's coming to pick you up today!" Her effusiveness ignited a roar of barking and banging. "You won't have to stay in a cage anymore!"

Of course, I did not know what a foster family was at the time, but Jen's bright face and high-pitched squeals had me spinning around in circles. She opened the cage door and tussled and wrestled with me for a moment. I sensed a strong change for the good in Jen's demeanor, a more pleasant positive energy she meant for me, and I felt more hopeful than I had at any time since Al's death.

Jen returned a short while later with a halter and leash. "She's here! She's here, Charlie! She can't wait to meet you!" I jumped out of the cage into Jen's arms as soon as the cage door opened. "Hold still, you silly dog!" She laughed as I wiggled and gave her kisses of gratitude for freeing me.

I led Jen upstairs, I knew the way out, and greeted Dr. Deaver's other helpers with jumps and whistles of glee. I had hoped to see Claire. I looked for a familiar face and searched for her scent but found none. Instead, in the area humans and their animals waited to see Dr. Deaver, a short woman with lots of blonde, curly hair waited for me dressed in a dark blue shirt, denim jacket, and blue jeans. The scents of several different animals clung to her clothes and piqued my interest.

"Hi Charlie!" she said. I ran over to smell the woman's clothes. She knelt on one knee and offered me her hand to sniff. "I'm Sam. You'll be coming to stay with me for a little while until we find you a forever home."

Her hand smelled strongly of soap, but her clothes carried the scents of multiple dogs, a trace of a cat or two, and the robust odor of a sweaty horse. I had encountered horses in my time with Mira. In the city, the men in striped pants sometimes rode them, or they pulled brightly painted wagons filled with humans. I often smelled a horse long before it came into view. Intertwined with the animal odors was the blonde-haired woman's own natural scent like wet grass. The combination was intoxicating.

Jen handed my leash to Sam. "Sam has a farm, Charlie! You'll make lots of new friends there." With a last scratch of my head, she said, "Come back and see us!"

Out in the parking area, I found no trace of Claire either. As we walked past the outside runs, I barked my farewells to the dogs still behind the fencing. I remembered the same walk the day Jen took me back to Al and it seemed like such a long time ago. This walk had a different feel to it, like I was headed in a new direction.

Sam led me to a big silver truck with "CHEVROLET" emblazoned on the back. The back of the truck did not have a roof or seats. It was all metal and looked very uncomfortable to ride in. Sam opened a door on the side of the truck and lifted me up onto a leather seat that also held many of the same scents that were on Sam's clothes. No cage. No hospital rules to follow this time. I was going to ride up front alongside her. Despite my anxiety over a ride in any vehicle, if a ride in Sam's truck meant I was leaving the veterinary hospital, I was willing to take my chances.

XXII

I pressed my nose against the glass the way I had on that first ride in Mira's car. As soon as I remembered the rush of wind in my nostrils and the frenzy of smells, the glass slid part way down as if I had been granted a wish. With my front paws on the truck's door and my hind legs still on the seat, I leaned out as far as I could until the edge of the glass pressed against my throat and permitted me to go no further.

We passed houses and stores and sometimes stopped for colored lights at street corners to let other cars and trucks have their turn. The further away Sam drove from the veterinary hospital, the fewer houses and stores I saw. Instead, fields lined with wooden fences and rich with the smells of dirt and droppings of horses and other animals stretched out along the road. It was the time of year when the trees were blossoming, and their fragrance added to the splendor. It seemed every turn brought with it a new smell to question or a familiar one to recall.

Sam turned onto a narrow road lined on each side with budding trees. Before we reached the end of the rows of trees, I smelled in the air the same scents of the dogs and the horse that clung to Sam's clothes. Over the rumble of the engine, I heard a chorus of excited barking and the whiney of a horse. Sam's animal companions were welcoming her home. When I answered with my own greeting, the horse's whiney stopped, but the dogs' barking grew louder.

The narrow road ended in a parking area in front of a big, white house with a large front porch. More trees, some as tall and thick as the ones along the river, stood around and behind the house as though they were guarding it from the sun. Their branches stretched out over its roof and promised shade when their leaves came to full bud.

Two more buildings stood where the parking area ended. The small one was square and twice the size of Al's shelter while the larger one was long, rectangular, and even bigger than Sam's white house. Both were painted bright red with white trim. They had tiny windows, black shingled roofs, and metal boxes on top with arrows and a large, painted bird that moved in the breeze.

Wooden post fencing and rails with wire in between extended from the rectangular building past the parking area, along the back of the smaller building, and past a stand of trees before it turned left and headed down into a pasture. The horse stood by itself along the fence, but the four dogs were climbing over each other trying to be the first to get out and greet Sam … or inspect me. A fifth dog, a big Golden Retriever, lumbered off the front porch of the house and up to Sam's side of the truck. He appeared to be an older dog by his stiff movement. I heard more barking coming from inside the house, a higher pitch like mine.

By this time, I was racing back and forth on the leather seat trying to get out. I jumped up on Sam and licked her ear.

"Hold on, Charlie!" Sam said laughing. "I have to stop the car first."

The truck rolled to a stop and the engine went silent. Sam scooped me up in one arm and pressed me against her body even though I wiggled to get free. I was surprised at her strength. When she opened her door, I found myself face to face with the big Golden.

"Hey, Duke!" Sam said. "This is Charlie!"

Dogs have their own customs when meeting other dogs just as humans have when greeting other humans. It starts with a quick nose-to-nose sniffing and then we move around to the hind quarters. The stronger scents that identify us originate there.

After the nose-to-nose sniff with Duke, Sam set me down on the pavement and laughed more as Duke and I thoroughly familiarized ourselves. Duke walked a few steps away, lifted his leg, and spritzed the pavement. I promptly walked over for a polite sniff. Between Duke and I, it was the equivalent of a human handshake.

"Men," Sam said.

I was already pulling at the end of the leash toward the four dogs in the fenced-in area before Sam removed a handbag from the truck and followed me. They were younger dogs racing up and down along the fence and howling their frustration at their exclusion from the sniffing ritual. I led Sam to the fence while Duke wandered off.

At the fence, the four dogs and I pressed our noses together. A short, stocky dog growled and snarled at the other three until he had smelled me first. It isn't hard to identify an alpha male.

"Charlie, meet Keisha, Kermit, Caleb and Clancey," Sam said. "I'm trying to find homes for them, too. I hope you won't be as challenging."

The four dogs were of mixed breed like myself, but, in my humble opinion, not as handsome. Keisha, the smallest and the only female, was all brown, short hair, long boned and skinny. She was fast. When they ran, Keisha reached the end of the fence well ahead of the males.

Kermit was the alpha male and a canine bully. He also had short brown hair, but unlike Keisha, most everything else on him was short, too. He had a short, stubby tail, short ears, and a short, bulldog-like nose. Kermit was muscular and powerful and asserted himself after smelling me by urinating through the fence on my nose. The sensation was not a pleasant one. I backed away from the fence and rubbed my nose in the grass.

"Kermit! Behave yourself!" Sam barked, but the deed had already been done. Worse than the smell in my nose and the taste in my mouth was the humiliation of being marked by another male dog. It would take a while for his scent to leave me.

Caleb had black hair with brown spots, long droopy ears and droopy eyes. While he was bigger than Kermit, he was cowardly and clumsy. Kermit had only to look in Caleb's direction to make him back away. Clancey was the only long hair variety among them and stood as tall at the shoulders as Caleb. He was black and white with graceful curves. I noticed he had a crooked tail and half of one ear missing and wondered whether it was Kermit's doing.

"Let's go inside," Sam said. "I'll introduce you to Pierre and Duchess. You'll be staying with them." Sam scooped me up and carried me toward the house. The horse had been watching us for the duration of the canine introductions and spoke up for the first time when Sam walked away.

"I am not ignoring you, Gracie," Sam said to the horse. "I just didn't think you really cared." She carried me off to the house anyway.

As we walked across the parking area, a gray cat raced from behind the small, red building and went under the truck. It passed within several feet of Duke laying in the grass between the outbuilding and the house, but Duke did not even raise his head. I wiggled and squirmed to be let down. Sam's farm was a different world from Mira's apartment and the city park or the camp by the river, a world of more animals than humans as far as I could see, and a world in which I would have to compete for my place. I knew I could easily fit underneath the truck, evict the cat from its presumed safe haven and give chase. Surely, there had to be at least one animal on the farm that would give me deference. But I was not to have the freedom I had in the camp.

Sam carried me to the rear of the house and into a small enclosed porch. The porch's worn door squeaked on its hinges and did not fully close behind us until Sam reached back and pulled it closed. Inside, the porch smelled of dogs—Duke and two others I presumed were the ones barking behind another door from the porch into the house itself. Sam set me down on the floor.

The porch had a couch that sagged in the middle, two chairs with stuffing coming out of holes in several places, and a small, wooden table that looked like cats had used it for a scratching post. Green carpet covered the floor. Food dishes, water bowls, toys, and two crates too small for Duke, but big enough for dogs like me, waited for their owners. Ever since Sam and I had left the veterinary hospital, pressure had been building up inside my bladder. In the yard, the excitement of meeting new dogs and adjusting to my new surroundings had kept it bottled up. But when I saw the crates and feared Sam might lock me inside one, my bladder let go. I peed on the green carpet.

"Charlie, you were just outside!" Sam seized me underneath my front legs and held me up with my hind legs dangling and my underbelly and privates facing outward. Her sudden snatching and lifting frightened me. A stream of urine arced across the porch like water from the ropes humans use to put out fires and hit one of the chairs.

"Charlie!" Sam moaned. She turned and carried me out of the porch, but not before my nervous bursts struck several other targets along the way. Sam sat me on the grass. "Well, at least it wasn't in the kitchen."

I laid my ears back and huddled in the grass while what remained in my bladder drained away. I avoided Sam's gaze and emptied my bowels, too, and then wiped my feet in the grass.

"Are you finished?" she asked. Sam scooped me up again and carried me through the enclosed porch into her kitchen.

As soon as we entered the kitchen, Pierre, a beagle, and Duchess a tiny white poodle, threw themselves at Sam's legs. Pierre was intent on reaching mine. He flung himself into the air with back springs and somersaults, sometimes crash landed, but then threw his head back and howled before trying again.

Sam set me down on the floor and held Pierre at bay with one hand while she removed my halter and leash with the other. When she let go, Pierre was a little too effusive in his greeting for my liking. After the briefest of nose sniffing, Pierre moved around to my hind quarters and promptly mounted them. I had never experienced this behavior from another dog and I turned around and told Pierre in the strongest of terms he had better not do it again.

"Boys, behave yourselves!" Sam shouted. She separated Pierre and me with her foot. "Pierre, if you don't leave Charlie alone, you'll go in your crate." Pierre went under the kitchen table and lay in his bed while Duchess sat in her basket shivering.

The kitchen, as large as it was, was not going to be regarded as my space and sharing it with other dogs would take a bit of getting used to. I was accustomed to my own space. Outside, no dog had ever approached me without Mira's or my permission and, inside, whether it was Mira's apartment, Mary's tent or Al's shelter, another dog had not so much as shed a hair. In fact, Claire told me I was the first dog ever to pad down the hallways of Father Paul's church. To go from being the exclusive canine presence among humans to an interloper in another dog's territory was unsettling.

I wandered over to a rug in front of another door and lay down. The kitchen itself was much bigger than Mira's and held more furniture and things. Besides the big wooden table and its four chairs, a tall, wooden piece of furniture with drawers and shelves full of plates and cups stood along one wall. Wooden doors stretched above Sam's head and underneath counters separated by the gleaming silver and black doors of her appliances. The kitchen floor was the color of brown autumn leaves and hard and cool like stone.

Sam opened some of the wooden doors over her head or underneath counters and removed several pots and bowls. She placed the pots on top of one of the counters, emptied into them the contents of cans she took from the large silver door, and soon I smelled a sweet aroma that made my stomach grumble.

When Sam set three small bowls on another counter, Pierre and Duchess took notice. They hopped out of their baskets and took their places by Sam's feet. Sam brought out more cans and scooped the contents into the bowls. She took two of them and set them on the floor by

Pierre's bed and Duchess' basket. After they had begun eating, Sam brought the remaining bowl over and set it on the floor by me.

"I know what it's like to lose someone close to you," she said as she stroked my fur. "It does get easier."

The food was much better than the veterinary hospital fare. It was moist and succulent and meat flavored. I have always been a dog who enjoys the experience of eating as much as the sensation of a full stomach and perhaps it is well I have seldom had to fend for my food. I enjoy the aromas, savoring the taste on my tongue and the texture of the food in my mouth as I chew. Pierre, however, was a glutton.

I had barely digested my first bites of the chicken flavored clumps when I heard Duchess growl and saw Pierre trotting toward my dish. Sam had wandered off into another room. When the low rumble in my throat did not stop Pierre, I spoke up more forcefully. Brazenly, he crept closer, but I was not about to surrender my supper dish to any dog even if it was his kitchen. My raised lips and snarling and snapping jaws sent Pierre running under the table again.

Sam stomped her foot on the floor. I hadn't seen her come in and scurried into a corner of the room furthest away from her.

"Someone's going in a crate," she said. Thankfully, Sam picked up Pierre and carried him outside onto the porch. When she came in, I heard Pierre's howls through the door.

"Now you can finish your dinner in peace," she said.

I finished eating and lay on the rug with my head between my front paws while Sam prepared her own meal.

When she sat down, Duchess scratched at the chair leg until Sam picked her up. I sighed, but my sigh went unnoticed. Sam spoke to Duchess in soft tones and caressed her with one hand while she lifted a fork to her mouth with the other. Sam's lap was Duchess' place, not mine. For the time being, I could feel the gentle strokes of a woman's hand only in my memory.

When Sam went to bed that night, I learned the second crate on the porch was mine. I joined Pierre in a chorus of unhappy howls. Sam opened the porch door and Duke lumbered in. The couch belonged to him. Duke stretched out the length of the couch and promptly fell asleep, but I howled long after Sam had turned off the porch light and went inside.

Sam let Duke out the porch door early the next morning. I took note of how long it took him to move through the open door, down the few steps, and out into the grass, and how the squeaky door always stayed open just a little bit until Sam pulled it closed. Pierre was already in an uproar next to me by the time she turned around and opened the doors of our crates.

"Good morning, boys," Sam said cheerfully. She wore denim jeans and a short sleeve shirt and smelled like syrup and bacon.

Pierre raced in circles inside the porch and knocked over a water bowl before he collided with me in a flying leap off Duke's couch. We had words again.

Sam stomped her feet. "Keep it up, boys, and one of you will end up out in the barn with the big dogs." She grabbed me and fit me in my halter and leash. "You first,

Charlie." Sam put Pierre in a halter and leash, too, and opened the porch door. "Let's go for a walk."

Outside, I strained at the leash and pulled Sam toward her silver truck while the big dogs created an uproar behind the fence and Gracie whinnied a "good morning." The air was filled with the sound of Spring bird songs and the smell of budding trees.

"We're not going for a car ride today, Charlie," Sam said. "You'll have your first chance to charm someone this weekend. So, what are you thinking? Large family? Small? You seem a bit nippy to be around small children. Too used to having things your way."

Sam continued talking as we walked up the narrow road between tall trees. Ahead of us, squirrels foraging in the grass raced up the trunks and chattered from the lower branches.

"Duchess, Duke and Gracie are my family now," she said. "Not as large as it was before the kids moved away."

She stopped where the end of the narrow road met a larger one and pulled a rolled-up paper out of a yellow box on a post. Pierre trotted into the road toward woods on the other side, but Sam pulled him back.

"Pierre, get out of the road!" she said. "People don't pay any attention coming around that curve."

As we walked back toward the house, I zig-zagged across the narrow road with bursts of speed testing Sam's grip. She held fast. The halter created an invisible fence, a box I could move freely within, but not beyond. When we reached the porch, Sam did not remove our leashes and halters until she had pulled the door closed behind us.

"I don't imagine you'll be with me very long, Charlie," Sam said as she bent down and unsnapped the leash. "You'll forgive me if I don't become too attached." She looked at Pierre. "You could be here awhile," she said.

Sam came and went during the day and left me alone in the enclosed porch. Pierre went inside with Duchess leaving me in peace on one of the armchairs. Late in the afternoon, Sam returned with her arms full of bags and balanced one on her knee while she yanked open the porch door. As she walked in, the door remained open as it always did.

I went through the opening before Sam set the bags down on the porch table. Her shouts started Pierre and Duchess barking inside the house. Duke got up from the grass and seemed happy to have someone to play with, but I was far too agile for him. I led him in a game of "catch me if you can" until he tired and sat down.

Out by the barn, the big dogs were digging a trench with their running. Kermit was especially incensed by my freedom and his inability to do anything about it. His saliva turned to foam and his jowls quivered like shaken pudding. I trotted along the fence taunting him. When he stuck his nose through a square in the wire, I lifted my leg and peed on it.

"Charlie! Come here, Charlie! Don't do this!" Sam stood at the edge of the parking area and her shoulders rose and fell as she tried to catch her breath. She held up her hand. "Would you like a snack, Charlie? Come, get a snack!" I smelled the scent of moist bacon and, impulsively, took a few steps toward her before I stopped.

Humans call them crossroads, moments in life when one must decide to go in one direction or the other. It may be momentous, or seemingly insignificant at the time, but the choice is inescapable. Remaining in the moment is not an option, and the decision will alter the course of the rest of your life.

My crossroads lay in the parking area between Sam and me. If I returned to Sam, I would not see the camp again. Not ever. Perhaps it was time to consign Al and Claire to fond memories and move on? How long had I been in the veterinary hospital anyway?

The seconds ticked away. Sam took small steps toward me holding the bacon scented snack out in front of her. "Come, Charlie."

Instead, I chose the narrow road. I ran at full speed past chattering squirrels and did not stop when I reached the end. A car loomed around the curve to my left. The sound of screeching tires and a blaring horn drowned out all sounds of squirrels, birds, and even the pounding of my heart inside my chest.

XXIII

Sometimes knowing what you don't want gets you closer to what you want even if you're not entirely sure what it is. The car swerved wide and rushed behind me. I barely gave it a second thought as I weaved through trees in the woods across the road and entered a field of clover on the other side. Running with my face to the wind and a thousand scents coursing through my nose, I alone determined my direction no longer beholden to a leash or a fence or a human's will.

Night was approaching. A gentle breeze sent swells through the clover and brought with it the odor of horses, a familiar odor I recalled from the trip to Sam's farm. It was an odor that told the way home, and it beckoned me as much as if Claire had called my name. There were uncertainties, for sure, in returning to the camp, not the least of which was whether I would find Claire there, but the camp was where the last life I'd chosen had ended. I was sure a new beginning would start there.

I set out in the direction of the horses and did not reach their pasture until well after nightfall. By then, the moon overhead made the sky as bright as it was that night along the river even though I saw only the one. All around me in the meadow, the smell of the horses saturated the air. I meandered among their droppings until I reached the crest of a hill and saw lights on a long, rectangular building sitting atop the hill beyond. A stream trickled through the bottom of a shallow valley in between. In the moonlight, it glistened like one of Mira's jewel-encrusted designer leashes. I ran down to the bottom of the meadow, waded into the stream and lapped up my fill of cold water. All the running had made me thirsty. My stomach began to grumble, too, so I set off up the hill on the other side in search of food and a place to rest.

In the barn, horses were whinnying to each other. They had smelled me coming up the hill, and their conversation expressed their curiosity, but also irritation over the nuisance of an unwanted nighttime visitor. Their barn was built differently from Sam's. It was open at either end and had a wide corridor running through the middle. The horses stood in stalls on either side behind heavy wood doors with barred windows.

I crept along the corridor cautiously and stopped every few feet to sniff the air. Some of the horses snorted and pawed the floors of their stalls and then turned away and showed me their hind quarters. Others simply glared down at me. Their eyes reflected the dim light from a few bulbs dangling high overhead and made them look like little moons.

I detected a new scent and, at the same time, saw the silhouette of a cat hastily making its exit out the far end of the barn. I quickened my pace but stopped when I reached the place where the cat was. Bowls of food and water laden with feline scent sat on the floor by a wall covered with horse-sized leashes and halters and other things that smelled like Mira's leather boots. My conscience did not trouble me in the least as I crunched down the cats' food and even licked up the crumbs scattered around the bowls. I washed it down with their water and continued my trek along the corridor.

At the end of the corridor, I found a room filled with bunches of a sweet-smelling grass tied together with wires. Loose grass lay strewn across the floor. I recognized the smell as one of several that had come from the horses' stalls and the stalks as the same ones that extended from their mouths as they chewed. Nestled in among the bunches of grass on a bed I had made from loose strands, I felt warm, protected, full, drowsy and content. Something about freedom lends itself to a good night's sleep.

The next morning, I was aroused by a horse's loud neigh and the sun's first rays streaming in through the open door. I sat up and stretched with my forelegs out in front of me and my hind quarters up in the air, then finished with a good shake to rid myself of the stalks of grass clinging to my fur. A cat strode into view on its way to the empty food dish. When it saw me, it arched its back and spat at me before turning and running back the way it had come.

For a moment, I considered giving chase, but the desire to return to the camp and find Claire was stronger. I left the barn and followed a narrow gravel road through more fields until the gravel road ended at the edge of a large paved one.

The morning air was still. It lacked even the hint of a breeze that might carry along with it smells I could identify and refresh my memory of the route I had taken the day before. I trotted along the edge of the paved road covering as much distance as I could while the going was straight and level. Whenever I heard the sound of a vehicle's engine, I hid in the ditch alongside the road until the car or truck had passed.

As the morning lengthened, however, it seemed the road did also. The sun rose high in the sky and its warmth was magnified by the pavement underneath. Before long, I was panting and thirsty. The pads of my feet blistered, and my gait had slowed to a labored walk. I lifted my nose to the air, but still could not smell anything familiar nor the scent of moisture anywhere. Breathing in the air felt like it had when the fire burned the camp and its swirling black smoke entered my lungs. I gave up hiding in the ditch whenever a car or truck passed. I simply did not have the energy to climb out anymore.

By the time the sun began its descent, the colors of the landscape had begun to run together, and the shapes of trees and buildings became distorted. I became disoriented, wandered out into the road, and then ran in another direction at the sound of screeching tires and an angry horn. I stumbled along searching for a familiar scent until another horn blared and sent me running off in a different direction. In the heat, with my heart pounding and nostrils flaring, I felt the fire would finally consume me from within even though there were no flames around.

Out of the soupy landscape arose a shiny silver and glass shield ablaze in sunlight. It grew larger as it approached me, and its brightness became so powerful I had to look away. I heard the whine of heavy tires on the roadway, but I stood still, confused and disoriented, as though my paws had finally melted into the black top. The growl of an engine seemed to come from everywhere and nowhere. Even the sound of screeching brakes did not loose me from my paralysis. A large truck came to a stop beside me and let out a long, deep breath. The truck was so long its hind quarters blended in with the sky and its many wheels with thick flaps behind them seemed to extend to the horizon.

The body of the truck was all white and bore an emblem of a black flying bird with a long neck inside a gold circle. The door of the red cab bore the same emblem and, above it, the word "Wawa." As I squinted up into the sunlight, the door opened and denim clad human legs wearing white sneakers swung into view. The driver jumped down from the cab and revealed the rest of himself, a man half Al's size whose head wouldn't have reached much higher than the bottom of the open cab door if it wasn't for the tall hat with the wide brim he wore. The driver wore a white shirt with the same emblem as the truck and the same word "Wawa" stitched on it above the pocket. I figured Wawa must be his name. In one hand, Wawa held a clear bottle filled with water. He knelt in the middle of the road just several steps away from me and poured water from the open bottle into the other cupped hand.

I drank the water from Wawa's hand. I caught the drops that fell from his hand on my tongue and I licked the wet spots on the pavement. I drank until the last drops of water that fell from the bottle into Wawa's hand were replaced with my saliva. I looked up into Wawa's eyes and smiled and wagged my tail in gratitude.

"Hot, ain't it?" Wawa said. I wagged my tail again. "Whysa little guy like you hoofin' it along a stretch like this?" He held out his hand for me to sniff. It smelled like all the ingredients of one of those big, long sandwiches with meat and vegetables Al used to eat and it reminded me of him. "No collar. No name," Wawa said. "But you look like you belong to someone. How 'bout I give you a ride?"

Wawa stood up and opened the cab door as wide as it would go so I could see inside. "It's nice and cool inside," he said. "I'll take you down to the truck stop and see if anyone there recognizes you."

I understood his invitation. I limped over to a shiny, metal plate at the bottom of the cab and then looked back at Wawa. Even if I had enough strength left to hop up on the plate, the seat above me was too high for me to reach. Wawa scooped me up and set me down on the seat and then climbed into the cab beside me. He reached out with his left hand, grabbed the door handle and pulled it shut. With his right hand, he reached up and pulled a cord. A horn blared, the engine roared, and the truck began to roll forward.

The air inside the cab was cool just as Wawa had promised. Streams of cold air blew down from spaces on a long board full of knobs and buttons and glowing, round circles with painted numbers. Looking up through the glass as I lay on the seat, I could see the cloudless sky and the tops of trees that we passed. I licked my blistered paws to cool them while Wawa hummed along with the music playing in the cab. His voice was no better than Al's.

Wawa reached over and picked up a small black box on a cord hanging from the long board and began talking into it. "Break 1-9."

The box talked back. "Go 'head, break." I never heard anything Mira or Al talked into talk back to them.

"I just picked up a hitchhiker of the four-legged variety by mile marker 120."

"Come back?"

"Yeah, I found a four-legged hitchhiker with a long coat and a long tail wanderin' back and forth across six-eleven. A couple four wheelers nearly made a road pizza with him."

"You sure it ain't a pole cat?"

Wawa laughed. "No stripes down his back though he does smell ripe. I was wonderin' whether anyone's spoke of a lost dog in radioland?"

The black box was quiet for a moment. "Negatory," the voice said, "but I'll put an APB out there for ya. What's your twenty?"

"Seven miles from the Trexlertown choke and puke. I'll stop in and ask around. I just can't put the little guy back on the blacktop."

"10-4. I'll keep my ears open for you."

Wawa placed the black box on the long board. "I sure wish I knew what your name was," he said, and then he began calling out names. "Fred? Felix? Max? Murphy?" *Nope.* "Sam? Rusty? Ralph?" *Getting colder.* The names flew by with the scenery. "Alpha? Bravo? Charlie?" I barked. Wawa looked down at me. "Charlie? Is that it?" I barked again and wagged my tail. "Well, I'll be a bear's best friend," he said.

A little while later, Wawa pulled into a large parking lot where there were several trucks with as many wheels as his all lined up in a row. He rolled up next to one and the truck let out another deep breath when its wheels stopped.

"You best stay here," Wawa said. "This place has enough problems with the health department. I'll leave the fan on for you." He opened the cab door, hopped out, and closed it behind him.

I stretched out on the long, red seat and napped while the fan blew cool air on me. The pads of my feet still hurt, and the cool air soothed them. I don't know how long I had dozed off when the cab door suddenly opened, and I saw Wawa from the chest up with another taller man. The taller man's big, shiny belt buckle perched just above the edge of the seat. He had wispy gray hair, a gray beard and smelled like bacon. My mouth started to water.

"Looks like he's part fox," the gray-haired man said.

"He does in a way," Wawa agreed.

"Where'd you say you found him?"

"Wandering around in the middle of six-eleven near mile marker 120. Heat musta got to 'im. His name's Charlie."

"Now how do you know that?" the gray-haired man asked.

"He told me," Wawa said. The gray-haired man gave Wawa a look like Claire had given Al when she didn't believe him. Wawa explained how he stumbled onto my name.

"Just coincidence," the gray-haired man said.

"Go ahead and ask him yourself then," Wawa replied.

"Is that your name? Charlie?" the gray-haired man asked.

My ears perked. I barked and pushed myself up into a sitting position even though my paws were still sore. I was also curious to know where that strong smell of bacon was coming from.

"Didn't I tell ya?" Wawa said. He lifted a white bag into view. The bag oozed the odor of bacon, toasted bread, fries and melted cheese. Wawa had my full attention. He reached into the white bag and pulled out one of the largest burgers I had ever seen loaded with so much bacon it was falling out the sides. I licked my jaws to keep my saliva from dripping onto the red seat cover.

"Charlie, this is what I call a MasterCard burger," Wawa said. "It brings instant satisfaction, but it makes you pay later."

"Are you saying there's something wrong with my burgers?" the gray-haired man asked.

"Oh, no," Wawa replied. "Just that there's enough grease in this here burger to lubricate all the axles of my truck."

The gray-haired man scowled. Wawa ripped off a chunk of the bread and meat and held it out to me. I took it from Wawa's hand gingerly and backed up a few steps before I lay down on the seat with the burger section between my paws.

"He don't eat like any trucker's dog I ever saw," the gray-haired man said.

"He ain't a trucker's dog," Wawa said. "No trucker worth his sweat would've dumped him on the asphalt."

"So whatcha gonna do?" the gray-haired man asked. "I can't keep him here."

"I dunno," Wawa said. He ripped off another thick chunk of the burger and dropped it on the seat in front of me.

"I hear they have these new chips they can put under a dog's skin that have the owner's information in them, even the dog's medical history," the gray-haired man said.

"That so?" Wawa asked.

"Yeah, like an invisible electronic dog tag," the gray-haired man said. "But you have to have one of them fancy gadgets to read it. There's a doc over in Ainsley. He may be able to tell you whether Charlie has a chip in him."

Wawa frowned. "I still have a drop in Riverdale this afternoon. Maybe I'll look for one there after I'm off the clock."

The gray-haired man shrugged. "Good luck," he said. "If anyone asks for Charlie, I'll give 'em your handle."

"Much obliged." Wawa grabbed a silver bar and pulled himself up into the cab. He closed the cab door and the last I saw of the gray-haired man was his back as he walked across the parking lot toward the building. The truck engine roared. Wawa pulled a cord and the horn blared two short blasts before the truck slipped out of the parking lot onto the highway.

As the truck gained speed, I stood up on the seat with my front paws and my nose against the glass of the door on my side of the cab. Wawa took the hint and let the glass roll down until I stuck my head out far enough to fill my nose with the wind. In the cab, I was higher than I had ever been before, and I dared myself to face the turbulence and let my nostrils contend with the full jet stream. My ears bent back. My eyes were barely open. And my nose caught every scent like a giant web.

We were headed in the right direction. The scents I had gleaned from my ride in Sam's truck were still fresh in my memory like odorous signposts. I grew more excited as I counted down each one and anticipated the last, the smell of the river, the beacon that would guide me back to the camp.

I smelled the familiar scent of the river long before it came into view, a medley of the moist smells of earth and rock and moss and water. I had known no other river and its breath lingered constantly in the camp especially on the mornings when the mists crept up through the woods and slipped quietly along the worn footpaths between the tents. Even if I had not returned, I would have recognized the river's breath anywhere as much as I would have my mother's.

As we neared the river, I barked and whined and paced anxiously back and forth on the red seat in between Wawa and the window.

"What is it, Charlie?" Wawa asked. "You smell something familiar?"

The truck came to the end of one road and turned onto another. Past the window on Wawa's side I could see the river filling in between the trees. I knew where I was, and the camp was not far. I barked and whined and scratched at the cab door. It was time to leave my new friend.

The truck rolled forward slowly until Wawa pulled off the road into a parking area sheltered by trees. My brain matched the image of the parking area to the same one Mark had brought me to when he set my box on fire. From the height of the cab, I could still see a faint black stain on the parking lot where my box had burned. I began to shiver. How strange that I should come to this very spot on my journey back to the camp as if it was meant to warn me of trouble ahead.

For a moment, I considered curling up on the red seat and allowing Wawa to drive on. He was kind, and I imagined all the places I might see from the cab of his truck. But I desired a place I could call home with a food dish and water bowl, a toy or two, and a basket or rug all my own full of familiar scents that would comfort me. A rolling home did not appeal to me anymore than Sam's home did.

As the truck let out another deep breath, Wawa opened the cab door, grabbed the silver bar and swung himself off the seat. He stood quietly for a moment looking past the trees to the river, and then he turned and looked at me.

"I had a mind to keep you if you wanted to be kept," Wawa said, "but far be it from me to hold anyone against his will." He took a few steps backward while I tiptoed up to the edge of the red seat. Still up high, I fussed because it was a fair leap down for a dog my size. Wawa stepped forward, lifted me up, and set me down on the ground. I gave myself a good shake and stretched.

"May the road rise up to meet you," he said. I trotted off a little way, turned back, and gazed at Wawa standing beside his enormous truck one last time. I barked.

"You're welcome," he said.

The smell of fumes still lingered on the surface of the parking lot. It stirred the memory of the fire more strongly and my anxiety churned inside my stomach again. Yet, it was still daylight and I could hear the river off to my left. Home was not here. I ran off into the woods in search of the camp.

XXIV

The scents filled my nose more strongly the further I went, the smell of humans, their waste, their trash, their cars. I heard the familiar hustle and bustle of the activity around the shopping center and ran faster. I imagined Claire's surprise when she saw me, the tears she would cry, and all the hugs and belly scratches from the camp's residents who hadn't seen me since Al's death. When I wiggled underneath the last thicket into the gravel parking area, it made what I saw all the more stunning. I saw nothing. Not a tent. Not a shelter. Not a human. Just black signs with red letters on many of the trees. NO TRESPASSING. WATER CO. PROPERTY. VIOLATORS WILL BE PROSECUTED.

I sat down in the gravel confused. Could my nose have misled me? The scents were indeed fainter than I remembered, but they were still there. Claire's. Bruce's. Even Al's. I trotted across the parking area into the thin grass still speckled with rubbish. I found my own scent and followed it to a bare area of dirt crossed by tire treads.

A familiar strip of cloth soaked with my scent protruded from the dirt. I bit it with my teeth and pulled until the object under the dirt popped free. It was my chewy.

I lay down with my chewy and put my head between my paws. I had come home only to find home had gone elsewhere while I was away. My thoughts competed for priority, from wishing I had stayed with Wawa to wondering where everyone had gone, until renewed rumbling in my stomach brought with it another memory and gave me a glimmer of hope. I got up and trotted off toward the highway.

Along the highway, a tall, new fence stretched as far as I could see in both directions and had the same signs I saw on the trees. I ran along the edge of the fence until I found a place where the ground underneath the fence dropped off and left a gap wide enough for me to squeeze through.

I crossed the highway at the pole with the colored lights and made my way past the familiar storefronts of the shopping center. Mira's image no longer appeared in the window of the last store in the row. I went around the end of the building and did not change course even to chase the orange tabby who sat on the pavement out in the open. He arched his back and spat, ran a little way, and then sat down and licked his paws when he saw I had no interest in him. Cats always seem perplexed when they aren't the center of attention.

I barked and scratched at the backdoor of the deli. The man in the apron had been kind to me. And he had been kind to the camp's residents, too, giving them food when others mostly turned and looked the other way. When the door opened, a young woman appeared instead. She wore a black shirt, black pants and a white apron, too, but had red hair tied behind her head with a scrunchie like the ones Mira wore. When she saw me, she wrinkled her face in the way humans express disgust.

"It's just a stray dog," she said as she began to close the door. "Someone call animal control."

I sat in front of the closed door with my head down and my ears laid back. Had the man in the apron gone away, too? No, I was sure he was inside and would recognize me if he came to the door. I began barking and scratching again. I was still barking and scratching at the door when a white van appeared around the corner of the building. The orange tabby stopped licking its paws and ran into the thicket. The van stopped, and two men got out. They carried long poles with loops on the ends.

"We're not going to hurtcha, little fella," the man closest to me said as he took small steps toward me.

I scratched at the deli door harder, desperate to find a human who'd remember me, but the door did not open. When I turned to run, the man with the long pole stood even closer, too close. An instant later, he slipped the loop over my head and pulled it tight around my neck. I tugged and twisted and growled as I tried to slip free, but the harder I tugged and twisted, the more it hurt my throat.

I growled and showed my teeth. At any moment, I expected the man in the apron to burst through the back door and wave his gun the way he did at the man in the hooded sweatshirt. When they saw his gun, surely these men would drop their poles and run away, too. But the second man grabbed me. He wore thick gloves and held me firmly until he thrust me into a cage in the back of the van. The door closed and as quickly as my freedom had begun, it ended.

As I bounced along inside the cage, I imagined myself stretched out on the red seat of Wawa's truck with the sunlight pouring through the glass and the road stretching out ahead of me. I had dreamed inside cages before. Cage doors eventually open.

When the van stopped, I heard a chorus of dogs barking. The rear door of the van opened, and a woman appeared with the man who had lassoed me with the long pole. "Don't be afraid," she said to me in a soothing voice. Dressed in a blue shirt and baggy pants, she reminded me of Jen at the veterinary hospital. She bore the same smells of dogs and cats and disinfectant and wore her hair in the same pony tail fashion.

"He's not your typical stray," she said to the man. "I'll take him inside and see if he has a chip in him. Someone might be looking for him."

Bright lights illuminated a parking lot around a long, rectangular building. At one end, there were fenced-in runs like Dr. Deaver's veterinary hospital, but the runs were empty. The night had arrived and although the air was decidedly cooler, it was still quite pleasant to be outdoors. Inside the building, the woman with the pony tail took me into a small room and placed me on a metal table. Once again, I suffered the indignity of human hands pressing in places I prefer not to be touched. Another younger, blue-clad woman joined us and held me to keep me from wiggling.

"You seem to be in good health and well fed," the older woman said. "Where did you come from?" She opened a drawer and removed an object that looked like the black stick the news woman spoke into the day the men in striped pants tried to close the camp. She waved it around my head and it beeped.

"That's strange," the woman said when she looked at the black stick. "He's registered to Dr. Deaver at the Riverdale Veterinary Hospital. His name's Charlie." When I heard my name, I wagged my tail. "Better call Dr. Deaver and tell her we have one of hers over here. Then give him a bath and find him a bed," the older woman said.

I will never understand why humans insist on dousing me with water and rubbing soap into my fur every now and then to try to make me smell as they please rather than as I am. But the ritual makes them happy, so I go along.

After my bath, the younger blue-clad woman carried me down another hallway past offices, examining rooms and a glass-walled room filled with cats! These cats, however, were not confined to cages, but romped freely among carpeted posts with stairs and platforms and chased each other and batted balls hanging on strings from a bar overhead. Along one wall, a few cats slept in carpeted boxes stacked like blocks, but there were no doors on the boxes to restrain them. Inside the room, the cats were free to do as they pleased.

I soon found out dogs were not entitled to the same privileges. I ended up in a metal cage in another room with other small dogs. Why anyone would think dogs cannot get along together in a room of their own just as well as cats shows a complete lack of understanding of our species.

Dr. Deaver and Jen arrived the next morning. The woman with the pony tail came in the room with them. When I saw Dr. Deaver and Jen, I began to shimmy, shake and bark.

"Hi Charlie!" Jen said. She opened the cage door. I jumped into her arms and covered her face with kisses. "That's the Charlie I know! We were worried about you!"

Dr. Deaver walked up and scratched my head. "We sent him to a foster home in the upper county three days ago," she said to the woman with the pony tail. "He managed to get loose the next day, but it still amazes me how he was able to find his way back to the camp so quickly."

"I've heard of dogs traveling greater distances to find their way home," the woman with the pony tail said, "but two days from the upper county is impressive."

"Charlie would not have known all the residents had relocated," Dr. Deaver said. "When he left, there were still people living there."

"Isn't there anyone willing to adopt him?" the pony-tailed woman asked.

Dr. Deaver frowned. "He needs a permanent home as much as the people who were in the camp," she said. "The young woman Charlie was closest to now has a job in the city and lives with another woman in an apartment that does not allow dogs. The foster mom had planned to take him to adoption days at several local pet stores, but she is reluctant to take him back."

"We take some of our animals over to the PetSmart on Route 13 every Saturday," the pony tailed woman said. "He'll catch someone's eye there."

"I had intended to send him to your shelter when he first came to our office a couple years ago." Dr. Deaver glanced at Jen and sighed. "But I'm glad I didn't. Charlie was the perfect companion for the man who ran the homeless camp."

"Doesn't he want Charlie anymore?"

"He passed." Dr. Deaver sighed.

"You're welcome to leave Charlie with us," the pony tailed woman said. "We've found new homes for quite a few of our guests through the PetSmart program with very few returns."

"Thank you," Dr. Deaver said. "I think it's best for Charlie. He'll see more people there."

I was stunned when Jen placed me back in the cage. Surely, she knew how to find Claire. I barked and ran in circles and tore up the paper.

"Don't be upset, Charlie," Jen said through the bars. "I'll come back to see you."

"Actually, it would be best if you did not," the pony tailed woman said. "Seeing you and having you leave again will only increase his anxiety."

Dr. Deaver nodded. "Charlie needs a fresh start," she said.

Tears welled up in Jen's eyes. She stood in front of my cage for several more moments petting my nose through the bars. "Goodbye, Charlie," she whispered. She touched my nose for the last time and then hurried out of the room.

"We'll let you know when we've placed him," the pony tailed woman said. Dr. Deaver nodded again but did not speak. For a moment, she simply gazed at me until she, too, turned abruptly and left the room with the pony tailed woman right behind her.

When I tired of tearing the paper and my throat was sore from barking, I lay down on the cold metal of the cage and wondered what I had done to cause so many people to abandon me. Claire, the camp residents, and the man in the apron were gone, and now even Jen and Dr. Deaver did not want me. This was not the homecoming I had expected.

XXV

The wonderful thing about second chances is they often arrive at unexpected moments just when all seems hopeless. My days at the animal shelter dragged on longer than anyone had imagined for a young dog like me. At the PetSmart adoption days, plenty of people stopped by to pet me, give me treats, and tell me how handsome I was, but at the end of the day I still found myself in a cage in the van for the ride back to the shelter.

Theresa, the woman with the pony tail, did her best to lift my spirits each time we returned to the shelter. "Don't worry, Charlie," she said. "There is someone special out there meant just for you." *Really? But what if I already had my someone special? What if Mira, or Al or Claire was my someone special? Then what?*

I surmised Theresa ran the shelter much like Al ran the camp because everyone listened to her. She gave orders to the young women who took care of me every day just like Dr. Deaver had at the veterinary hospital. There were trips to the runs and exercise while my cage was cleaned and daily fresh food and water. But much of my time I spent in a cage just like the veterinary hospital, in boredom, dreaming of the day the cage door would close behind me and I would never return.

The seasons had passed through the summer and the return of cool temperatures and the time the leaves change color and fall from the trees. Not long after, the snow returned. I did not stay outside in the runs long or make many trips to PetSmart. Yet, it was an unusually warm day in the middle of the cold season when I met Lucy.

I had been out in the runs that morning enjoying the warm temperature when a shelter volunteer led me to the van instead of back to my cage. Since I had come to the shelter, the PetSmart trips were the only reason for a van ride. They were a welcome relief from the boredom of the kennel.

When we arrived at PetSmart, the sidewalk in front of the store was dry and warm. The shelter volunteers and dogs alike stretched out along its length to bask in the sun. I had been napping, absorbing the sun's warmth as I had the heat from the gray box in Al's shelter, when I heard heavy footsteps approaching intermingled with a lighter scuffling, metallic clicking noise and soft thumps. I opened my eyes and looked up into the face of a young girl. She was shorter than Claire, not full grown, and wore pink pants, a pink coat, and a white hat with a furry ball like a rabbit's tail on top. Her eyes were as blue as the sky overhead and she smiled at me. She leaned on a metal pole with a rubber tip and had metal bands wrapped around her legs from her knees down.

"Daddy, look at this one!"

I stood up and stretched and wagged my tail. "His name is Charlie," one of the volunteers said.

"Hi Charlie," the girl said. "I'm Lucy." She tried to lean over and pet me, but she was having a time of it because of the pole and the metal bands around her legs. "Could you pick him up for me?" Lucy asked the volunteer.

I sniffed at the bands around Lucy's legs and licked one before the volunteer picked me up and held me for her to pet. Despite the obvious obstacles to her mobility, there was a joy about her and she smelled of washed clothes, sweet syrup, and a cat.

A man with a square face and broad shoulders stood behind her. His chin and cheeks were dark with whisker stubble. Gray tinged his dark brown hair and there were bags underneath his eyes. I had seen his face before—in Mary, in Bruce, sometimes in Al—the look of a human for whom the unkindness of the world had taken its toll.

"He's a good-looking dog," the man said.

"Would you like to hold him?" the volunteer asked. I thought she meant Lucy, but she gave me to the man instead. I didn't spare any charm and wiggled and squirmed in the man's arms and licked his chin.

"He likes you, Dad," Lucy said.

"He is friendly," the man agreed. As I felt the man's arms tighten around me in a hug, my heart beat faster. He liked me back.

"Can we adopt him?"

The man shook his head. "We came here for cat food, Lucy. Not a dog. Dogs are a lot more work than Princess."

The Meaning Of Home

"I'll take care of him," Lucy said. "You won't have to do anything."

"Famous last words. You can't even remember to change the cat litter."

"It smells."

"So does a dog's poop. Who's going to walk him when he has to go out and pick it up?"

"I will," Lucy said. The man's eyebrows raised, and he frowned. "I promise," Lucy said firmly and crossed her heart with her finger. "Look at him! He's so much friendlier than Princess. He'll follow me around and we'll be best friends! C'mon, Dad, you said yourself it's been too long since you had a dog."

The man sighed, and his shoulders drooped ever so slightly. He did not speak for a few moments, but I could sense whatever silent thoughts were running through his mind were colliding with each other and causing him conflict. I took it as a good sign that he continued to give me scratches and hadn't given me back to the volunteer.

"We can't just bring a dog home," he said.

"Then let's bring Mom here," Lucy said. She sensed her father's will weakening and pressed him with subtle persuasion. "Mom will like him if she sees him. He's fluffy. And he's sooooo cute. Trust me on this."

When the man handed me to the volunteer, I barked and wagged my tail furiously. I wanted to go home with them. They had pleasant smells and I sensed in both a strong wanting, even in Lucy's father. He reached over and scratched my head again and sighed even louder. "Will he be here next week?" he asked the volunteer.

The volunteer pointed at Theresa and said, "You'll have to ask her."

While Theresa walked over, the volunteer placed me on the sidewalk. I shimmied and shook and jumped up on Lucy's legs. In my enthusiasm, I had circled Lucy and wrapped my leash around her.

"Be careful!" the man said sharply to the volunteer holding my leash. "I can't have her fall."

"Stop it, Dad," Lucy snapped. "I'm not an invalid."

"Are you interested in Charlie?" Theresa asked.

"Yes," Lucy answered.

"Maybe," the man said. "Will he be here next week? I'd like my wife to meet him before we commit to anything."

"If we know you're coming to see him, we'll be sure to have him here," Theresa said. "Or you can always stop by the shelter." She handed Lucy's father a glossy piece of paper. "Here's our address. And some things to think about when adopting a dog. Have you ever adopted before?"

"No," the man said. "But I had several growing up."

"If you adopt him, we'll come visit your home a couple times to make sure it's a good fit," Theresa said. "It's as important for Charlie as it is for your family."

The man stared at the paper. "Please, Dad?" Lucy asked.

"You ask your mother," he said.

"Yessss!" Lucy squealed.

When Lucy and her father began to walk away, I whined and fussed and tugged on my leash. What had I done? Why were they walking away?

"Don't worry, Charlie," Lucy said. "We'll come back and get you. I promise"

I did not understand. I watched them until they got into a big white car and drove away. The ride back to the shelter that afternoon was the longest ever.

I don't know why I am partial to human females, but I am. Perhaps it is because my first experience with a human male was not a good one. And it took me quite a long time before I completely trusted Al. When Lucy entered my room in the animal shelter, I was ready to go with her anywhere, even into a home with a deranged cat. I shimmied and shook and barked the happiest of barks. I knew she had come for me.

Lucy's father and mother entered the room behind her. Theresa was with them. Lucy's mother's scent was strongest of all, a uniquely sweet aroma of fragrances I had not smelled before and likened most to the scents of some of the women I had passed at Al's funeral. I could easily see the resemblance between Lucy and her mother. They were short with brown hair, and both had the same round cheeks and blue eyes.

"This is Charlie, Mom!" Lucy said. Her eyes were wide and hopeful. When she opened my cage door, I jumped into her arms and showered her with kisses. "Isn't he wonderful?"

The woman reacted tentatively. She reached out and touched me the way Mira used to touch the bath tub water to gauge its temperature. Sometimes, the only way to get love is to give some first, so I turned to Lucy's mother and gave her my full attention. I wiggled in Lucy's arms and she gave me to her mother to hold. In her mother's arms, at first, I felt tension, but as the moments passed, the tension melted away. I tried to give her kisses, but she turned her face away from me. I licked her hand instead. She laughed.

"He is sweet," she said.

Lucy's face beamed. "Can we adopt him, Mom? Please? I've always wanted a dog."

"We don't know anything about him," Lucy's mother said.

"What's there to know?" Lucy asked. "Look at him! He's love with fur!"

"Is he housebroken?" Lucy's mother asked. "Will he chew my nice things?"

Theresa had been standing in the doorway closely observing the interaction between myself and Lucy's mother. "Charlie is meticulously clean for a male dog," she said. "He has never pooped in his cage as long as you stick to a schedule. He needs to go out first thing in the morning, in the afternoon, and last thing before bed. He is neutered so you need not worry about some of the more annoying habits of a male dog.

"As far as chewing, I can't really say. We don't leave toys with them in their cages. He listens well, so if scolded, I believe he'll get the message. If it doesn't work out, we'll take him back. It has to work for everyone. The last thing we want is to have unhappy clients with an unhappy dog."

For a few moments, no one said anything as if they were waiting for Lucy's mother to speak first. Then Lucy finally said quietly, "Please, Mom?"

"How are you going to take him for his walks?" Lucy's mother asked.

"I can do it!" Lucy insisted. "I'm getting stronger."

Lucy's father spoke up for the first time. "When she can't, I will." Lucy gave her father an adoring, thankful glance and then looked anxiously at her mother.

"I guess we can give it a try," Lucy's mother said, "but I can't have him chewing my nice things."

Lucy squealed so loud, she started all the dogs in the room barking including myself. What a racket we made! She was so excited, I was sure it meant I was going home with her.

"If you'll come with me," Theresa said to Lucy's parents, "there is some paperwork to fill out."

Lucy's mother gave me back to Lucy who hugged me and buried her face in my fur. "I told you we'd come get you," she said.

Soon, I was wearing a new halter and leash Lucy's father had purchased from the shelter and was tugging with all my strength as we walked out of the shelter toward the big white car. My days as a shelter dog were over.

XXVI

Lucy's family lived in a modest two-story home in a neighborhood of similar homes with patches of brown lawns showing through a receding blanket of snow, leafless trees, and white mailboxes decorated with icicles. For a time when I first came to live with her, I was confined to two rooms on the first floor, the kitchen and a family room with a soft couch and armchairs that were delightful for napping. At night, however, Lucy's father, Justin, would pick me up, take me downstairs into their basement, and put me in a box not unlike the one Mira had for me in her kitchen. I howled and barked and scratched at the metal bars of the box door for the first several nights, but not even Lucy came to my rescue.

My mood did not improve when Princess the cat showed up to satisfy her curiosity. Upstairs, I had seen but a fleeting streak of white and gray whenever I smelled her close by. When I was confined inside the box, however, she came down into the basement and sat just a few feet away, watching me and licking her paws, until she grew bored and went back upstairs.

One night, Justin fell asleep on the couch while watching the TV. Lucy's mother had already gone up to the second floor of their home where I was not allowed to go. I lay next to Lucy on an armchair big enough for the both of us, nestled amongst plump pillows, and pretended to be asleep. Lucy stood up with the help of her pole, turned off the TV, and then turned and gazed at me for a long time. I had one eye open just enough to see her standing there in the dim light of a lamp on the end table by the armchair and sensed her wrestling with her thoughts. Finally, she walked over to me, bent over, and stroked my fur so gently I could feel the affection flowing from her hand.

"Be a good dog, Charlie," Lucy whispered in my ear before she stood up. She turned off the light and went upstairs.

I heard Lucy's father get up later and go upstairs, too, but in the darkness, he did not see me curled up on the big armchair among the pillows.

Princess didn't either. After Justin went upstairs, she crept into the room with her eyes aglow and her tail twitching. No doubt, she had already been down to the basement and discovered I was not in the box. She suspected I was still in the house and came looking for me in the area I had carved out of her territory. I waited until she was directly below me before I poked my head up from among the pillows and grinned. It was gratifying to see her instantaneous look of shock, alarm and disgust, ruffled fur, and rigid tail, before she bolted out of the room, but I did not pursue her. Lucy's whisper still tickled my ear. *Be a good dog, Charlie.* I had the good sense to know that giving Princess her comeuppance would, at best, land me back in my box or, at worst, back in my cage at the shelter.

Sunlight was just beginning to filter in through the kitchen and family room windows and birds were singing their morning songs when Lucy's mother came downstairs. My heart raced as I listened to her footsteps approach. She entered the family room dressed in a white robe, walked over to the TV, and turned it on. When she turned around, she saw me laying among the pillows on the armchair. I smiled at her and wagged my tail.

"Justin!"

A few moments later, I heard the heavy, rapid footsteps of Lucy's father coming down from the second floor. I heard the softer sounds of Lucy stirring, too.

"What's wrong?" Justin appeared in the doorway between the family room and the front hall. He wore dark colored pajamas and sleep was still in his eyes.

"The dog. You left him upstairs all night!"

Justin rubbed his eyes. "I fell asleep on the couch," he said. "I completely forgot he was still upstairs." Justin looked at me and then around the family room. "Did he do anything?"

"I don't know. I don't smell anything."

Lucy's mother and father walked around the kitchen and family room for several moments inspecting every inch. By this time, Lucy had come downstairs, too. She watched her parents for a few moments in silence, and then said, "Charlie behaved himself, didn't he?"

"You left him upstairs on purpose?" her mother asked.

"He was so unhappy in the cage, Mom," Lucy said. "I knew if he had a chance, he'd prove himself."

"But this was just one night… you're lucky."

"Let him stay upstairs, Mom. Please?" Lucy pleaded. "If he misbehaves, I'll clean it up."

"What if he chews something?"

"I'll pay for it out of my allowance."

"Your allowance isn't going to buy a new piece of furniture."

"I'm not worried," Lucy said.

I never spent another night inside a box after that. Justin, on rare occasions, did put me inside the box as punishment whenever I forgot myself and pooped inside the house in the excitement of having company or when anxiety overcame me during a thunderstorm. But I never spent more than the length of a TV show or two in punishment. Lucy and her mother were sympathetic.

Yes, I soon won over Lucy's mother, Nancy, with my good behavior and irrepressible charm. I made it a point to curl up next to her and rest my head on her lap whenever she sat down on the couch to watch the TV. A few wide-eyed puppy looks up at her face brought her hand to my head, and then to my belly when I rolled over. Women simply can't resist a handsome dog. I followed her around the kitchen and family room when she was alone in the house during the day. Soon, Lucy's mother herself took the barriers down and gave me permission to follow her anywhere on the first floor. I went into the basement with her when she washed clothes, past the dreaded punishment box that still stood in a corner. I became her shadow to the point that when I didn't follow her, she often called to me.

Justin loved me, too. I sensed I had opened a door into his past and helped him remember a forgotten joy, the companionship of a dog. He often came home late at night after Lucy and her mother were asleep, and he carried the same small, flat box with a handle that he left the house with each morning. It was filled with papers. Justin would set the box down, then ruffle my fur and make a big fuss over me.

Justin always shared his dinner with me just like Al did. And then we went for our walk through the dark and quiet streets of the neighborhood. On our walks, Justin sometimes talked to me.

"Where'd you come from, Charlie?" he'd say. "How did you know where to find me?"

He made up little songs using my name and sang much better than Al.

More often, Justin would look up at the sky and talk to God out loud just like Al did. Justin asked God many questions like why Lucy wasn't getting better and why his father had to die from cancer. But I never heard God answer Justin either. I wondered whether it was the same God Al spoke to and whether Justin had ever been to his house.

Perhaps because I had my own anxieties, I recognized the symptoms in Justin. He was always drumming his fingers on something, usually me. And when he sat down, he'd cross one leg with the other and twirl his foot in the air. He seldom sat perfectly still unless he fell asleep on the couch or in the big armchair. When he did, I curled up next to him and his hand would find me.

The surest sign of Justin's anxiety was the telltale tension in his facial and body movements. Even when he smiled, it seemed forced. Justin was a man immersed in his thoughts, wrestling with them, and sometimes trying to flee from them unsuccessfully.

Besides Justin, Lucy and her mother, Nancy, I smelled the scent of another human in the home, fainter than the rest but strong enough to tell he had spent a good deal of time there. It was a masculine odor. Yet, for the rest of the cold season, no one entered the house whose scent matched the scent I had detected.

As the days grew longer and the air warmer, Justin and Lucy lengthened our walks. I could not walk as fast with Lucy as I could with Justin on account of Lucy's braces and the pole with the rubber tip. Lucy constantly implored me to slow down and stop pulling against my leash.

The earth was moist with melted snow and carried so many scents I wanted to stop and smell each one. The deep rich smell of dirt, the fresh smell of new growth pushing up from underneath, and the scents of Lucy's human neighbors and their dogs all deserved inspection. The warmer temperatures had also awakened rabbits from their burrows and brought them out to nibble on the new Spring grass. When a foolish one hopped out of brush directly in our path, my foxlike instincts took over.

I leaped toward the rabbit and pulled the leash right out of Lucy's hand. With a nose full of scent and a lack of restraint to hold me back, my feet kept moving as long as the rabbit did. I did not see Lucy fall.

Looking back on it now, had I known the pain it would cause Lucy, I would not have run. But then, I was completely unrestrained for the first time since the dog catcher had lassoed me. I had no intention of running away from Lucy as I did from Sam and her dogs when I left their farm. I only wanted to explore a bit like I did at the camp when Al wasn't around. No matter where my roaming had taken me, I had always made my way back to Al's shelter and my food, water bowl and my rug before nightfall. Home is home, and I had one now I did not want to give up.

The rabbit disappeared underneath a neighbor's porch I could not squeeze under. I paced back and forth for a little while and barked, but it wasn't coming out and I wasn't getting in. I wandered off through one yard after another creating a new scent trail for myself through the neighborhood and leaving my mark next to other dogs' scents. A woman came out of her house, stood on her porch, and called my name.

"Charlie! Charlie! Come here, boy!"

Though her voice sounded kind, I did not know who she was and had no interest in going to her.

At the end of the row of houses, I came upon woods that reminded me of the woods around the camp. I ventured in and startled a fine smelling animal with long, thin legs and a big, white tail. It snorted and pawed at the ground when it saw me, and then bounded away in a succession of great leaps. All I could see was its white tail waving back and forth.

My leash still trailed behind me and snagged on a log forcing me to backtrack to untangle myself. I was tired of running and started back the way I had come thinking it was time for a cool drink and a long nap in the armchair. When I reached the street, I saw Justin's big, white car coming toward me. I ran toward it wagging my tail, and circled it leaping and barking when it slowed down and stopped. But I stopped leaping and barking when Justin got out.

I recognized the face of human anger, the glaring eyes, the deeper color, the raised ridges underneath the skin. I had seen anger many times in Mark's face, and sometimes even in Al's although never at me. Justin was angry with me. I lay down on the street by the car with my ears back and head down and looked away from him.

"Charlie, do you know what you've done?" Justin shouted. "You hurt Lucy!" He walked up to me and grabbed my leash. I closed my eyes and waited to be picked up by the scruff of my neck the way he had once when he was angry with me for pooping inside the house. But he didn't. He sighed and gathered me up gently. "Of course, you don't," he said and shook his head. "You're just a dog who ran after a rabbit. Let's hope Nan sees it that way." I wagged my tail, but I still could not bring myself to look at him.

"C'mon, let's go home," he said. "Lucy's more concerned about you than she is about herself."

He put me in the back seat of the car. As he began driving, I heard Justin talking to Nan, and he didn't even use a little black box like Wawa did or hold anything to his ear. Apparently, Justin could talk to Nan the same way he spoke to God, but I heard Nan's voice.

"Did you find Charlie?"

"Yeah, I have him. How's Lucy?"

"She has bruising all down her left side, Justin. She's lucky she didn't break something."

"What did the doctor say?"

"He gave her anti-inflammatories. She'll have to use ice until the swelling goes down and then we'll just have to keep an eye on her. She'll miss a few days of school. Justin, I can't have her walking Charlie anymore."

"I'll do it."

"How are you going to come home in the middle of the afternoon?"

Justin paused. "Can't you find time to walk him once a day?"

There was another pause. "And what if he runs away from me?" Nan asked.

"Then he does," Justin said. "I won't be angry with you, but if we give him back to the shelter, it will hurt Lucy a hundred times worse than anything she felt because of her fall."

Nan paused again. "I never said anything about giving him back," she said.

"Then you'll walk him in the afternoons?"

"I suppose."

"Thank you. I'll see you when you get home."

When I entered the house, Lucy and Nan were not there. Justin removed my leash and halter and stood there looking at me. "You've stolen our family's hearts," he said. "Be careful you don't break any."

XXVII

When Lucy came home, Justin carried her to the couch in the family room and set her down with her legs raised on the cushions. I promptly jumped up in her lap. Lucy bundled me in her arms and squeezed me so tightly, I grunted with satisfaction.

"Promise me you'll never do that again?" she asked. Lucy's affection flowed from her body and soaked into my fur as strong as ever. All those lonely nights in the veterinary hospital kennel and the shelter, I had longed for moments like this, to be someone's dog and to love and be loved unconditionally.

"I wish I could run like you," Lucy said to me after her parents left the room. "I just want to be like everyone else and not be treated like a cripple." She stroked my fur. "What I wouldn't give to take these things off and run around the yard or climb a tree." Lucy lifted her leg and winced. "I'll run one day. They'll see."

Lucy recovered from her fall slowly. Every day, her mother took her to see a doctor and every day Lucy came home exhausted. "They make me do so many exercises, Charlie," she complained before she stretched out on the couch and fell asleep. However, I liked having Lucy home in the afternoons. Now I had someone to nap with.

One afternoon while I lay on the sofa napping with Lucy, I was awakened by the honk of a horn followed by the thud of a car door closing. I jumped off the couch, rushed to the front door and barked to let everyone know a visitor was coming. Nan was right behind me and almost stepped on me in her haste to open the front door. "Tommy's home!" she shouted.

A few moments later, a young man walked up the steps of the front porch with a big bag slung over his shoulder. He was dressed in a red and blue uniform with shiny buttons that looked just like Al's. When Nan opened the door and I caught a nose full of his scent, I instantly recognized it as the unknown masculine odor I had not been able to identify since my arrival. If this man belonged here, why was I meeting him only now?

Tommy entered the house, dropped his bag, and embraced Nan in a big hug.

"It's so good to have you home," Nan said.

"It's good to be home," Tommy replied. Then he looked down at me. "Who's this?" He bent down and held out his hand for me to sniff. "This is Charlie," Nan said. "Lucy and your father saw him at a pet adoption day and … well … I couldn't say no."

"Hi, Charlie," Tommy said. "You must have some exceptional charm if you were able to persuade my Mom to take you in. I asked for a dog for years."

"But you always wanted a big dog, Tommy," Nan said. "What was it?"

"A bulldog."

"And they slobber. I couldn't have that in the house."

Lucy appeared in the front hall leaning on the pole with the rubber tip. Tommy stood up smiled broadly, walked over to Lucy, and gave her just as big a hug as he gave Nan, perhaps bigger. "I heard you got a little banged up," he said.

"It's nothing," Lucy said. "I've missed you."

"I've missed you, too. Thanks for posting on Facebook. Otherwise, I'd have no idea what's going on around here."

"You can always call," Nan said.

"How long are you home for?" Lucy asked.

"Ten days."

"That's all?"

"At my rank, I was lucky to get that much."

"Are you hungry?" Nan asked.

"Starving," Tommy said. "And I'd like to get a shower."

"Your room is waiting," Nan said.

Tommy gave Lucy and Nan each another big hug, picked up his bag, and went upstairs.

Justin came home early that evening in a lighter mood and beamed when he saw Tommy, now dressed in denim jeans, a dark green tee shirt, and sneakers. Tommy took after his father. He was just a bit taller than Justin with Justin's broad shoulders and square head, but much thicker arms and legs. And where Justin was normally tense and reserved, Tommy was relaxed and playful. He picked Lucy up in his arms and spun her around in the family room.

"Tom, be careful with your sister," Justin said.

"Stop it, Dad," Lucy snapped. "I'm fine."

"You're getting stronger," Tommy said to Lucy. "I can feel you have much better muscle tone than the last time I was home."

"Thank you for noticing," Lucy said. "No one else seems to." She shot an annoyed glance at her father.

"That's not fair, Lucy," Nan said. "We just don't want you to have another setback. You have missed enough school as it is."

The dinner table conversation that evening was more boisterous and cheerful than any I remembered since my arrival. For the moment, whatever concerns each of them carried they set aside, whatever troubles lay outside the walls of their home would stay there. This family's bonding was a fascinating aspect of human behavior I had not witnessed before. Their home wasn't just a physical shelter, but an emotional one. More than rain or snow, it provided a respite from the world's unkindness.

I sat quietly at the foot of Justin's chair waiting for his hand to drop to nose level with a juicy morsel. He did not disappoint me. Nan had made succulent chicken and delicious rolls. There were other smells I recognized, ripe tomatoes, leafy lettuce, and the sauce from a bottle they poured on top.

Lucy recounted the story of how I came to live with them, and how she left me upstairs all night by myself.

"That's my Luce!" Tommy said. "Always willing to take a gamble."

Justin reached down and lifted me into his lap. It was the first time I had been elevated to dinner table level anywhere and my heart swelled as much as my nose. Right in front of my eyes were the remaining chicken breasts and rolls, and Justin's plate was closer still, streaked with sauce and juices. I stretched out my neck and licked the plate.

"Justin!" Nan snapped.

"What?" he said. "It's going in the dishwasher anyway."

After dinner, everyone moved into the family room. Tommy sat down in the big armchair and I took the opportunity to jump in his lap and introduce myself.

"Welcome to the family, Charlie!" Tommy said. He gave me a vigorous scratching. Tommy had great strength in his hands and it felt oh, so good.

"He's a good dog," Nan said.

"Did they tell you anything about him?" Tommy asked.

"Just that he was a stray," Lucy replied.

"He didn't grow up a stray," Justin said. "He was already housebroken, and someone taught him manners."

"I'm glad Lucy has you to keep her company," Tommy said to me. I rolled over and let him scratch my belly.

"How are things at the office, Dad?" Tommy asked.

Justin's face tensed, and his foot started twirling again. "Same," was all he said.

"Didn't you just get employee of the month or something like that?" Tommy asked. "I thought I saw Lucy post it on Facebook?"

"So I had my picture pinned to a bulletin board, but not a dollar extra in my paycheck."

"I don't know why you don't just quit," Lucy said. "Why do you work there if you're so unhappy?"

Justin sighed. I sensed there was more he wanted to say but he kept silent.

Nan stood up. "Would anyone like to play a game?" she said as she moved toward the kitchen. "I'll have the dinner table cleaned up in just a moment. Tommy, I bought a gallon of your favorite ice cream for desert. Moose Tracks. I bought a gallon for the rest of us, too." Nan laughed at her own joke.

"Thanks, Mom," Tommy said. "But I was planning on going to Erica's in a little while. I'll have some of that ice cream, though."

Lucy made a scrunchy face. "Why are you seeing her again?"

"Don't worry, sis," Tommy said. "Your still my number one." Tommy stood up and winked at Lucy before he walked into the kitchen.

When Tommy stood up, I moved over to Lucy's lap. I sensed her mood had changed from her body language. The lack of attention she gave to me meant her mind was preoccupied, but I could not tell if she was still annoyed with her father or wishing that Tommy would stay home.

"How 'bout a game, Lucy?" Nan asked. "Your pick."

Lucy pushed me off her lap and pushed herself up on the pole with the rubber tip. "No thanks," she said. "I still have all that homework to catch up on." When she walked by her father, she did not even look at him.

During the time Tommy was home, I grew to be fond of him. He roughhoused with me like Daniel had, although he never held a sock in his teeth and shook his head. He took me for long walks all the way to the woods. Tommy was never impatient with me and always gave me plenty of time to sniff along the way. He rolled a ball in the house for me to chase and he gave the best scratches. Yet, ten days in human time isn't very long. It passes by as quickly as a cool breeze on a hot day. The last meal at the dinner table found my new family all seated together again, but in noticeably different moods.

Tommy tried to keep the mood light. He complimented Nan's cooking, asked Lucy questions about her school work, and recalled family times together before my arrival. Nan, Lucy and Justin answered, but gone was the boisterous laughter that had rolled around the table at the first meal. I suppose the problem with humans and their homes is the world won't let them stay there forever.

After he finished eating, Tommy wiped his mouth with a cloth and then sat back in his chair. He took a drink from his glass and said, "We're being deployed to Afghanistan."

XXVIII

Nan's eyes widened. She held her hand to her mouth and glanced back and forth from Justin to Tommy. Lucy stared at her brother in a mystified incomprehension while Justin simply stared at his plate as though it was a book he was reading. A discomforting sentiment pervaded the silence and bothered me so much I went into the family room and curled up on the armchair.

"Don't worry," Tommy said. "I know guys who did several tours in Iraq and Afghanistan and came home without a scratch."

"Why?" was all Nan could manage to say.

"Orders," Tommy said. "There are a lot of bad guys over there who want to hurt us. Better we get them first."

"Where's Afghanistan?" Lucy asked.

"North of India and Pakistan. South of Russia," Tommy said.

"That's far," Lucy said.

"Yes, it is far," Tommy agreed. "But I'll be able to call you on a sat phone and see you on Skype just as often. You'll never know I'm in Afghanistan instead of Texas."

"When?" Justin asked.

"The end of next month," Tommy replied. "It will be my first trip on a C-130. I'm excited."

"Excited? You think it's exciting to go risk your life?" Nan was shaking.

"I'm excited to serve my country," Tommy said sternly.

"You could have served your country just as well in the Navy or the Coast Guard," Nan said. She took her napkin and dabbed her eyes.

"Mom, we've been over that," Tommy said. "I didn't want to join the Navy or the Coast Guard. I wanted to become a Marine. Besides, I get seasick."

Nan's lower lip started quivering. She got up from her chair and left the room.

"Dad, you understand, don't you?" Tommy asked.

Justin nodded his head slowly. "I understand, but I don't have to like it."

"You and Mom have always taught us to have faith in God," Tommy said. "Isn't this a time to put your faith into practice?"

Justin didn't have an answer. In the silence that followed, the humming of the refrigerator gave a sound to the tension in the room, an incessant *whrrrrrrrrrr* that nibbled at my nerves.

"There's still some of the Moose Tracks left. Would you like some?" Justin asked.

Tommy smiled, and his shoulders relaxed. "Sure."

Lucy started to get up from her chair and Justin went to help her.

"I can do it myself," Lucy said. I saw a sadness in Justin's eyes as he watched her push herself up on her pole and leave the kitchen.

The next morning, Tommy was up before the sun. I heard him moving back and forth upstairs and the sound of water running in the bathroom. Nan was the first one downstairs in her white bathrobe and slippers. She did not stroll over and sit down next to me in the armchair as she often did to stroke my fur and chat with me as casually as she did a friend. Instead, she stalked around the kitchen preparing breakfast. Her movements were tense. Occasionally, she stopped, leaned against the kitchen table and fought to keep her composure, and then she launched herself into her next task. After a few moments, I smelled the aroma of that wonderfully strong-smelling beverage humans never share with dogs.

Tommy came downstairs dressed in his uniform. Nan fought back tears when she saw him, and then walked up to him and kissed him on his cheek. "I'm so proud of you," she said. Tommy embraced her, and they both stood in the family room locked in the embrace for several moments.

"I'll be okay, Mom," Tommy said.

Lucy shuffled into the family room in her pajamas rubbing her eyes. "What time is it?"

"5:30," Tommy replied.

"Why do you have to leave so early?"

"I have to be at the airport by seven, Lucy. Our flight leaves at nine."

Justin appeared behind Lucy and placed his hand on her shoulder. He followed her into the kitchen and patted Tommy on the back along the way without saying a word. When they sat down, Nan slid a plate of pancakes and sausages onto the table. I positioned myself in between Justin and Lucy, and although I received an occasional offering of the warm, buttery cake and tangy meat, this morning it was just food.

"I washed all your clothes and packed your duffel," Nan said to Tommy. "I wish you would have told me earlier. I could have bought you more underwear. I don't suppose they have a Wal-Mart in Afghanistan."

"I still don't understand why you have to go all the way over there," Lucy said.

"To keep the terrorists from coming over here, Lucy," Tommy said.

"When will you get leave again?" Justin asked.

"I'm hoping maybe Christmas, but I don't know."

"We won't see you for seven months?" Lucy moaned.

"We'll Skype, sis," Tommy reassured her. "I won't forget you."

As I watched them eat breakfast, I thought of the conversations I had observed between Al and Claire at the table in his shelter. Especially with Claire, there was so much more on her mind she did not say. Now, my new family was engaging in the same complicated human behavior. They all had thoughts and feelings they were unwilling to express openly to each other even though I could sense the conflict through their body language. I had always sensed a measure of sadness at moments of separation for humans who were fond of each other, but in this moment, I sensed a strong fear from Justin, Nan and Lucy behind the usual sadness. Yet, not one of them wanted to let it show.

The inevitable moment of Tommy's departure came at last. They all followed Tommy into the front hall where his heavy green bag lay propped up by the front door. Nan and Lucy began to cry. Justin shoved his hands into the pockets of his sweat pants and looked down at the floor. There were individual hugs, and then my family stood in a circle with their arms around each other until a car horn beeped and Tommy said, "I have to go." He knelt down next to me to say goodbye.

"Be the best watchdog ever, Charlie," he said. "Keep an eye on things while I'm gone." He rumpled my fur, then picked up his bag, and he was gone.

Nan and Lucy cried on and off for much of the morning. Justin was silent, and later left for work. Justin had that way about him. When the emotion of situations at home overcame him, he thrust himself into his work, not as a sanctuary, but simply as a distraction.

I believe Nan, Justin and Lucy did the best they could not to dwell on Tommy's whereabouts as the summer lengthened, but I could always tell when Tommy called home. The phone call brought so much more excitement and temporary relief than any other caller. When Nan pressed a button, I could hear Tommy's voice, and then everyone started talking over each other at once. Tommy laughed until the conversation settled down. On occasion, Nan, Justin and Lucy gathered around a screen in

Justin's special room just off the family room. I call it Justin's special room because it is the only room in the house I have been in that has just his stuff. There isn't a petal from a floral arrangement, a feminine color, or a hint of fragrance other than the honeysuckle that comes in when he opens a window.

Tommy's "Skypes" were one of the few times I saw Lucy or Nan enter the room. Lucy sat in the big, burgundy armchair behind Justin's desk and Nan and Justin stood behind her. Lucy held me in her lap so I could see the screen, too. When Tommy's face appeared on the screen, I barked and fussed and wagged my tail. I did not understand how I could see and hear him, but not smell him or jump into his arms.

Their conversations always started in the same boisterous manner as it did on the phone with each one speaking over the other until Tommy had answered questions about how he was (always "super"), how was the weather ("hot"), and what was he doing ("working with the local Afghanis and meeting nice people"). Sometimes, Tommy's friends appeared behind him in the screen and made faces and funny shapes with their hands that made Lucy laugh. The Skypes always ended with questions about when Tommy was coming home ("I'm not sure, maybe Christmas") and then long goodbyes from Nan and Lucy. I saw Tommy's hand fill the screen with his fingers spread and Nan, Lucy and Justin would each take a turn pressing their hands against his as they said goodbye. Lucy lifted me up and pressed my paw against the screen, too.

When the screen went dark, the familiar sense of sadness mixed with fear hung in the air like a chill. Nan often went into the family room and turned on the TV while Lucy went upstairs, and Justin sat in silence in front of the dark screen for awhile until something motivated him to move and focus his thoughts elsewhere.

On our walks, Justin's conversations with God often centered on Tommy. "I know you gave him to us. I knew the sacrifice we might be asked to make when he joined the Marines. And I know this is a selfish request, but please don't let anything happen to him. He has his whole life ahead of him."

Home was a quieter place without Tommy in it. A home changes when a member of the pack leaves. A piece of the fabric is torn away, and the impact depends upon which part of the fabric it is. While I believe humans and dogs often dream of a home that is constant and un-changing, a place we can return to that will be the same as it was when we left, it seldom is.

Tommy did come home for Christmas. It was a happy time filled with music in the house including some of the songs Al used to sing off key. Nan and Justin bought a real tree bigger than the fake one Mira had in the apartment and set it in a stand in the family room. It smelled like a forest inside the house. They waited until Tommy came home to decorate it with bright, blinking lights, shiny ornaments and a human with wings perched on the top like the one I saw in Father Paul's church. The rug underneath the tree became another favorite of mine for napping.

Underneath the tree, Nan piled many boxes wrapped in brightly colored paper just as the ladies at the church had done for the residents of the camp, but she did not give them to anyone right away. I sniffed each one curiously trying to identify its contents without much success. I have always found the human behavior of gift giving fascinating as it often seems to bring as much pleasure to the person giving the gift as it does to the one receiving it.

The feeling on the morning of Christmas was as close to what I imagined it had been like in my family before Tommy entered the Marines. For a time, the sadness mixed with fear had disappeared again like the fog along the river when the sun rose. There was laughter. There were hugs. There were relaxed postures and serene expressions. When they opened the wrapped boxes, I went to each one to inspect the revealed contents and memorize the smells. Lucy received plenty of new clothes and a box of the sticks and creams human females use to decorate their faces. Nan gave Tommy lots of new underwear.

As I lay on the family room floor amidst the wrapping paper and bows with the smell of pancakes and sausage and the strong-smelling beverage humans won't share with dogs wafting in from the kitchen, I wondered why all humans' Christmas days were not like this one. I remembered the pain in Claire's expression when she talked about hers and how Mira's Christmases were always subdued and overshadowed by Mark's unhappiness. I wondered why each day could not be like this one. And then I wondered how many Christmas days had passed by without my knowledge while I was in the camp or in a cage. I supposed I should be grateful for this one since many dogs never get the opportunity to share even one Christmas with humans.

The seasons had turned, once again, into warmer weather, and I heard Nan and Lucy talking excitedly about the possibility that Tommy might be coming home soon. One day, however, a car pulled into the driveway unexpectedly. Only Nan was home. I, of course, ran to the front door barking to alert Nan that someone was approaching. Nan came to the front door and told me to hush. When she opened it, there were two men standing on the porch in uniforms like Tommy's. Nan's eyes widened. She clutched her hands to her chest and began shaking her head even though the men hadn't spoken a word.

"No. No. Please! Not Tommy!"

She slumped against the door and slid down until she landed on her knees. An indescribable pain welled up from inside her and threw her body into convulsive sobbing. I immediately rushed to Nan and nuzzled up against her. Her hand clutched my fur. One of the men in uniforms opened the clear door to the outside and both men stepped inside the front hall. The first one knelt beside Nan and tried to comfort her, although he withdrew his hand when I growled.

"We're very sorry, Mrs. Thompson. It is our sad duty to inform you your son, Tom, gave his life in the service of his country."

Nan did not find his words comforting at all and her cries filled the front hall.

"Is there someone we can call for you?"

There was more anguish as the day went on. The men in uniforms made phone calls for Nan who was too distraught to speak. Shortly, friends of Nan's arrived to cry with her and the men in uniform left. Then Justin came home. Nan's friends left the living room while she and Justin clutched each other on the sofa and sobbed. The worst was still to come. Lucy had not been told of Tommy's death before she came home from school, but she knew instantly what had happened when she walked in the house and saw her parents' faces.

She screamed. Justin and Nan hadn't uttered a word. Lucy screamed in a shrill, terrified voice the echoes of which sometimes still ring in my ears to this day. Even when Justin dropped to his knees and held her, she kept on screaming until her voice was hoarse and she had no tears left in her. Justin carried her upstairs to her bedroom while Nan laid down on the sofa. I jumped up beside Nan even though she normally did not allow me on the living room sofa. Nan reached down and clutched my fur. I heard Lucy upstairs still crying and wanted to absorb her pain, too, but I was afraid of angering Justin and Nan by going upstairs.

As I lay next to Nan and felt her fingers dig into my skin, I perked my ears listening to the sounds—Nan's deep breaths, Lucy's crying, muffled voices of the visitors—and felt helpless. I felt helpless because I couldn't do more and guilt because I didn't feel my family's pain in the same way.

Shared pain is different from personal pain. It is not as severe. When I look back, I still see the day I lost Al as the worst day of my life. I loved Al deeply. Not that I didn't love Tommy. I simply didn't know him as long and had not bonded with him as I had with Al. Tommy's loss was not a personal loss to me as Al's was, and yet I shared my family's pain and felt deeply for them in a different way. Unquestionably, Tommy's death was the worst day of their lives and I could only love, comfort, cuddle, kiss, and dry tears as best as a dog can.

Over the next few days, the house was filled with people coming and going and staying all hours of the night. So many, in fact, that I was pushed away, kept from my family, walked by strangers. There was a funeral, but I was not invited to go. I remember the day of the funeral because my family came downstairs together all dressed in black clothes and they left the house without speaking to me. I watched through the clear front door and barked as they stepped into a long, black car in the driveway. I wanted to go with them. I should have gone with them just like I had accompanied Claire at Al's funeral. Out in the street, men in uniforms like Sergeant Mike's sat on motorcycles. As the car pulled out of the driveway, the men on the motorcycles escorted the car down the street until it was out of my sight.

Someone who's smell I recognized but whose name I have long since forgotten stayed with me in the house all day. I lay in the armchair and listened for the garage or the front door to open. When I heard the front door open, I jumped down and ran into the front hall. Some of Nan's friends came in first. The lady who had stayed with me in the house all day picked me up and would not allow me to rush to my family despite my efforts to wiggle out of her grasp. When I saw my family, I could tell from the expressions on their faces that they were simply exhausted. They went upstairs and slept.

As time passed, people stopped coming by. Justin returned to work in a worse mood than ever and Lucy went back to school even though she argued she was not ready.

"There is no point in laying around the house crying," Justin said. "Tommy wouldn't want that."

"Why not?" Lucy asked. "That's all Mom does."

Lucy was right. Nan fell into a deep depression and nothing I did would make her smile. It continued for quite a while. Even after she began doing things around the house again and driving Lucy places and going shopping, Nan was never the same again. I have never seen her have a moment of pure joy since. Not once.

And Justin became an angry man. On our walks, he took his anger out on God.

XXIX

"Why? Why?" Justin shouted at the sky and then hurried me off down the street when a porch light came on in a nearby home. "Why Tommy? Wasn't it enough my daughter has been deprived of a normal childhood because of her illness? You had to take my son, too? Why didn't you protect him?"

I could not see Justin's face in the dark, but I was frightened by the strong emotions that poured out of him, emotions reminiscent of Mark's anger, the kind of emotions that may cause someone harm. I had seen Al angry before, of course, but he seemed to control his anger better. And I never heard him talk to God the way Justin did for a time after Tommy's death.

Every morning when Justin left for work, he left abruptly without speaking or even saying goodbye to me with the usual pat on the head and belly scratches. When he came home late at night, he seemed to be boiling like the shiny pots Nan placed on her stove, and then it all spilled over on our walk. When we went inside, Justin went upstairs to his bedroom often without eating.

The grief in the home was stifling, more so than the fear that pervaded Mira's apartment after Mark lost his job or the grief everyone felt upon Al's death. It suffocated conversation and muted my family's desire to do much of anything. Each day, they were just going through the motions.

Humans take much longer to resolve grief than dogs, perhaps because they feel it at a much deeper and more complex level. Some humans never come to terms with their grief and all humans need help to do so. I did the best I could. When they were home, I never left my family alone. I always followed them around and divided my time between laps sharing my smiles, kisses and tail wags. I loved them during long hugs. I even followed them upstairs and discovered they rarely scolded me.

Princess, on the other hand, was not pleased with my permitted territorial expansion. To discourage me from coming upstairs, she would often hide in a closet or some other nook and cranny and then leap out, hiss and spit at me, and swat me on the nose with her paw before running away. Fortunately, she was declawed.

I tolerated her behavior for a while. I was pleased to have more freedom to roam and did not want to give Nan or Justin a reason to restrict me. But one day when no one was home, I went upstairs looking for Princess. Justin and Nan kept the door to Tommy's bedroom closed so I went into Lucy's bedroom first. Her room had pretty, blue walls with pictures of horses and dogs, a bed just her size with white posts, a tall piece of furniture with drawers and a mirror, and a short stand next to her bed. Princess often liked to hide underneath Lucy's bed because the sheets reached all the way to the floor, but I did not find her there.

There were two other rooms down the hall. The first was a large bathroom. Just inside there was a large, white bathtub to the left and next to it a tall shower. Sometimes, Princess sat inside the shower with its clouded glass doors. She also liked to crouch behind the laundry basket in the closet on the other side of the room. I had to pass both to reach the covered sandbox underneath the bathroom window where Princess relieved herself. She hated it when I marked her box with a spritz of my own urine, and she often lay in wait to ambush me on the way there, but I did not find her in the bathroom either.

Justin and Nan's bedroom was at the end of the upstairs hallway. As much as I know she loves me, Nan's desire for my company ends at her bedroom door. Besides, Justin said, Princess came to live with them first. She should be entitled to some sanctuary.

Their bedroom was larger than Al's entire shelter with light green colored walls and a separate bathroom twice the size of the one down the hall. There were so many places for Princess to hide, under the monstrous bed, behind any one of several pieces of furniture, even in a clothes closet that was a room unto itself.

I made my way into Justin and Nan's bathroom with its own large tub, shower with clouded glass doors, and laundry closet. There were clothes spilling out of the laundry basket in the closet and onto the floor and towels hanging from a rack on the shower soaked in Justin's and Nan's scents. When I returned to the bedroom, Princess attacked from the clothes closet. I smelled her on the way into the bathroom and I was ready for her. Instead of docilely absorbing her abuse, I bared my teeth and a brawl began.

I had never fought a cat before and I figured a skittish housecat without claws could not be as much of a threat as the cats I had seen in the city or around the camp. I didn't consider that Princess might have had a life like me before she came to live with my family. Princess fought with the fury of an alley cat to protect this last undefiled portion of her turf. If she had had claws, she may have given me several new places to breathe through.

We rolled across the bedroom floor snarling and swatting and biting. She broke off her attack and went underneath the bed. I followed and soon learned that it was not the wise thing to do. Underneath the bed, my mobility was limited, but hers was not. When she met me head-on in a renewed frontal attack, my only option was an inglorious retreat. Princess remained underneath the bed hissing and daring me to come get her. I walked around the end of the bed to the other side. When I peeked under, I saw Princess in her crouch, her ears flat, eyes sparkling, and her tail swishing back and forth. She showed me her gleaming white teeth. I chose to leave her claim the large space underneath the bed as her own and considered the matter of my presence upstairs settled. Just to be sure, I left the bedroom, went into the hall bathroom again, and peed on her sandbox before I went back downstairs.

I always have anxiety when humans argue. Loud voices and anger disturb me as much as thunderstorms and fireworks even if I am not the cause. After Tommy's death, Justin and Nan argued more.

"Why did you allow him to enlist?" Nan shouted one evening. "You know I didn't want him to enlist!"

Justin sat in the armchair reading. I lay on the carpet by his feet. He dropped the book into his lap and stared straight ahead. "He was a grown man."

"He was only eighteen!"

"And he was a grown man," Justin repeated. "He graduated high school. He was entitled to make his own decision and he decided he did not want to go to college right away. You never like it when I try to make decisions for you."

Nan paced back and forth in the kitchen. "You should have done something more."

"Like what?" Justin asked.

"I don't know," Nan said. "Something. Found him a job. Anything. He could have joined the National Guard if he felt that strongly about serving."

"He also could have left on his own and legally enlisted in the Marine Corp without our permission. He had his mind made up and was strong-willed enough he would have done just that. Would you rather he left us resenting us, or worse, for attempting to control him, or knowing he had our love and support no matter what?"

Nan sat down in a kitchen chair and started crying. "I can't open his bedroom door. When the phone rings, I keep thinking it's going to be him, that we've all been through some hideous nightmare and when I pick up the phone, I'll hear his voice on the line. Hi Mom, I love you." Justin sat perfectly still, his face expressionless, staring ahead at nothing in particular as if his mind had momentarily left his body. "Aren't you going to say anything?" There was silence. "Justin?"

"What?"

Nan looked at him in a pain-stricken disbelief. "I'm sorry I interrupted your reading!" she said and stormed out of the kitchen.

Justin sat in his trance for a few more moments before he lifted his book and tried to read. A few moments later, I noticed his hands were trembling and the trembling had spread to the book. Justin tried to steady the book in his lap, but the trembling would not stop. In one swift motion, he raised his arm and then slammed the book on the floor next to me. I jumped up and ran into the kitchen.

"I'm sorry, Charlie," Justin said. "I forgot you were there." He stood up and followed me. In the kitchen, he grabbed my leash and halter and said, "C'mon, Charlie. Let's go for a walk." Although I was frightened, I did as I was told.

Outside, the insects played their night music and a nearly full moon bathed the trees and lawns in silver. A light breeze stirred the humid air and smelled like approaching rain. Justin and I walked at a steady pace down the street in the direction of the woods. When we reached the end of the street, Justin looked up at the sky through the tree branches overhead and wept.

"My boy! My boy!" Justin walked back and forth in the road. "Am I to blame? The sins of the father? Why didn't you take me instead? You should have taken me!" I watched helplessly while Justin punished himself with his thoughts. Finally, he sat down on the curb in the darkness which gave me the opportunity to squirm into his lap. He wiped his eyes with the back of his hand and then scratched my head.

"You know, Charlie, it is harder to watch Nan and Lucy grieve than to grieve myself. We're all grasping for answers and there aren't any. We all want to blame someone but there isn't anyone. War is Hell." I licked the back of Justin's hand while he spoke.

A flicker of light up the street caught my attention. Behind it, a dark silhouette loomed coming toward us. I barked sharply to alert Justin and then gave a low, throaty grrrrrrowl.

"Who is it, Charlie?"

The flicker of light turned into a flashlight beam accompanied by the jangle of a small bell on a dog collar. I recognized the smell of a neighbor's dog, Jake, a big, clumsy, but friendly Golden Retriever I didn't particularly care for. Whenever we met on our walks, he always invaded my space and, in his youthful exuberance, thumped me with a massive paw or drooled on my fur. The flashlight swept back and forth along the curb line and settled on Justin.

"Justin, is that you?" a voice called.

"Evenin', Fred," Justin replied.

"Are you alright?"

"I'm okay," Justin said. "Just needed some fresh air."

I heard Jake's labored breathing and the sound of his toenails scratching the pavement as he pulled Fred toward us. The curve of his back and his big block of a head took shape in the moonlight and I braced myself for the onslaught.

"Whoa, Jake," Fred said. "Heel." His words did little to slow Jake down. Moments later, Jake and I were nose to dripping-wet-nose. His breath filled my nostrils and his saliva seeped into my facial fur. "Looks like we may get some rain tonight," Fred said to Justin while Jake urged me to leave Justin's lap and play with him. I declined.

"Does look that way," Justin agreed.

Then Jake pressed his nose against Justin's face and stepped on me in the process. I snapped at him. Fred yanked hard on Jake's leash at the same time Justin swatted my nose. "Behave yourself!" he said. I lay my head down in Justin's lap and sulked. I had only been trying to rid us of the interruption.

"Sorry," Fred said to Justin. "Jake is still learning boundaries."

"I don't mind," Justin replied. "It's his nature."

"Are you sure you're okay?" Fred asked, but then he followed up with "I'm sorry. I can't imagine what you must be feeling."

Justin sighed and shrugged his shoulders. "I wouldn't know what to say either."

"I read the story about Tommy in the paper," Fred said. "It said he went back for a wounded buddy."

Justin nodded. "That's what they told us. His squad was ambushed on a patrol. A couple guys were hit right away and Tommy, he … he was trying to drag one of them to safety behind an armored vehicle when he …"

At that moment, the music of the insects in the woods stopped and stillness prevailed. Even Jake grew calm as if all the natural world was honoring the memory of Tommy's selflessness with a moment of silence.

"He was a hero."

"Yeah."

"There is no greater love than to lay down one's life for a friend," Fred said.

"Tommy's friend died, too," Justin replied. Anger had seeped into his voice again. Jake seemed to sense it and backed away. "So what did he die for?" Justin asked. Fred bowed his head. "Look, I know you mean well," Justin continued. "I just have to work through this on my own."

"I have two tickets to a ball game in the city next week," Fred said after the insects resumed their chirping. "A co-worker was going, but he had to back out because of some family obligation. Why don't you come with me?"

Justin thought for a moment. "I haven't been to a ball game since I took Tommy and Lucy to a family night at the park with my firm when he was still in high school."

"Come with me," Fred urged.

"I'll think about it," Justin said.

"Are you walking back?" Fred asked. "I'll walk with you."

"Thanks, but I'd like to sit here a little while longer," Justin replied.

"Call me," Fred said. Justin simply nodded.

As Fred and Jake made their way back up the street toward home and the beam of the flashlight grew dim and then disappeared, I felt the first drops of rain.

XXX

Justin did not go the ball game with Fred. Though Fred invited him a few more times, and others made offers as well, Justin always found excuses not to go. *Too much work. Not feeling well. I want to spend time with Lucy*, although he spent most of his time at home sitting in the armchair in front of the TV or in his special room staring at nothing in particular. He nourished his anger and allowed its roots to grow deep.

All humans and dogs experience anger. I was angry at the man in the hooded sweater who hurt Mary and I harbored anger toward Mark for many years. Yet, my anger never changed who I was on the inside. Justin's anger took over and changed him the way the cool air changes the color of leaves in the Fall. In his moodiness and general unpleasantness, he became more like Mark everyday with one big difference: Justin directed most of his anger at himself. I often think his refusal to join in anything fun was a way of punishing himself for not living up to his own expectations.

Nan didn't help. She was awash in enough grief of her own looking for someone to blame for Tommy's loss and Justin was a convenient outlet. Her grief took the form of irritation with just about everything he did ... or forgot to do. *You left your dishes on the kitchen table again. Do you think I'm your maid? Has it ever occurred to you once to put them in the dishwasher so I don't have to walk in the kitchen all the time to a pile of dirty dishes?* Nan's criticisms only worsened Justin's opinion of himself and drove them further apart.

Lucy floundered around somewhere in between them waiting for her parents to comfort her. In their absence, she confided in me.

"Charlie, what's happening to us?" Lucy whispered one night while I lay next to her on her bed. She sat with her back against the curved white board at the top of her bed and her knees up against her chest. She rested her chin on them. "I still can't believe Tommy won't ever be coming home again. And Mom and Dad hardly talk to each other anymore except when they argue. I don't know what I'd do without you. You're the only one I can talk to."

She reached over and scooped me up in her arms. I lay in her arms, belly up and head against her shoulder, and grunted while she gave me scratches. She spoke into my ear.

"Even before Tommy died, Mom and Dad always did what they thought was best for me without really listening to what I had to say myself. Tommy listened. I told him how sick and tired I was of Mom and Dad always worrying about me hurting myself. He said you can't go through life afraid of what might happen. You just have to live. But now he's dead."

I licked her cheek. Of course, I could neither understand everything she said in human words nor speak to her in her language, but I sensed her deep-down sorrows and conflict and did what I could to reassure her and give her hope. I was there to be her friend and companion just like I was for Claire when it seemed her life couldn't get much worse. When you have a friend, there's always hope.

I wondered why Justin did not seem to have many friends. Before Tommy died, Nan often had friends visit. They sat at the kitchen table and talked and drank that wonderfully strong-smelling beverage humans won't share with dogs. Sometimes, Nan had parties in the kitchen with several women where they passed around all types of plastic bowls, boxes and trays and tasted a variety of foods. They filled the house with talk and laughter. And Lucy's friends were just as many and noisy, although they usually went down to play in the basement or upstairs to her room. After Tommy's death, Nan's and Lucy's friends still visited even though there wasn't as much noise anymore.

Justin left the house early and often came home late at night. I did not know any of his friends. And after the initial hubbub surrounding Tommy's funeral, no one came to the house to visit him.

The seasons turned once more, past the time when the air grew cooler and the leaves changed colors, until the trees were bare and my fur grew in thick again.

I have noticed that humans feel the absence of others most keenly around their holidays, and their loved ones most of all. So it was around Christmas, the first one after Tommy's death, my family's grief which had submerged somewhere beneath the activity of their everyday lives, returned like an undigested meal.

Nan was unable to decorate the Christmas tree. Justin and Lucy managed to do it, but not without several stops in which Lucy, more often than Justin, cried and they stood there in front of the tree embracing. Unlike the times I had watched Mira and Al decorate their trees, I noticed that almost every one of the objects Justin or Nan or Lucy placed on the tree had a special meaning and evoked memories. The last Christmas when Tommy was home, the memories often brought smiles and laughter. This time, the same object often caused pain and brought tears almost as soon as it was lifted out of its box.

On the evening before Christmas, Lucy and Nan retired early instead of staying up late as they had with Tommy, playing games at the kitchen table and singing along with the Christmas music coming from the box in the family room. Justin sat alone in his armchair. The house was dark except for the glow coming from the lights on the Christmas tree. Justin brooded until the contents of the glass in his hand were gone. Then he got up and went upstairs also.

On Christmas morning, before anyone came downstairs, I heard water running, closet doors opening and closing, and footsteps in the hallway. When they came downstairs, Lucy, Justin and Nan were already dressed.

Nan gathered up the few brightly colored packages that lay underneath the tree and put them in bags.

"Can't we take Charlie with us?" Lucy pleaded.

"No," Nan replied. "Aunt Joan has cats and she won't appreciate Charlie disturbing them."

"Charlie never starts anything. He …"

"I said no."

"I'll hold him."

"I said No!"

Lucy looked down at me forlornly. "I'll miss you," she said.

After a brisk walk with Justin, I returned to the house. I barked and ran back and forth in the front hall begging Justin and Nan to take me with them, and I followed Lucy's sad gaze until the door closed behind her. I was alone. No brightly colored packages to inspect. No laps to lay in. No delightful smells of food to savor and anticipate. While I was often alone in the house during the day, being alone on this day was unexpected and it hurt.

Shortly after Christmas on a gray and gloomy day with a cold drizzle streaking the window panes, Justin came home very early, before it was dark. I, of course, was delighted to see him. I ran into the front hallway and barked to greet him. Justin shuffled past me, threw the box he always carried on the floor of the family room, and took off his dripping wet coat. Nan had been upstairs, but the look on her face when she entered the room and saw Justin did not mirror my happiness. I sensed a deep unease in her.

"Why are you home so early?" she asked.

Justin did not reply immediately. He stood at the open door of the refrigerator, removed a bottle, and then sat down at the kitchen table.

"Justin, what happened?" Nan asked. I felt her anxiety increasing.

"I lost my job," he said.

Nan's expression changed from one of unease and concern to a confused bewilderment. "Why?"

"Downsizing," Justin said.

"But you have been their controller for over twenty years!"

"So? That just made me a bigger target."

Nan began to pace. "What are we going to do?" she asked. "How will we survive without your income? Did they give you any severance?"

"Five months."

"Five months?! After twenty years of service?!"

"One week for every year I was there. They don't have to give any."

"And our health insurance! What about Lucy's doctors?"

"There is COBRA."

"But we have to pay for that!"

"I didn't ask to be laid off," Justin said. "I'll find another job."

"I think you should talk to a lawyer, Justin. It's not right!"

"They threw in a couple thirty somethings from other departments. They know what they're doing."

"So that's it? You're just going to take it?"

Justin looked up at Nan. "No, I'm going to look for another job."

Nan turned abruptly, picked up her car keys lying on a lamp stand, and went into the front hall. I heard the closet open and the shuffling of coats before she left through the door to the garage.

Justin remained seated at the kitchen table drinking from the bottle. When he finished, he went upstairs, and the house became eerily quiet.

I sat in the kitchen for a moment bewildered by their behavior. Why wasn't Justin's coming home early a happy occasion? I went into the family room, jumped up on the armchair, and tried to nap. Though Nan had left, I still sensed a lingering tension in the room and, in Justin's mood, a quiet despair that was equally upsetting. I sat up, perked my ears, and listened for the sounds of Justin moving about in his bedroom. The humming of the refrigerator, once again, seemed as loud as the buzzing of insects in summer until a male voice interrupted.

"Charlie, go upstairs and find Justin."

Al? I heard the voice as clearly as if the man had been standing beside me, but there was no one in the room.

"Charlie, go find Justin now." The voice was sharp. Firm. Urgent. The tone of voice a human uses to give a command. I jumped down off the armchair and obeyed.

At the top of the stairs, I peeked into Lucy's room. No sign of Princess. I padded past the bathroom door and entered Justin and Nan's bedroom expecting her to pounce at any moment. I found Justin sitting on the edge of the monstrous bed, head down, eyes closed, holding something in his lap. I heard him murmuring, just barely above a whisper and not nearly loud enough for me to hear his words. I crept over to the bed still expecting Princess to attack from underneath, but there wasn't a sound to alert him to my approach.

When I pawed at Justin's pant leg, it startled him. He sat up straight as if I had awakened him from a dream and revealed what he had been holding in his lap. It was a gun. It smelled of the same faint odors of oil and smoke like the one I had seen lying on the floor next to Mira the night she made Mark leave the apartment.

"Charlie, what are you doing in here?" Justin whispered. "Nan will have a fit."

Justin held the gun with his right hand wrapped around the wide end and resting on his leg. The short end with the small opening pointed toward the alarm clock on the nightstand. I remembered the fear I felt from Mark when Mira pointed the object at him. The object scared me, too.

"Shoo. Go on downstairs."

I did not obey Justin. Instead, I jumped on the bed and, with my tail wagging and as bright a face as I could muster, scooched toward him until my body lay overtop his right arm. Though my body quivered, I forced myself to look away from the gun in Justin's hand and only at his face. I barked.

Justin's face began to wrinkle. Then he began to sob. His whole body shook. I felt his right arm jerking underneath me, but I did not get up. He bent over and laid his head against my body.

"Did he send you to stop me?" Justin asked. "I just want to be with him right now."

The Meaning Of Home

As I lay sandwiched between Justin's head and his right arm, I turned my head and looked at the gun he still held in his right hand. I hoped he would drop it on the floor like Mira had.

When Justin's sobbing finally subsided and the fur against my ribs was a warm, wet mass, he sat up and wiped his face with the tie he wore around his neck for work. I still lay draped across his right arm and leg. "I don't want to die, Charlie," he said. "I just want to stop the pain."

Justin sat quietly for a few moments taking long, deep breaths. Then he began to pet me with his left hand. "If I promise not to do anything, will you get up?" He gently nudged me with his left hand until I reluctantly backed off his arm and sat on the bed beside him. Justin leaned over, opened the drawer of the nightstand, and put the gun inside. He stared at the gun for a moment before he closed the drawer.

"My son was a better man than me," Justin said. He looked up at the ceiling. "He died doing something he believed in. He died in the midst of a selfless, heroic act. Just imagine what he might have accomplished had he lived?"

Justin turned his head and looked down at me. "What have I accomplished, Charlie? What have I done for the last twenty years except balance someone's books? And now they don't want me for that anymore.

"Do you know what I wanted to do? Do you know what I dreamed of doing when I was a kid? Acting. I wanted to be an actor. I wanted to play roles that would make people laugh or cry and feel all the different emotions that make us human. I wanted to entertain. I loved the applause. I wanted approval.

"You know the sad thing, Charlie? I have become an actor. These last twenty years, I've been acting as though I'm satisfied and fulfilled with my life. But I haven't been very convincing, have I?"

Justin reached over and began scratching my head. I rolled over and offered my belly, and he obliged.

"Too much pain can make us do horrible things. What was I thinking, Charlie? What kind of a man bails out on his wife and daughter? I would have disgraced Tommy's memory."

Justin stood up and began walking around the bedroom. I jumped off the bed and followed him. He paced back and forth running his hands through his hair. "I need to get out. I need to talk to someone. Maybe the pastor."

As Justin turned and walked toward the bedroom door, Princess entered the room. I stood between her and her sanctuary underneath the bed. She arched her back and hissed and spat at both of us. Justin picked up a sock off the floor and threw it at her, and she ran.

Justin shook his head. "If I ever act like her again, Charlie," he said. "throw a sock at me."

XXXI

In all my seasons in the camp often exposed to the weather outside, and in my days confined in rooms with many dogs, I had never come down with an illness more troubling than a cough. When the warmer weather returned once more, and Justin took me for longer walks, I began to feel a discomfort in my belly that eventually turned into pain. It was a knot inside my stomach that never went away. Whenever I moved in certain ways, it felt like Dr. Deaver had stuck me with a pin from the inside. I did not look forward to our walks anymore and even short distances became something to endure. One day, I simply laid down in the street when the pain became too much for me.

"Charlie, what's wrong, boy?" Justin asked. He bent down beside me and scratched my head. He tugged gently on my halter, but I would not stand up. "You've been acting funny, lately. Aren't you feeling well?" When he reached under my belly and began to lift, I cried out.

"Okay, okay, Charlie. I didn't mean to hurt you," he said, "but I can't leave you lying here in the middle of the street. I have to get you to a doctor."

Justin gently rolled me over onto my back and slid his arms underneath me. When he lifted, the jostling again caused some pain, but I felt better laying on my back in his arms.

When Lucy saw Justin carry me into the house, I sensed from her the same fear she expressed when Tommy said he was going to Afghanistan. "Dad, what's wrong with Charlie?" she asked.

"I don't know," Justin said. "He's having abdominal pain. Get a laundry basket and throw some towels in the bottom. I have to take him to the veterinarian."

"I want to go, too," Lucy said.

"Fine. Fine. You can go. Just bring me a laundry basket so I can make him comfortable."

Lucy brought the laundry basket and Nan came up the stairs from the basement with her. When Nan saw me, her lip quivered. "Poor Charlie," Nan said. "Was it something he ate?"

Justin shook his head as he laid me in the laundry basket. "I don't know."

"You're such a good dog, Charlie," Nan said as she stroked my fur.

Justin carried me out to the car and slid the basket into the back seat. It occurred to me I had not laid inside a laundry basket since Mira had lifted me out of the basket with her folded clothes and it comforted me to lay amidst the folds of the towels soaked with Justin and Nan's scents as though they were holding me in their arms.

Everyone climbed inside the vehicle for the ride to the veterinary hospital. Lucy held the laundry basket on her lap. On the few occasions I had been to the hospital previously for a check-up, I had always been bouncing around the back seat with Lucy holding onto my leash instead. She did not want me to leap out of the car the moment the door opened. Car rides were still a source of anxiety. I never knew whether the ending would be good or bad, and I had often whined and whistled and paced back and forth until we reached our destination. While I did not take kindly to the poking and prodding and occasional pin stick at my check-ups, this veterinary hospital was right next to an ice cream shop. I learned that my good behavior during the examination earned me a dish of vanilla ice cream afterwards.

On this trip, however, I lay still in the laundry basket and did not make a sound. When we reached the veterinary hospital, Justin carried me inside into a room with a silver table. We did not have to wait for our turn in another room like we usually did.

The veterinary hospital was very small compared to Dr. Deaver's. It was only one store in a shopping center, no bigger than the pet store in the one across the highway from the camp. The entrance was narrow with nothing more than a couple chairs, a plant, and a large, square bowl filled with water and fish on top of a wooden stand. From the entrance, a narrow aisle led past a counter on one side and shelves along a wall stacked with cans and bags that smelled like food. On the other side of the aisle, three doors opened into examining rooms. Justin carried me into the last one. There wasn't space enough inside the examining room for more than two or three people.

"I'll go have a cup of coffee next door," Nan said.

Moments later, the doctor entered. Dr. Carey, as the people in the office called her, was much taller than Dr. Deaver, and younger, with long, brown hair spilling down around her shoulders onto the white coat she wore. She had dark brown eyes and a smile as bright as my own. Like Dr. Deaver, she had a soft, soothing tone to her voice that put me at ease.

"Hi Charlie!" she said enthusiastically as if it was any other visit. "I hear you're not feeling well?" I managed to raise my head and give her a few wags of my tail.

"He hasn't been moving around much lately," Justin said. "This afternoon on our walk, he just lay down in the street and would not go any further."

"Let's get him out of the basket," Dr. Carey said. Justin lifted me up with Dr. Carey's help while Lucy pulled the laundry basket out from underneath me. The movement caused a sharp pain in my belly and I yelped.

"Easy, Charlie," Dr. Carey said. "Let me find out what's bothering you." While I lay on the table, she began pressing her hand firmly against different parts of my body. When she reached my belly and pressed firmly at a point just behind my ribs, I felt a shooting pain and yelped again. Dr. Carey frowned, and both Justin and Lucy noticed.

"Has he been vomiting?" Dr. Carey asked.

"Not to my knowledge," Justin said. "But he hasn't had much of an appetite lately."

"Have you noticed any blood in his stools?"

"They have been dark," Justin acknowledged.

"What's wrong?" Lucy asked. I could hear the alarm in her voice. I tried to get up to go to her, but Dr. Carey held me still.

"I don't know for sure," Dr. Carey said, "but I want to take him back for an ultrasound. Hopefully, that will tell us what is going on inside his belly. It may take a little while. If you'd like to wait out front, I'll come get you as soon as we have the results."

Justin and Lucy bent over the table to give me scratches and kisses before they left the room. "Please get better, Charlie," Lucy said.

Other women in blue shirts and pants placed me on a small, rolling table and wheeled me back through another door into a room at the rear of the veterinary hospital. The room was as big as the rest of the veterinary hospital beyond the door. Against one wall were the familiar metal cages, now empty. Along other walls were cabinets and counters, and across the room from the cages stood a large white machine like the one I had seen at Dr. Deaver's.

The women in blue rolled me up to a counter next to an object that looked like one of the computers in Mira's studio. Dr. Carey came in. She pushed buttons on the machine and waved a long, white stick over my belly. White shapes appeared—streaks and circles and swirls—but Dr. Carey didn't like the picture she drew. She frowned again. Soon, the women in blue took me back to the tiny examining room where Justin and Lucy were already waiting.

When Dr. Carey entered the room, I sensed from her a deep concern. I have always had a keen intuition for human emotion and knew what she had to say was not good before she spoke the words.

"Charlie has a mass in his abdomen," Dr. Carey said.

"What kind of mass?" Justin asked.

"Most likely a cancerous one," she replied. "He will have to have other tests done and surgery to remove the mass soon, but we're not equipped for that sort of thing here. There is a hospital over in Riverdale about an hour from here I'd like to send him to. We can transfer him there tonight."

Justin sank into a chair and Lucy began to cry. "Is he going to die?" she asked through her tears.

Dr. Carey hesitated, then put her best face on. She knelt beside Lucy and placed her hands reassuringly on Lucy's shoulders. "Dr. Deaver is the best surgeon I know," she said. "Plenty of dogs go on to live full lives after having tumors removed. Don't worry."

Lucy spent several minutes by my side stroking my fur, scratching my head and whispering into my ear. "Please don't die, Charlie. You must get better. I love you." I licked the tears from her cheeks as fast as they fell and managed to wag my tail. I did not understand the problem I had inside my belly and wanted to go home with Lucy. I barked and tried to get up as Justin led her out of the examining room, but a woman in blue kept me still.

Beyond the open door, Dr. Carey stood behind the counter speaking to someone on a telephone. "Dr. Deaver, we're transferring a patient to your hospital tonight. His name is Charlie."

XXXII

When I arrived at the veterinary hospital with the familiar sign of the dog and cat, Dr. Deaver was waiting for me. "I always hoped we would meet again, Charlie," she said, "but not under these circumstances." She scratched me behind my ears and I managed to wag my tail for her. A young woman I had not met before carried me into the Quiet Room and lay me inside a cage. I did not whine or fuss very much or care whether there were any cats in the room. My belly hurt too much to do more than lie as still as possible.

I did not know what cancer was or how big the growth was inside me. However, I had heard the word "die" often enough in my lifetime and associated it with such times as Mary's and Al's and Tommy's deaths to understand it meant the possibility of a permanent separation from my family when Lucy spoke it to me. I also understood the person or animal that died went somewhere else while everyone else stayed behind. And separation caused sadness and pain. While I was curious about what lay ahead

The Meaning Of Home

if I did die, especially whether I might see Al again, I did not want another separation to cause my family any more grief than they had already suffered in just one cycle of seasons. If I had anything to say about it, I wanted to live.

Dr. Deaver came into the Quiet Room very early the next morning. "Good morning, Charlie," she said softly. "We'll be coming to take you into surgery soon." She opened the cage door and pet me for several moments. I lay still and grunted. With her hand still touching me, Dr. Deaver did something I never saw her do before. She closed her eyes, bowed her head, and spoke softly to God. "Father, guide my hands today and help me heal this very special dog."

The young woman who put me in my cage the night before came to take me out. She handled me gently and spoke soothingly, but I missed Jen. I believe dogs as much as humans would rather face trouble with friends beside them. She brought me into a large room with bright lights around another silver table. Several humans stood around the table dressed in blue clothing tied with string in the middle and wore blue hats to hide their hair, blue masks over their mouths and noses, and clear, shiny glasses over their eyes. I did not recognize anyone, and that frightened me. I began to squirm and whine when they put me on the silver table until I heard Dr. Deaver's voice.

"We'll take good care of you, Charlie," she said. "Don't be afraid." Dr. Deaver placed a clear plastic cone over my nose and said, "Sweet dreams."

I don't know whether I dreamed while I was on the silver table or when I was back in my cage in the

Quiet Room, but I dreamed. I was walking with Al again around the camp. He looked much younger and stronger, more like the man I saw in the photographs he showed Claire. He walked briskly and kept moving further ahead.

We turned a corner along the path that lead through the camp toward the woods and the river beyond. I saw Mary standing by her tent with the young boy from the photograph. She was much younger, too. Her clothes were tidy. Her hair was groomed. She had her arm around the boy. "Hi, Charlie," she said and smiled. "Thank you for helping me find Billy. You always were a good dog." I wanted to stop for hugs and kisses. I had never had a chance to thank her for saving my life at the expense of her own, but Al kept walking.

Further on, we came upon Daniel lounging in a camp chair by his tent. He waved to Al and then to me. "Whasssup, Charlie? I heard you saved the camp. Awesome!" I was confused because I had a memory of returning to the camp and finding nothing but trash and my chewy, the only trace of Al's shelter. What had happened? I wanted to stop and talk to Daniel, but Al only walked faster. I barked at him to slow down.

When Al was almost to the woods, I looked out into the gravel parking area and saw Tommy standing there in his Marine uniform. "Please don't go with him, Charlie," Tommy said. "Not yet. Mom and Dad and Lucy still need you, Charlie. Be the best watchdog ever."

I looked back at Al. He had stopped by the edge of the woods and turned to face me. "He's right, Charlie,"

Al said. "Your tour isn't over. The camp will still be here when it is. Go on back, now."

Tommy raised his hand to his forehead in a salute to Al the same way Jeremy had and yelled, "Semper Fi!"

Al returned the salute sharply. "Semper Fi," he said. He turned and disappeared into the woods as the tents all around me dissolved into the gray of four cage walls. I heard someone tapping gently on the metal bars of the cage door and calling my name. "Charlie? Charlie, can you hear me?" My eyes would not focus and everything in between my ears was pounding. I managed to raise my head off the cage floor and thump my tail once.

"Welcome back," Dr. Deaver said.

For a time after the surgery, Dr. Deaver kept me on strong medicine. It made my hair fall out in clumps inside the cage and I did not feel very handsome anymore. The medicine also made me sick to my stomach. I did not feel like eating very much and lost weight. Dr. Deaver set up a pole next to my cage and hung a bag of clear liquid on it. A line went from the bag into the skin on my right front paw. She said it would keep me fed until I was able to eat on my own.

Dr. Deaver also frequently checked a long line of little knots on my belly. I was embarrassed to discover that nearly every part of me underneath had been shaved as bald as my water bowl. Eventually, Dr. Deaver took a sharp metal object and snipped all the knots off. She told me how pleased she was I had left the knots alone and had not tried to pull them out myself.

During my long recovery, Justin, Lucy and Nan stopped by regularly to visit me in the Quiet Room. Seeing them helped reduce my anxiety about ending my days in a metal cage or wandering through woods or along roads. I knew they would take me home with them when I was well enough to go. I realized I was wanted … and loved … by everyone. Their home was my home, and it made me more determined than ever to get stronger and eat on my own. Lucy often sat in a chair next to my cage and told me about school, and her own therapy and doctors, and how she had decided she would like to help other shelter dogs like me find good homes.

When my zeal for barking returned and it upset the cats in the Quiet Room, Dr. Deaver's assistant moved me into the kennel downstairs. I had stated my case to go home. I was eating and gaining weight. My fur was growing back as soft and luxurious as ever. The day Dr. Deaver's assistant entered the downstairs kennel carrying my leash and halter was one of the happiest days of my life.

Justin, Nan and Lucy were waiting for me upstairs in an examining room. I was barking. I was leaping. I caused quite a stir. The dogs in the kennels were in an uproar and the more vocal cats were pleading for quiet to return. In the examining room, Dr. Deaver was all smiles.

"All his tests have come back negative," she said. "It was a large tumor, but it appears we got it all before it had a chance to metastasize."

"What's that mean?" Lucy asked.

"It means none of the cancer cells from the tumor in Charlie's belly travelled to other parts of his body to grow tumors there."

"Oh."

"He has a clean bill of health, but I'll still want to see him back in six months," Dr. Deaver said. "We should keep an eye on him."

Justin nodded. "Thank you for everything you've done, Doctor," he said. "C'mon, Charlie. Let's go home."

As Lucy lifted me off the examining room table, Dr. Deaver handed Justin a piece of paper. "Next month, there will be a pet fair at the county park and the proceeds will go to benefit homeless pets and homeless people."

"Can we go, Dad?" Lucy chimed in. "Please?"

"Are dogs allowed?" Justin asked.

"Of course," Dr. Deaver said. "In fact, I was hoping you would bring Charlie. We'll have a booth at the fair, but there is someone else coming I think Charlie will be very happy to see."

XXXIII

The day of the pet fair was a bright, sun-soaked day like the ones I enjoyed so much along the river. The air was pleasant and breezy and filled with scents. Overhead, the blue sky promised not to allow so much as one puffy white cloud spoil the picture.

During the ride to the county park, I raced back and forth in the back seat from one window to the other. I whined and fussed and heard "Settle down, Charlie!" from Lucy and Justin more times than I could count. I suppose I'll never be perfectly calm on a car ride even though nothing bad has happened on one in quite a while. I became an optimistic sort, and my behavior in the car with my family was more motivated by the excitement of what may lie at the end of the ride than the fear of it.

The county park was an expanse of green fields circled with towering trees still clothed in a canopy of green leaves and sprinkled with spots of red and gold. And there were tents! Big tents and small tents of assorted colors, shapes, and sizes, but no shelters. When I saw the tents, I wondered if this could be where the camp had moved, and whether Claire might be here, too. But there were obvious signs it wasn't. This camp was too clean. I did not see trash on the ground anywhere. And there were children. And dogs. Lots of dogs.

I barked and scratched at the window as Justin stopped the car. I wanted out. I wanted to run, but Lucy had a tight grip on my leash. Oh, the smells when Justin opened the door! Hundreds of them! I inhaled the scents of other dogs crisscrossing the park leading their human companions. The smell of burgers, fries and the warm, chewy dough with white powder mixed with less pleasing smells of cars and the funny outside booths humans use for bathrooms. Lucy handed my leash to Justin and he lowered me to the grass. Between Justin's hand and my back, my leash went as stiff as an angry cat's tail. It was all that was holding me back from food.

"Do you see Dr. Deaver's booth?" Justin asked.

"Over there," Lucy said and pointed to a small blue tent in a row of smaller tents. On the blue top of the tent in white was the familiar sign of the dog and cat.

In the grass, Nan walked as slow as Mary and we had to wait for her to catch up. I spied a man in a white hat handing ice cream cones to children and urged Justin and Lucy to follow me, but Justin tugged me toward the veterinary hospital's tent instead. Dr. Deaver and two other women stood behind a table covered with papers, toys, leashes, halters, and jars of snacks. When she saw us, Dr. Deaver smiled and came out from behind the table to greet us.

"Hi Charlie! Hi Lucy! I am so glad you could come."

Dr. Deaver shook hands with Justin and Nan. She knelt beside me, rumpled my fur, and offered me treats she took from a pocket of her white coat. "Thank you for bringing them," she said to me and winked. I sniffed each treat and took them politely before walking a few steps away to eat them as was my custom.

"He looks strong," Dr. Deaver said.

"He has been eating well," Justin said. "Perhaps too well," he added and glanced at Lucy. "He loves his snacks."

"He is at a good weight, now," Dr. Deaver said. "Don't let him get too much heavier, Lucy. It is not good for dogs anymore than it is for people." Lucy nodded.

"There is someone I'd like you to meet," Dr. Deaver said, "an old friend of Charlie's who has not seen him in quite a while. Come with me. Her tent is just across the way on the other side of the main exhibition tent."

"Someone from the shelter?" Justin asked as we began to walk with Dr. Deaver.

"Oh, they are here, too." Dr. Deaver said. "But this friend goes even further back. I told you when Charlie came to me for his surgery that I knew him from the shelter, but I did not tell you the rest of his story from his time before the shelter. You had a lot on your mind."

"How far back?" Justin asked.

"A few years," Dr. Deaver said. "Charlie was living in a camp of homeless people down along the river not far from my hospital."

"A homeless camp?" Justin's eyebrows rose, and he and Lucy looked at each other. Nan scrunched her nose.

"Yes," Dr. Deaver replied. "He first befriended an elderly woman in the camp and then the camp's director when she died. He also became particularly close to a young woman in the camp whose name is Claire."

When I heard Claire's name, I perked my ears and looked up at Dr. Deaver. Was Claire here? I could not smell her.

"Why isn't he still there?" Lucy asked.

"Unfortunately, the director died, too. He was a wonderful man named Al whom I respected very much. And then the Township closed down the camp and forced all the residents to move, including Claire. She gave Charlie to me thinking he would be better off with a new family. Eventually, he wound up at the shelter."

"So, I'm guessing we're about to meet Claire?" Justin asked.

It was the third time they had spoken her name. I knew she must be here and began to whine and fuss because I still could not smell her.

"Yes," Dr. Deaver replied.

"Why didn't they tell us all this at the shelter?" Nan asked.

"Because not all people are prepared to hear that the lovely dog or cat in their arms at the shelter has had an uncertain past. Some of the pets at the shelter come from good homes where the family is simply no longer able to keep them for any number of reasons. They have been loved and well taken care of. Other animals have been abused and mistreated almost since birth, but through much love and care from the shelter staff, they have been rehabilitated to the point we are comfortable placing them in new homes with the right owners. We don't want an animal's past to prejudice its opportunity to find a new home anymore than a person's past should prejudice his or her opportunity for a fresh start."

As I trotted along ahead of Justin around the side of the large, white exhibition tent at the center of the fair, I inhaled a familiar scent that stopped me in my tracks. It was there briefly but faded before I could be sure. I turned toward the tent with my nose in the air and pulled Justin away from his intended path.

"No, Charlie," Justin said. "We are not going in there now. Dr. Deaver has someone she wants us to meet."

"Hey, look, Dad!" Lucy said. "They're having a doggy fashion show later!"

"Now that's something I'd like to see," Nan said.

"It doesn't start for another hour," Justin said. "We can come back. We have all day."

On the other side of the exhibition tent stood another row of smaller tents. Dr. Deaver led us to a white one with large black letters that read "ICPH." The tent top bore a black silhouette of a man sitting by a shelter with the outline of tall city buildings in the background.

I smelled Claire before I saw her, a scent as fresh as vanilla ice cream. I heard her calling my name, "Charlie! Charlie!' as she came running toward me past the line of tents. Tears were streaming down her face.

We met at the point where my leash would go no further. Claire dropped to her knees, scooped me up in her arms, and buried her face in my fur. I felt a bit awkward because everyone around us was watching.

"I thought I'd never see you again!" Claire said. "Let me look at you." She held me up underneath my front legs which was even more embarrassing. My fur had not fully grown back since the surgery and my privates were exposed.

"You are still so handsome! Dr. Deaver told me all about your new home. I am so happy for you, Charlie." Claire pulled me into her chest and hugged me again. "I just hope you can forgive me for giving you up for adoption."

When my paws were back on the ground, Claire walked with me the few steps further to my family. She introduced herself, shook my family's hands politely, and gave Dr. Deaver a big hug.

Claire suddenly became shy. I noticed her hair wasn't colored purple any more. It was long and dark and glistened like grass in rain. She wore a pretty blue shirt with white, lacey designs and shiny leather boots, but her jeans had holes in the knees. I hoped someday Claire could afford to buy clothes without holes in them.

"Thank you for doing what you did for Charlie," Justin said to break the awkward silence.

Claire smiled. "No thanks necessary. I love him. He did a lot for me first."

"Claire is the director of the Interfaith Council on Poverty and Homelessness," Dr. Deaver said proudly. "She has started a new initiative to pair homeless animals with homeless people in transition to new housing. In fact, this pet fair was her idea. She has organized them in many of the surrounding counties."

"I'm impressed," Justin said. Claire blushed.

"Claire did a study in college," Dr. Deaver continued. "She found that homeless people in transition to housing who were paired with pets had a much higher success rate in holding onto jobs and avoiding a relapse into substance abuse than the ones without pets. Frankly, it is not surprising."

"When someone bonds with a pet, it gives them something extra to live for," Claire said. "It motivates them. I noticed it myself with Charlie."

Justin looked down at me and nodded. "He is a remarkable dog,"

"Very well behaved," Nan added.

"He deserves a good home like yours," Claire said. "I can tell you have bonded with him and he with you. Would it be alright if I stopped in to visit him on occasion?"

Justin looked at Nan and Lucy. "Of course," Nan said. "I don't see why not."

"Thank you," Claire said. "I enjoy coming out to the burbs. I grew up around here, and it's still home even though all my memories of growing up here are not pleasant."

"Visit whenever you like," Nan said.

"I've been spending too much time in the office lately," Claire said. "Our bookkeeper just quit, and I've been trying to do what I can to keep up while trying to hire someone at the same time. It hasn't been working out very well."

Nan nudged Justin. "I might be able to help out," he said.

"Really?" Claire said. "That would be awesome! Here's my card. Give me a call on Monday and let's talk. It's funny how these events always seem to bring with them new opportunities!"

Claire dropped to her knees and gave me another great big hug. "I am so happy for you, Charlie! It has worked out well for both of us."

As I breathed in her scent, I wondered what my life would have been like if Claire had kept me. Would I have lived in a camp? An apartment or a house? Would it have been just the two of us? Or would she have loved another? Would I have been at home wherever she was?

I sensed Lucy's impatience behind me. How lucky I was to be loved by so many, and how silly it seemed to wonder about what might have been when I already had what I wanted.

"Oh, I almost forgot to tell you!" Claire said. "I'm getting married in the Spring! Can you believe it? And by Father Paul!" She looked up at my family. "I hope you will come and bring Charlie."

Claire's happiness was contagious. I was so happy I could not stop myself from doing my shimmy-shake and barking.

"I wish Al could be there to walk me down the aisle," she said quietly. I wished Al could be there, too. I wanted to see him again.

As Claire said her goodbyes, there were hugs all around. No more handshakes. Dr. Deaver left us and returned to her tent with Justin's promise to bring me to her office for a check-up in a few months. We wandered past tent after tent of pet displays and stopped in to see the folks from the shelter. Theresa, the pony-tailed director, was there and I sensed from her, as I did from Claire, a deep inner satisfaction from seeing my contentment with my family.

We entered the main exhibition tent in time for the doggy fashion show and sat down on long, metal benches. There were three large boxes out in the center of the show ring colored red, white and blue. I smelled the same scent I had detected earlier when we walked past outside, but this time the scent was stronger and unmistakable. Mira was somewhere nearby.

I whined and fussed in Lucy's arms and looked for Mira. Finally, I saw her enter the tent at the far end of the ring. Several men and women of various ages came in behind her each with a dog on a bejeweled leash and sporting one of Mira's fashionable designs. I barked in my highest pitched, most excited of voices to attract her attention, but with several other dogs barking inside the tent, she could not hear mine over the hubbub.

Mira looked just as I had remembered her, slender, confident, and fashionably dressed in jeans (with no holes) and a leather jacket. She stood at a tall box at the far end of the arena and spoke into a black stick she held in her hand. One by one, she introduced the other men and women and the dogs that accompanied them. One by one, each of the men and women trotted around the ring with a dog. Taking turns, the trainers led the dogs into the center of the ring as Mira called each dog's name. When a dog jumped up onto one of the colored boxes, Mira told the audience about the dog and described the clothes it wore while the dog posed on the box or performed a trick. She said all the dogs in the show were rescues.

At the end of the show, all the men and women with the dogs lined up at the far end of the ring as they had done in the beginning. However, this time, Mira herself led them and waved to the audience as they processed around the ring.

I watched her come closer and closer and struggled mightily in Lucy's arms.

"Charlie, stop it! What is wrong with you?"

Mira walked along the inside of the railing until she was directly beneath me, only several rows away. I barked repeatedly with all the sound my lungs could produce and, this time, she saw me. She looked right at me and stopped, stopped waving, stopped walking. She just stood there and stared at me with her mouth open. The men and women and the dogs behind her had to stop, too. While other members of the audience were already spilling out the sides of the tent, Mira and her trainers and my family and I were all frozen in the moment.

With a few more vigorous twists, I managed to free myself from the halter and the leash attached to it. I ran down the rows of seats straight to Mira. Although I heard Lucy's panicked cries, and Justin and Nan shouting, I had to go to Mira once more to let her know it was me, that I survived, and did not blame her for what had happened. I wanted her to have that peace.

Mira fought back tears as she bent down and gathered me in her arms.

"Ay, Pequeño? Como es posible?"

It did not take long for Justin, Nan and Lucy to reach the side of the show ring.

"Ma'am, we are so sorry!" Justin blurted out. "He has never behaved like that before. I don't know what got into him."

But Mira did not reply, nor immediately hand me over. Lucy watched the interaction between Mira and me. "He knows you," she said. "That's why he ran to you. He wasn't running away from us, Dad. He was running to her."

Justin and Nan looked at Lucy strangely, then glanced at Mira who was still holding me and whispering "Forgive me" in my ear. I licked her cheek.

"Is that true?" Justin asked.

"How many more lives has Charlie had?" Nan wondered aloud.

"Is that what you named him? Charlie?" Mira asked.

"We didn't give it to him," Justin replied. "That was the name he had when we adopted him from the shelter."

"It's a good name," Mira said.

"What did you call him?" Lucy asked.

"It doesn't matter," Mira replied. "He's Charlie now. We were separated a long time ago. I thought he was dead."

I saw worried expressions like shadows darkening my family's faces and I knew what they were thinking. The longer I remained in Mira's embrace, the more uncomfortable they became. I loved Mira, but I had no intention of turning back the clock. With a few final kisses, I turned and wiggled and communicated my wish to be returned to Lucy's arms. Mira complied, and the shadows on their faces vanished.

"I want to give you something," Mira said. "Wait here." She walked to the far end of the show ring and began to rummage through some boxes there. By now, the trainers and their dogs had wandered off to various parts of the tent, exchanging conversation with curious members of the audience and allowing their children to pet the dogs.

When Mira returned, an older gentleman accompanied her. He was much taller than her, crisply dressed in brown pants, polished leather boots, a black shirt underneath a leather vest, and a broad hat with a big, blue stone and feathers on the front. He had a kind face, round and bearded, with dark, brown hair. His moustache and beard were neatly trimmed. He exuded pride as he accompanied Mira, but not just pride in himself. He was proud of her.

Mira carried several garments in her hands. "Here," she said as she handed them to Nan. "Please take these for Charlie. He'll be fashionable for every season."

"Thank you," Nan said.

"Look, Charlie!" Lucy said. "Look at all the clothes you'll have to wear. You'll be the best dressed dog on the street!"

"This is my husband," Mira said introducing the older gentleman. "Carlos. It is Spanish for Charles. He wanted to meet the dog that shares his name."

The older gentleman stretched out his hand and shook my paw. "The pleasure is mine," he said with an accent like Mira's. He shook my family's hands as well. A moment of awkward silence followed, the kind I've seen so often among humans when their minds are bubbling over with thoughts, but no one will allow the thoughts to form words and leave their lips.

Mira looked at Carlos and broke the silence. "We have a long ride back to the city and still have to load the truck." He nodded. They exchanged another round of handshakes and well wishes with my family and finished with me.

"Goodbye, Charlie," Mira said. A tear escaped her eye. *"Vaya con Dios."* Go with God.

As they walked across the show ring, Carlos placed his arm around Mira and drew her tightly to him. I relaxed in Lucy's arms. And then it occurred to me. Mira had been given a second chance of her own.

EPILOGUE

I am old now. I spend most of my days napping in a large wicker basket Nan bought for me after I became unable to jump up into the big armchair. The basket has a soft cushion in the bottom, padding around the side, and an extra blanket for colder days. In the evenings, I lay in the basket by the armchair at Justin's feet while he reads or watches the TV. During the day, on occasion, I still follow Nan around the first floor of our home, but I tire easily. I do not navigate stairs well and rarely go upstairs anymore even though Princess is no longer there to harass me.

I sometimes think how fortunate I am that my life has come full circle from one comfortable basket to another. What more can a dog ask for than to end his days in warmth and comfort in a home where he is wanted?

Lucy is in a place Justin and Nan call college, although she comes home often. She doesn't have to use the pole with the rubber tip anymore and she takes me for short walks, although I can't go very far. Even the rabbits and squirrels sense my frailty and barely make the effort to move as we approach.

When she is home the longest in the summer, Lucy works at the shelter. She took me with her once, but I became so upset I pooped and peed everywhere. You might think by now I would be secure in my family's love, but at my age, even the thought of being left in a cage again brought back a strong anxiety. I shivered and shook until Lucy finally took me home to curl up in my basket.

Lucy told me how she trains the dogs at the shelter to have manners and listen to humans so people will want them. She says she wants to be a doctor like Dr. Deaver when she finishes school. I think Lucy will make a fine doctor.

Claire still lives in the city with her husband and they have a child. She stopped by to see me not too long ago and brought her child with her. All it wanted to do was pull my ears and tail, so I made myself scarce after Justin, Claire and Lucy started talking. Claire still helps homeless people in the city and Justin and Lucy volunteer for her organization. Justin did work for the Interfaith Council in the city for a while after the pet fair, but eventually found a job closer to home. He never liked working in the city. I heard Justin and Lucy talking with Claire about helping her again with the next pet fair. I like to think I had something to do with it.

I never saw Mira again after the first festival. I don't know why. Perhaps I reminded her of a time in her life she wished to forget. Sometimes a memory of a loved one brings too much pain and it is better to simply let go.

Justin had a difficult time working through Tommy's loss. I cannot imagine a deeper pain for a human than the loss of a child and I still recall how terribly it affected Mary. The sadness never goes away entirely, and I can tell the days when it bothers him most. He becomes silent and withdrawn again.

Not having Lucy home saddens him more. His mood brightens when she comes home. I see Justin come closest to real joy when he is spending time with Lucy and volunteering for Claire's organization. He tells me how much better helping people makes him feel than balancing books even though he earns all his money doing one and nothing from the other.

Nan walks me during the day. I have noticed she tries to get out of the house more and have her friends over for snacks and that wonderfully strong-smelling beverage I still have never had the pleasure of tasting. I still love company and her friends always coo and dote over me and give me belly scratches. Yet, there are days she will walk by Tommy's room and start sobbing. I always get up from my basket and go sit at the bottom of the stairs. She must pick me up now to lay in her lap if she wants to run her hands through my fur.

I sense there will be a day in the not-too-distant future when I will close my eyes forever in this world. May it be in my bed just like Al. It will be a bad day for Justin, Nan, and Lucy when I do. Yet, unlike Tommy, I have had a full life with many second chances and dogs simply don't live as long as humans do. Separation when there has been love, whether between humans or humans and dogs, is always painful. One always seems to come with the other. But I would never trade all the love I received from my human companions in this life to avoid the pain of missing them.

I wonder if I will open my eyes again in the better place called Heaven I often heard Al speak of, and whether I will see him there. Al said it was the best home of all, a home we'd never have to leave. It is a wonderful and reassuring thought, and I hope for Justin and Nan and Lucy, they will see Tommy again, too. For my family, I also hope they will find another dog from the shelter when I leave and give him the home and the love they gave to me. There are still plenty of lost dogs waiting to be found.

ACKNOWLEDGEMENTS

No accomplishment can be achieved solely through one's own effort. I am grateful for the assistance of author Joyce Magnin, my content editor (The Bright's Pond Novels and Cake), and to Chandi and Shahid at ArcManor, my copy editor and publisher, for being very patient with me.

I owe a tremendous debt of gratitude to my test readers. In 1979, Marilyn Soufer was my 11th grade AP European History teacher at Hatboro-Horsham High School. She is the most compassionate and inspiring teacher I have ever known. I do not believe it was a coincidence that our paths crossed again thirty-nine years after I left her classroom. She has inspired and encouraged me to pursue my dream of becoming a published author I dreamed even then.

Pamela Herlong and Michele Cayemitte are dear friends from church who have also shared in my journey from dreamer to writer to author. Before *The Meaning Of Home,* they took the time to read and give me their frank opinions on two earlier novels which were my learning projects in the school of hard knocks. Despite multiple setbacks, Pam and Michele have always encouraged me to keep writing, for my own and others' enjoyment. Hopefully, three's the charm.

Betty King, a fellow Mitch Albom fan, read the manuscript and fanned my ego by telling me how close to Mitch's writing mine has come. Thanks, Betty, for the vote of confidence.

Thank you to my wife, Carolyn, and my daughters, Courtney, Diana and Gabrielle, for their patience, love, and tolerance of the many hours I spent in my home office writing after the many hours I'd already spent in the law office. And thank you, Charlie, for telling me your stories. I know Sancho sent you.

Yet, most of all, I owe a debt I can never repay to my Lord and Savior, Jesus Christ. I know I am his unfinished project, a story in progress in desperate need of his editing. Thank you for my gift and may the words of this novel fulfill Your purpose.

Coming
from
Scott I. Fegley

CATSEQUENCES

Never Displease Your Cat

Made in the USA
Middletown, DE
09 February 2019